Ghost Music

A Marcus Brace Mystery

Patrick Linder

Oak Tree Press — Hanford, CA

Oak Tree Press
Publishers Since 1998

GHOST MUSIC, Copyright 2013, by James Patrick Linder. All rights reserved. Printed in the United States of America. No part of this book may be used or reproduced in any manner whatsoever without written permission except in the case of brief quotations used in critical articles and reviews. For information, address Oak Tree Press, 1820 W. Lacey Boulevard, Suite 220, Hanford, CA 93230.

Oak Tree Press books may be purchased for educational, business, or sales promotional purposes. Contact Publisher for quantity discounts.

First Edition, October 2013

ISBN 978-1-61009-127-5
LCCN 2013949916

For Cleta Stevens, who always delighted in having a family full of readers.

For JL Linder, who equally appreciated a literary turn of phrase and a truly bad pun.

Chapter One

I almost stepped on a piece of skull. My foot neared the ground at the same moment my mind recognized the silver-white shard for what it was. I short-stepped, shuffling like an old man, to keep my shoe from disturbing the splinter of bone.

I turned to the woman at my side and shook my head to share a moment of exasperation. We were the last ones here, tardy only because it shouldn't have been our scene at all.

I let out a quick, sharp whistle. "You missed a piece," I hollered as heads turned our way. I pointed toward the skull fragment I'd nearly crushed.

"You Detective Brace?" a gaunt officer asked, annoyance in his voice. He might have been the skinniest guy I'd ever seen. I'm thin as well, but I like to think I'm athletic-thin. I'm a runner and have the lean body type and ropey muscles that go along with it. He didn't. His version of skinny made me think of someone too busy to be concerned with eating. Someone who probably didn't like wasting his time waiting for us.

"That's right. How you doin?" I replied, hand outstretched as a gesture to smooth things over.

"Be better after I hand this one to you," he replied. "You must be doing something right. The dead are asking for you by name, calling out for the great Marcus Brace."

"I take it they didn't call for me as well?" the woman next to me asked, pouting slightly and feigning hurt. "Detective Ashlynn Rivers," she said, extending her hand.

Her coy response bothered me more than the derision dripping from the officer's words. She did that to me. "Let's see what we have," I muttered.

The scene was brutal. The extreme damage done to the woman's head drew our immediate attention and wouldn't let us go. Half of her face was missing, the features disappearing where her skull caved in, like an overripe cantaloupe. She had been struck above the left eye, the blow destroying her forehead, the skin collapsing within the hollow, the eyeball flattened into the pulverized socket. Blood had run down her cheek before pooling on the ground beneath her neck, where it matted her once-curly brown hair to the asphalt. Then I saw it. My business card, with my name circled in blood, had been laced between the dead woman's fingers, creating a flag for whoever found the body.

Ash turned toward me. "The dead aren't calling you. A killer is."

I looked again at the woman's flattened face. There wasn't much to see. What was there didn't spark my memory. I didn't recall giving my card to a woman with brown hair in the last week or so. I had no idea why it was woven into her fingers.

"Look at this," Ash said, pulling my attention back to the body. She pointed beneath my business card, to the middle of the woman's hand. A small, blackened circle stared up at us. "See how precise it is? It's perfectly centered on her palm."

I looked closely at the circle. "Makes me think it was made postmortem. I can't imagine her holding absolutely still otherwise." I bent closer. "Any guesses on what made the mark?"

Ash bent closer. A wisp of auburn hair escaped from her tight, natural curls and tickled the back of my neck. As she examined the mark, her mouth opened slightly in surprise, then quickly closed. "It's a cigarette burn," she said, her statement definitive, her voice shaky.

"A cigarette burn wouldn't be black, would it?" I asked. "A burn would be pink or red. Maybe white with scarring if it's old."

"It's been filled in with something black." She looked again at the darkened circle. Her eyes flitted from side to side before resetting in the center. "The wound itself is a burn from a cigarette. I'm sure, absolutely positive." She raised her shirt a few inches to expose a mark on the right side of her belly that was in line with her navel. Her own scalding from a cigarette.

I wanted to ask her about it. Her scar drew a part of me toward her in ways that I had been able to push away before. She was tough and didn't need me to rescue her, but that impulse stirred in me nonetheless when she showed me the burn. I saw someone else who was in pain, someone else who had been damaged by somebody they had probably trusted. I checked myself, realizing that my thoughts said more about the sorry emotional state I was in with my marriage ending than anything the mark necessarily said about her. I fought to push the image of her stomach away and quash a pity party of comparing injuries and licking one another's wounds.

I shouldn't have even been at this crime scene. I also shouldn't have been here with *her*. My partner, Ryota Hisada, had been gone the last five days on vacation. That part didn't bother me: Ryota and I didn't get along very well and hadn't exactly gelled as partners. On the other hand, I feared that I got along too well with Ashlynn. We'd danced around each other for months, moved by whispered music that neither of us had ever acknowledged to the other. I looked at her face, transfixed by freckles spaced at random, splashed along high cheekbones that reminded me of apples. Forbidden fruit. I might have been tempted, but I hadn't yet fallen.

I turned away, moving so my eyes could make a full circuit around the crime scene. We were under the Alaskan Way Viaduct, across from the waterfront, a hundred feet or so below the main entrance to Seattle's Pike Place Market. The body rested in a space comprised of parking spots and the filthy backsides of shops that put their better looking portions forward. Traffic from the viaduct above brought a constant rumbling, punctuated at regular intervals by the clunk-clunk of tires as they passed over a joint in the roadway. Behind us, a brick wall threw off scars of graffiti, foreign symbols or tags that I didn't recognize. It was an ugly, liminal space, caught between the water on one side and the tourist-friendly front of the market on the other side. It was a space that should have been a natural repository for scraps of paper, bottles, cigarettes, maybe even the odd condom wrapper. Nothing.

"Looks like the place has been swept clean," Ash remarked.

"It's *too* thorough," I said. I paused, processing the cleanliness the killer had left us with. We looked at each other in frustration. We had no name, no history, no momentum to move us forward, nowhere to start. Just a brutally beaten body that the killer further degraded by turning it into a holder for my business card.

My phone rang, momentarily interrupting my frustration. "Marcus Brace," I said into the phone. I heard only silence in return, as though my words were in a time delay or the other person were trying to figure out if he or she had the right number.

"Marcus," a gravelly voice finally replied, "it's Mike. Mike Brey." I recognized the name but not the voice. Mike Brey was my best friend growing up. More of a brother, really, than friend. I hadn't heard from him in years. "My dad's dead," he told me as soon as he had identified himself. No small talk, no preliminaries. "He left a few things for you. We need to . . . Call me when you get to town. I'll be at the old house."

I paused in silence and tried to figure out where to go, what to do. Mike made the decision for me, hanging up before my mouth could move. I continued to hold the phone next to my ear, shocked. Mike hadn't been a part of my life for years. He'd disappeared after college. Even his father hadn't known where he was. The raspy and harried voice that had just spoken to me sounded less like that of the friend I remembered from our youth and more like something that should belong to a recently rescued castaway with sunburned skin and long, straggly hair. Someone who had almost forgotten how to speak.

I brought my phone down in front of me and ended the call. I stood like that for a moment, head down and body frozen except for my thumb, which kept rubbing back and forth over the face of the phone. In my head, I heard the Mike from my youth, the guy who would have given me shit for developing an unhealthy obsession with the feel of my phone's touchpad. Then he would have punched my shoulder, hard. I forced my head up and put the phone away. I caught Ash watching me.

"You okay, Marcus?" Her voice was softer than I had ever heard it. Her hand started to move toward my shoulder as she asked her question. She caught it about a third of the way up and it fell back by her side. Her feet shuffled a half step closer to me. I wanted to tell her all of the crazy stuff running through my head and have her help me sort it out. Like her arm, though, I only made it about a third of the way there before collapsing and re-establishing the self-contained state we were each more familiar and comfortable with.

"Yeah. Hell of a day is all. This case dropped on us and I just got a call about a funeral I need to be at. Just need a sec to clear my head."

Her mouth didn't change; her body didn't move. But her slate-green eyes lit up, filled with something simultaneously healing and needy, full of comfort for me and overflowing with what I thought was her own aching and an echo of the pain I saw when she had shown me her cigarette burn. They called to me, and scared me, with their intensity. A contagious desperation sparkled in them, infecting me with its combination of hunger and hurt. I felt something smoldering in the space between, waiting to erupt and burn us, leaving only scorched ground where we once stood. Part of me was willing to burn with her. The last few months, as my own marriage fell apart, I'd worked ridiculously hard to push aside thoughts of immolation with Ash. I feared that once the flame erupted, I wouldn't be able to extinguish it. Then that look was gone, and her eyes filmed over with the look of the everyday.

"Sure, Marcus. I'll double-check with the techs, see if there's anything else to know."

I turned, heading for the water. I grew up in Kansas, as landlocked as you can get. Seeing Puget Sound always amazes and calms me. I looked back to the crime scene. The back of Pike Place Market peeked down at me. Up above, the smells of local produce and fresh fish and stale body odor and greasy floors mingled together in a specifically Seattle stew that visitors could take back home in their memories. Tourists up above, on a different level. I thought of them moving among the vendors, crammed among the stalls, buying flowers and mesmerized by fish flying in front of their eyes.

Seeing the Market and thinking of tourists enjoying themselves up above while a murder investigation took place below made me think of Seattle's Underground Tour, another big draw for visitors. You move through several blocks of subterranean pathways that sit directly below present-day Seattle. There are spots where you look up and see people walking above you, can holler at them and see if they hear you. It is Seattle history, buried: you move among earlier streets and stores that were, literally, built over to form the Seattle I now know.

I think of Seattle's underground often. It reminds me of my job, walking among the ugly layers that others prefer remain buried and hidden. Days like today, however, allow those layers to burst forth, force you to recognize the voices that drift up from your feet, pleading for you to acknowledge them. We live on top of a palimpsest, choosing to believe that the thin crust on which we walk is all that there is, preferring to overlook what came before us and no longer easily fits within everyday life. We construct our experiences atop buried strata whose origins, we hope, remain obscured. It's easier, more comfortable, to look around and see where we are than to dig to find where we came from. Surprises wait to burst forth from what we choose to ignore, from layers we don't really want to uncover.

I reached the end of the pier, the water lapping at the support post beneath me. Even this seemingly absolute margin was a false front, the apparently native Seattle topography shaped by massive early twentieth-century regrades. After the hills were sliced to more manageable levels, the extra dirt had been purged into Puget Sound, forming the boundary I now stood above.

The sun momentarily moved from behind the clouds, replacing the wintry Seattle gray with fractured, diffusive light. Amber skies shined from the direction of the Olympic Mountains, and purple waves ran toward the pier. Sea salt air hit my nostrils. The mood I was in, I could only think of giant teardrops.

I knew exactly where my next move would take me. The killer might have left a calling card, my business card, but I had to be there for Mr. Brey's funeral. I owed him that. He was more a father to me than my genetic father had ever been. I looked down at the water, the waves moving in toward the pier, then rebounding against the support post and rippling back, with less energy this time, to sea. I needed to get back to the Breys' house; I needed to get back to Kansas.

Chapter Two

Sweat broke out just below Captain Markeze's close-cropped, graying hair when I told him I needed to leave town for a few days. I anticipated a fiery response. That's how he is. Small in height but large in determination, he possesses an iron-will that coordinates nicely with his iron-like biceps. He climbed the ranks, I think, because he views life as a contest and turns everything he can into a personal affront; then he goes and beats that challenge, demolishes whatever perceived slight he has found until he's the last one standing. I imagine him talking trash to the curl bar every morning at the gym, feeling insulted so that he can squeeze the bar into submission.

He's blustery, but he's also a hell of a leader. He'll stick up for you no matter what, fight as doggedly for anyone under his command as he would for himself. He transfers his simultaneously reactive and aggressive posture toward life onto anyone in his department, so that anything bad that happens to you is something he wants to help you crush into the dirt. He's soft like that.

He's even softer and more protective toward those of us he knows well, and I've known him for nearly fifteen years. He's almost teddy-bear cuddly once you pass the ten-year mark. He knew how important Mr. Brey had been to me. My partner Ryota would be back from vacation today. After sweating and swearing for a bit, Markeze decided that Ash, who at the moment was partner-less and floating around as extra help, could fill Ryota in on the new case and cover my desk until I got back. So here I was, on a plane back to the Plains, leaving one death behind to head home for another.

Giving me time away temporarily solved another of Markeze's current challenges. I'd managed over the past eight years to keep work and a cop's life from damaging my marriage and had always been proud of that, only in the end to have my marriage start to screw up my work. A life in irony. Other detectives were whispering about my work slipping. Judging by the sarcastic comments from the officer at the crime scene yesterday, word had slid down the ranks quicker than I had imagined. Maybe Markeze thought a few days away would help me get my head on straight, let me come back as a more effective detective and a better partner to Ryota.

"Can I take those for you, sir?"

"Not yet," I mouthed. The rail-thin flight attendant wore her long, slightly greasy black hair in a loose ponytail. I never run across those gorgeous blonde flight attendants that movies assure me will be present to satisfy my need for blankets and drinks and crisp flirtation. Kind of like nurses. Movies always oversell those too.

She'd already asked me twice if I had finished. I admired her efficiency, but maybe her perseverance was a flight regulation to ensure that turbulence wouldn't transform mini-liquor bottles into missiles destined to land in some kid's animal crackers. I had three such potential missiles arranged in a triangular launch pattern on my fold-down tray. All empty.

Saying yes to her repeated efforts to take away the bottles felt like I would be acknowledging my fear that, lately, I had started drinking too much. I'd never been much of a drinker, never the drunk detective hiding from the ugliness of crime in a bottle of bourbon. My old man was a lush. I didn't want alcoholism to be the one thing he passed on to me. I'd always believed that I was better than my parents and never wanted the ugliness I saw within them to stick to me. Their failures, including a marriage that dramatically crashed and burned, wouldn't be mine.

My ears popped. The light from outside the plane momentarily dampened as we moved through a cloud. The air felt stale around me. I sometimes wonder, given what I grew up with and what I've seen on the job, if everything isn't built on a rotten core that slowly eats its way out, leaving only mushy debris that you can't ever put back together quite right. But I always refused to use that anxiety as an excuse to short my marriage with Paige. I never cheated on her. I never wanted to be the cliché of the burned-out cop who had nothing left at home, who sought some nameless woman for a sweaty, meaningless escape from the shit I saw other people do. I had always been desperate, I guess too desperate, to carve my marriage into a nook on a cliff and protect it from everything I witnessed as a detective. And as a child.

The flight attendant, who in both front and back was as flat as a washboard (do they say that anywhere besides Kansas?), tapped me on the shoulder. "Sir," she said, "I'll take those now." She grabbed my triangular life-art sculpture of bottles. "And, your seat needs to be upright for landing." Her plastic smile cracked fractionally.

Paige had the affair. Not me. Paige demolished, from the inside, what I always wanted to keep safe from the outside. Even then I chose to keep it on life support, taking heroic measures to try and save something ready to die.

I reached up again and turned the air as high as it could go, hoping the blast would cool my face. I felt claustrophobic. Nothing like being confined in a metal tube, I thought, as I pushed away an image of Mr. Brey's impending entombment in his own metal-lined tube.

I felt the plane start its descent, noted the hydraulic rumble of the landing gear lowering. Shielding my eyes, I looked past 11F's fat stomach and out the scratched Plexiglas at my birth-land. The Kansas topography was as flat as my new friend, the efficient flight attendant: no bumps to be seen anywhere. Cars moved in slow motion beneath us, inching along the rectilinear geography. Roads that never snaked formed geographical boundaries laid out in perfect squares. It was a modeler's dream. I could see why religion flourished here. Even the geography seemed preordained, orderly, complete. Nothing to complicate the picture. Its own clockwork set in motion by an unseen hand.

Creeping down toward Wichita's Mid-Continent Airport, I distinguished, through my plastic reflection, the streets from my youth peppered with buildings both remembered and unknown. An uncanny moment, it felt both home-like and not at all like home, familiar for what I saw and remembered from my childhood and foreboding for what I failed to recognize beneath me.

I'd felt that same sense of the uncanny when I understood that Paige had willed our love to die. Nothing like divorce to force self-clarity, even if you don't like what you see. I saw for the first time my own damaged state, witnessed what I had avoided knowing within myself. Paige stripped away my blinders, erased my sense that I was better than my past. Fractures, previously hidden, glared at me. I had constructed a life made of rock candy: what appeared solid, with sharp and clear edges, dissolved under the slightest heat, melting away, leaving me with only the faint aftertaste of all that is fragile and transitory. Inside, we're all Humpty-Dumpty, nervously awaiting our fall.

I felt cramped. My knees bumped into the seat in front of me. I fought the sun again to look once more at my native ground. There were few trees anywhere below, a stark contrast to the towering conifers of the Pacific Northwest. It looked bare, open, vulnerable. Kansas might be sandwiched geographically, and perhaps even culturally, but it is also climatically exposed. Baking heat and freezing cold, bright sun and strong wind. Always the wind, whipping things up, blowing things down. The Dustbowl had ravaged this land, dirt and sand blowing in through windows believed to be sealed, leaving a loose skin of loam atop things that otherwise would have remained clean. An epidemic of erosion stripped the land, laying bare what had previously been buried.

We landed with only the faintest trail of smoke from the burning rubber floating delicately upward for a brief, almost unseen moment. Then the Kansas wind quickly blew that away. No facades here. The sturdy Plains, formed by the wind. Nothing shallow or empty withstands the stress of this environment. The sun glared off the tarmac. The airport windsock shot straight, almost military in its salute. Good, I thought. Let the wind blow and the sun shine. I could use some clarity.

Chapter Three

I had a headache right behind the eyes and halfway up my forehead. Sinus. And tension. Pressure changes and divorce and death will do that. I wanted a hot shower, an aspirin, and a nap. But I couldn't wait any longer to see Mike and learn more about Mr. Brey. I decided to skip the hotel and head straight to the house.

My drive took me about twenty minutes, short for a Seattle trip and a bit long for Wichita. Open spaces everywhere. To my Seattle eyes, the buildings all looked wide, stretched sideways and squished flat with ample grass all around.

I pulled into Mr. Brey's driveway. A one-story, gray-red brick house. The old basketball hoop still stood; I wondered if Mr. Brey ever came out to shoot by himself. Sun and rain and wind had yellowed the backboard. I saw tightly clipped bushes near the house and neatly trimmed grass around the trees. Clearly defined edges marked the boundary between yard and driveway, yard and curb. A few red winter flowers sat in a container near the front door, looking a little weepy and in need of water but obviously planted by someone who wanted to see them on his way in and out everyday. It was Mr.

Brey everywhere I looked: thoughtful and detail-oriented, careful and caring.

I climbed the two steps to the front porch. They looked older, more worn than I remembered. More cracks in the concrete. More cracks in my face now too. The shrill tone of the doorbell echoed inside the entryway.

I shifted my weight from left to right. Nervous. I felt love and a profound respect for Mr. Brey. It embarrassed him that I could never get myself to call him anything less formal. But I sent him, not my birth father, my police academy diploma. I felt I owed him. He took me into his home when I was in high school, after it became apparent I had no desire to move from Wichita to a small town in Western Kansas with my old man. My mom was already gone. My dad, always laconic and distant, didn't put up much of a fight over the *de facto* change in guardianship to Mr. Brey.

Mike finally answered the bell with a quick jerk of the door, startling me. My weight shifted as I took a small, sudden step back.

"MB, in the flesh. Back at home. Back at home." He spoke in a rush and his voice created a tinny, metallic echo in the tiled entryway. He often called me by my initials. I hadn't heard that in years.

"Mike. How you been? Besides your dad, I mean."

"You know. Gettin' by. Come on in." He spun abruptly on bare feet and went straight toward the family room, leaving me to close the door. Not exactly the tears-of-joy moment from the After-School Special Mr. Brey would have liked. But not a catastrophe either.

I followed Mike to the family room but stopped along the way to glance at the kitchen. Mr. Brey had always liked to cook, and I knew he was proud of how he had upgraded his kitchen over the past year. He and I had stayed in close contact over the years, with letters and calls at first and then emails and texts as technology made the distance between Seattle and Kansas shorter, and the emotional distance between my birth father and I seem even greater. Standing once more in his kitchen, I liked seeing the new range and refrigerator he had told me about over email. Some sort of top-of-the-line equipment. That's all I could remember. Didn't seem important at the time. It did now.

I entered the family room but had to stop immediately so that I wouldn't run into Mike, who sat on the floor, hunched over something.

"Go around. Around." He jerked his head up at me before turning back in concentration to a pile of electronics on the ground. I gingerly stepped around Mike and three sets of screws, arranged neatly from smallest to largest. He remained focused on his project. I took a seat on the sofa, the same brown one I remembered from years ago, and waited.

I wanted to see what else Mr. Brey had or hadn't changed around the house, but I couldn't pull my eyes away from Mike long enough to glance around the rest of the family room. He looked terrible. Sallow skin. Gaunt face. Bags under his eyes like he hadn't slept in ages. Pimples popping out on his forehead. A shell of the person I remembered, he appeared at least ten years older than he should have. A body abused and showing the wear.

"What are you doing, Mike?"

Instead of responding, he grabbed a screw from the middle pile and worked on reattaching one piece of electronics to another, larger piece.

"Mike," I asked again, "what are you doing?" Still no response. The entertainment center showed an empty space where the cable box should have been. "Cable not working?"

One final twist and he finished with the last of the middle pile of screws. "Dad had a dish, not cable. It's the satellite box. The lights on the front blink when the TV's not on." He still hadn't looked up, his attention devoted to reassembling the box.

"It's probably the DVR," I said. "They record even when the TV isn't on." This wasn't how I'd pictured our homecoming conversation.

He finally turned to me and opened his mouth to speak. Then he closed it, held up his index finger to gesture for me to wait, and turned back to the satellite box once more. Opening his mouth had revealed a set of teeth yellowed and rotting to black at a few points—they would've made the most hardened of dentists squirm. I'd seen it before. Meth mouth. It always reminded me of pictures we had seen in 5th Grade Health Class illustrating what chewing tobacco could do to your mouth. Except meth mouth looked like those pictures on steroids and fast-forwarded.

I'd run across tweakers on the job before, seen their entire sense of existence directed toward cleaning something already clean or taking something apart or, like Mike, putting something back together. A state of concentration an anchorite would be proud of. Mike was down to about four screws, two from the largest-sized pile and two from the smallest-sized pile. I decided to wait him out and hope he wouldn't immediately start taking it apart again.

The sofa groaned every time I moved. A loose spring poked into my left thigh. I've always subscribed to the theory that an old couch, like an old pair of jeans, makes up in comfort for what it lacks in looks. But waiting for Mike with a spring in my thigh had me reconsidering that assumption.

I stood up, stepped carefully around Mike, and went to the kitchen to get water for both of us. Mr. Brey had never mentioned Mike and meth. I debated whether he kept it from me or whether he didn't know at all.

I passed a finger along the top of Mr. Brey's range. Viking, I suddenly remembered. That was the name from his email. I picture Vikings in the midst of pillaging more than epicurean adventures, but what do I know?

The appliances might be new but the kitchen organization wasn't. Mr. Brey hadn't moved the glasses from where I remembered them from my youth. I filled two glasses from the water dispenser on the outside of the fridge and turned to head back to the family room and Mike's epic quest with the satellite box. My dress shoes left a black smudge on Mr. Brey's linoleum as I pivoted. I stopped, put down one of the glasses, wet my finger on my tongue, and rubbed the mark away.

When I made it back to the family room, I cleared my throat to let

Mike know someone else was there with him.

"Got some water for you."

He turned his head, revealing a cheek whose skin sagged off the bone, like wax partially melted and in the process of cooling and hardening. He rubbed at his throat four times in rapid succession. "Good idea, MB. Be right there."

He closed the glass door on the electronics cabinet, stepped to me, gulped the water, then wiped a few loose drops off his cracked lips with the back of his hand. He handed his empty glass back to me and used his now free hand to scratch at his left forearm. He kept scratching, stopping momentarily only to shake his arm violently, before his nails went back to work.

"Mike," I called softly, "this isn't how I hoped we'd meet again." He didn't reply. "You didn't say much on the phone when you called. When's the funeral and where's the service?"

"No funeral. No service. I cremated him."

He had more to say but I exploded, the anger at losing Mr. Brey, the stress of traveling, my disappointment at seeing Mike as a meth-head, and thoughts of my own unraveling life all bursting free. I shoved him and he flew like a rag doll onto the rickety old sofa, which seemed to groan louder than Mike at the impact.

"You called me out here after you'd already cremated him?"

He cowered on the sofa, in a seated version of the fetal position, right leg bent and drawn up near his chest and the side of his head tucked into the crook of his right arm. He looked like he weighed all of a buck thirty.

I felt the anger wash out of me as I stared at him. My shoulders slouched in sadness. My hands shook as the adrenaline slowed its course through my veins. He was bigger than this in high school, and he never would have cowered from me back then. I felt utterly, profoundly tired. And sad. And, though Mike was right in front of me, alone. I pulled his arm away from his face and sat down next to him. "Why'd you do it, Mike? I would've liked to have seen him and said goodbye." My voice cracked at the last.

His dull eyes glistened momentarily. "Couldn't risk it. They killed him. They would have stolen his body too. They're after me now. I don't sleep. So they can't sneak up on me."

I inhaled through my nose as deeply as I could and closed my eyes. I wanted to keep them closed and forget about all of this. But I found pictures of Mr. Brey stitched on the inside of my eyelids. I opened my eyes as wide as they could go, then blinked several times.

Mike's reedy voice whispered toward me. "I've seen them watching me. Watching the house. Small guy, dark hair yesterday. Small guy, dark hair today. I've seen 'im on the sidewalk."

He suddenly jumped up, faster than I would have guessed possible. "And check this." He ran toward the kitchen, turned a right angle as soon as his bare feet slapped the kitchen linoleum, and dashed toward where Mr. Brey's office used to be and, I assumed, still was.

I stopped at the kitchen, not very excited about whatever it was that had Mike so animated. Not so excited about Mike, in fact. This time I walked past the fridge to the sink. I put my glass down on the beige Formica counter top and paused to look out the window at the backyard. The afternoon sun shone like a spotlight into the right side of the sink through a gap in two oak trees, standing like sentinels on the lawn. I closed my eyes, took another deep breath and opened the cabinet above the sunbeam, where I knew the liquor would be. I grabbed the bottle of Jack. I turned my water glass upside down and let the few remaining drops of water trickle into the sink, then poured myself three fingers and went to see what Mike was busy tearing apart this time.

I found him in the office, again scratching at his arm. Blinking fast, he pointed first at a file box on the desk and then immediately to a National Geographic calendar on the wall.

"There it is, MB. Look. You'll see. It's right here, right in front of us. All of it. You'll see."

I ignored Mike for what was behind him. When he moved his finger from the file box to the calendar, he traced an arc that passed directly in front of the computer. I felt a quick shiver, then grimaced and slugged a big drink of Jack as I realized that all my emails wound through cyberspace only to end up right in front of where I now stood. I saw my academy diploma, framed in cherry, sitting near the printer. I took another drink.

Mike's voice came back to me in mid-sentence. "The same day, MB!"

"What?" I had no idea what Mike's meth musings were about at this point.

He punched his bony finger at the calendar. "The *exact*," he said hunching down into a half-ball for emphasis as he spoke, "same day he died. It's right here. Starred for us, MB. It's why I called you when I figured it out."

He pointed at last Friday, five days ago. So now I at least knew *when* Mr. Brey had died. "Mike, how did he die?" My voice was firmer than I'd intended but it brought Mike back, momentarily.

"Heart attack. But it wasn't. Look at the calendar."

Mike again pointed below a picture of big-horn sheep with a dusting of snow on their coats and steam escaping from their nostrils, at the box with last Friday's date. The wall calendar evidently doubled as a day planner and last Friday had reminded Mr. Brey of a 2:00 p.m. appointment: "meet here with Willie J." Mr. Brey had scribbled an asterisk on each side of the note. Beyond that, I didn't see what Mike was seeing.

Mike remained animated. "All we got to do is find Willie J. and then you do your cop thing and we beat him down or shoot his ass."

I pinched the bridge of my nose tightly and squeezed my eyes shut. Thanks, Markeze, for letting me leave. This was so much better than Seattle.

"He wouldn't tell me what the meeting with Willie was for. I asked, you know. Thought it might be a rehab meeting or intervention or something. Dad didn't understand I have it all under control. Perfect control. Perfect."

"Wait a minute," I shook my eyes open. "You've been living here?"

"It was Willie. I know it. Get him MB." He was excited, keyed up on the idea of chasing down the infamous, anonymous Willie J.

"You've been living here?" I repeated in disbelief.

"Just the last week or so. It was Willie, man. Had to be."

My three fingers of bourbon were down to a pinky. "What did you want with your dad, Mike? Why'd you come back home?"

"You're not listening!" He slammed a sweaty palm on the desk, leaving a handprint that slowly receded from out to in until only a few dew-like drops remained. "It's not about me. It's about Willie Mother-fucking J!"

"Fine, Mike. Tell me what Willie looks like. How tall is he? What color hair? What did the mysterious Mister Willie want with your dad?"

"You're the cop, MB. That's why I called *you*." His bony finger pointed at my chest.

I finished the Jack in one final gulp and experienced a final feeling of being played like a chump. "You shitball," I growled, reverting without thinking to our favorite teenage insult. "You weren't even here when the mysterious Willie J. showed up, were you? You weren't here when your dad had his heart attack, were you? What the hell are you doing, man?"

I braced myself for the dissembling that I knew was coming. "I had to step out, MB. I ran to the grocery store. Give the old man a little privacy, you know."

I didn't say anything. Just waited and held myself from blinking for as long as I could. My silence and solid eyes, usually directed at greasy criminals, were now pointed at my greasy best friend/brother.

He shifted his weight from one foot to the other and started scratching at his arm again. "Fine, fine, fine," he sputtered. Spittle clung to his top lip. "I had my own appointment to keep." He paused for a moment but I remained silent. "To score." The last was spoken quietly. He looked at his feet and then shifted his gaze to the file box.

"So you called me, not so I could say goodbye to your dad. Not to help bury him. But on some wild theory that Willie J., who we know only from a calendar reference with asterisks, killed Mr. Brey. But how, Mike? And Why? Did he say 'Boo' so loud he had a heart attack?" Mike stared at me, the first time he hadn't moved since I'd seen him. And then it hit me. Why I was here. "Mike, you jackass.

You brought me all the way back here so you wouldn't feel guilty about getting high while your dad died, didn't you? You could've called 911 and maybe saved him if you hadn't left. And *that's* why you called me." I jabbed him hard in the solar plexus with my finger. He crumpled in half.

He popped back up, though. Went straight to the file box and grabbed something off the lid. "What about this, super cop?" He shoved a picture and a scrap of paper into my free hand.

I set my glass down on the desk and rotated the picture ninety degrees. The black and white photo showed a young Asian woman at some kind of celebration. It wasn't at a church but it looked like maybe a wedding. She had flowers in her hair, a smile on her face. A few other Asian people, groomed but not perfectly so, filled in the background. Something seemed a little off. I couldn't put my finger on it. She was happy, no doubt about that.

I placed the picture under the other scrap of paper, which had nothing on it except foreign writing that looked like it could have been taken from a Chinese take-out menu. It meant nothing to me.

"He had the picture in his hand when he died," Mike said. "And the other thing was in his shirt pocket. And Willie J. was starred on the calendar." He was so desperate to be absolved of the guilt he felt that he was almost pleading.

I didn't say anything. Couldn't say anything. My airplane booze and three fingers of Jack melted into melancholy at being back in this house with Mike in such a bad way. But the melancholy quickly tumbled into a landslide of anger at Mike for cremating Mr. Brey and the thought of never seeing him again. And all of this gathered momentum until it caught up with being rejected by Paige. And suddenly I felt dead tired. I had reached a point where physical and emotional exhaustion came together and beat every ounce of remaining strength out of me. Skipping the hotel was a terrible decision. I wanted to sit on the shower floor with hot water beating on my face and then go lie on some anonymous hotel bed and sleep for days and days.

"I have to go." My words sounded distant to me, as though I

experienced them as a reverberation.

"MB! Look at the picture. It's like my tenth grade history project all over. Remember? MB? MB? You listening to me?"

Willie J. and projects from the tenth grade. I didn't have the energy for Mike anymore. I didn't respond. He stopped scratching at his arm.

"He loved you more than me, MB. Superstar basketball player. Superstar cop. Super fuckin' you." He spit the last with venom, aged and held back for years. I turned my eyes to the picture again, not because I believed him or felt embarrassed, but because I missed Mr. Brey.

"Remember how close you and I used to be?" I asked. "We were more like brothers before I moved in than after, weren't we?" He didn't respond. "I know it changed things for you when your dad took me in. I wasn't trying to take your place. I needed somewhere to belong and you gave me that. But that's it. I don't know exactly what happened with you and your dad, but I was never a substitute for you or better than you."

Mr. Brey had never spoken to me about why or how his relationship with Mike deteriorated after I moved in. He never blamed me for the corrosion that developed between the two of them; he also never made me think that he loved Mike any less or blamed him for any tension in the house. It was like a broken-home version of an ABC After School Special: the good father who loved both sons (genetic and damaged impostor) equally. Love would conquer all and eventually reunite the prodigal sons with their father and with each other as best friends once more. At least in the television version.

Mike again started scratching his already raw skin, bringing a trickle of blood onto the surface in irregular drops. I looked up to see him scowling at me, one side of his top lip curling toward his nose.

"My dad had an affair with your mom before she ran away. I know it. You have to find Willie J., MB. Your dad knows about the affair. I'm sure of it. Maybe you're a love child, a bastard of my dad and your mom. Your dad knows something about that picture too, count on it. He knows. Shared a woman, shared secrets. Your dad probably knows Willie." His words were rushed as he screamed his rambling incoherence at me.

I punched him. A quick left jab. He fell in a heap to the floor, blood dripping in viscous globs out of his nose and his mouth. He laughed as he wiggled a loose black tooth with his tongue. He looked happy to have been hit, happy to find a loose tooth, happy to accept physical punishment as penance. I couldn't take it. I turned my back on him to leave.

He laughed again and choked briefly on his own blood. He cleared his throat, blood thick like phlegm rattling around as he did so. "MB, I got the house. Dad left the house to me, Super Cop. He left you the folder on the desk." He laughed once more. "I got a house and you got a folder. Take the picture and the scrap of paper too. Like a bonus inheritance."

I grabbed a legal-sized, brown folder from the desk. Emblazoned in red ink, the front read "To Our Detective, Righter of Wrongs." It looked as though it had been scrawled quickly. The title sounded so far-fetched to me. I almost chuckled along with Mike. All they needed to add was "Defender of the American Way" to the bottom of the inscription and we'd be set. Mike's idea of a joke, I suspected.

I pulled one of my business cards out of my pocket and dropped it where the folder had been. "I can find you a good program." I stayed facing the door, fearing I'd beat him again if I saw him smiling and laughing and bleeding in the office where Mr. Brey should have been. "I'll help you when you're ready. You shitball."

I navigated back to the front door, down the cracked, worn concrete steps and to my rental. The cold Kansas wind hit my face and added to the weight I carried inside. I tossed the picture and folder, face-down, on the passenger seat and gunned the rental toward my hotel.

Chapter Four

I woke early the next morning. No alarm set and bad sleep and God knows I didn't want to get up early. Too much to drink and too much had gone bad with Mike.

My head hurt and my mouth felt as though it were full of cotton whose wispy strands had sucked away all moisture and threatened to choke me. The physical manifestations weren't fun, but the emotional regret from drinking too much yesterday weighed heavier. I'd been here before. Self-loathing rides piggyback on the pathways of addiction, so that those things calling to you with warm arms, promising comfort, simultaneously trigger repulsion.

I had felt that same attraction and disgust when I went through a series of meaningless one-night stands to try and fill in, temporarily, what disintegrated like magic when Paige left and showed me our relationship had been based on smoke and mirrors. I would wake up, repulsed by sensual curves that drew me in the night before, only to leave the stink of day-old sex and used latex waiting for me in the morning. Between the alcohol and the cheap sex, I'd found myself falling almost effortlessly into everything that I easily resisted when I thought my marriage was sound: super cop turned cliché cop. I hate myself for that, for finding myself weak after all those years of thinking I was strong.

I sat on the bed, preparing to get the day started. My legs felt heavy, my muscles reluctant to move, my fitful sleep not enough to wash away my exhaustion. I pushed my feet into my running shoes and headed for the door. Nothing I do yesterday becomes an excuse for not running today. I made that deal with myself years ago. If I'm hurting from drinking too much the night before, I'm reminded of that error with each step on the pavement. My fault, my pain.

I'm good at pursuing things too far, until the good transmutes into the bad, becomes over-taxing and emotionally draining or even damaging. I tell myself that enduring a little pain, witnessing or experiencing suffering, is a prerequisite for making something better in the end. I turn running into my cleansing ritual, my act of atonement for the moments when I'm disappointed in the way I've been living and the decisions I've made.

This time I ran until sweat left my shirt clinging like Saran Wrap to my torso. The Kansas wind made everything even more difficult but I didn't stop. I wanted a runner's high to burst my capillaries and flood my brain with so many chemicals that it would shut down. I wanted to sweat out the toxins from my life, the alcohol and the disappointments and the feeling that everything solid was melting away.

Back from my run, my stomach heaved as I exited the elevator and turned toward my room. A man, fairly young and gym-membership muscular, leaned against the wall by the door. Before he said a word, I knew he was local police, probably a detective.

He wore a brown suit, relatively new but slightly wrinkled, like it had been worn a few times and hadn't made it to the dry cleaners. The suit itself looked like pretty good quality. The shoes and the shirt were what gave it all away. The shirt looked thinner and cheaper than anything a lawyer or banker would wear. And the shoes were chosen for comfort and durability over fashion. They were shoes that a man on his feet for long hours each day would select. Their scuffmarks went well with the wrinkles in his suit.

"Morning detective," I grunted as I slid my key in and out of the door lock. "What can I do for you?"

He didn't answer right away. He took a slow, deliberate sip from a large, stainless steel mug he held in his left hand. He seemed determined to make me wait, maybe as payback for however long he had been waiting at my door while I purged demons by pounding pavement. A wisp of steam escaped as he lowered his coffee mug. His top and bottom lips crept momentarily toward his gums in a grimace, like they do when scalding coffee hits your tongue and your throat. Patient with me but impatient with his coffee. I figured his patience with me was the anomaly and took it as a forced move, a plan to gain the upper hand in whatever conversation we were about to have.

I had my door open and he still hadn't said anything. He looked me over and furrowed his brow slightly. Maybe I smelled from the run. Maybe he was worried that I would drip sweat on his suit. I wasn't concerned either way. "I need some coffee. Come on in."

Inside the room, I took the coffee carafe into the bathroom, rinsed it out, then filled it. I returned to find that the detective had been joined by his partner, a man in a suit more wrinkled and more out of date, but with shoes that looked almost exactly the same. Detective shoes, without question. It wouldn't have surprised me if the old guy had recommended them to the young guy. The partner had a fair-sized paunch. Bald on the top, he wore a dark brown beard flecked with gray that reminded me of pictures I'd seen of Sigmund Freud. But his eyes lit up with a mirth that I would never have associated with the German psychologist.

"Detective Brace, good morning. Caught you on your morning run, Jake tells me. And you caught me on my morning run when you got back. Too much coffee and too big a prostate. I've learned to put my detective skills to work locating all nearby restrooms wherever I go." He chuckled at himself, warmly and with a note of comfortable self-deprecation. "I'm Detective Angstrom. You and Detective Harper have already made acquaintance," he tactfully added.

He was an easy guy to like, I could tell. He reminded me of Sean, my previous and recently retired partner. Sean taught me that being likable was a valuable skill for a detective. "Get more bees with honey than vinegar, Marcus," he would quip when we first started together. All of this made Angstrom more interesting to me but also more worrisome because Sean was a hell of a good detective and could get whatever information he wanted with an effortless grace.

"What can I do for you fellas this morning? And at the risk of overloading your prostate, Detective Angstrom, can I start some more coffee for you? And please," I concluded with my most honey-filled smile, "call me Marcus." I hadn't completely tuned Sean out all those years.

Angstrom chuckled again and, in a gesture of surrender, raised both hands, the right one about half a hand higher than the left. "No, no, no. I'll never make it back to the station if I have more coffee." He lowered his right hand and held it out in my direction. "Jim," he said as we shook hands.

His young counterpart followed the lead and offered his hand. "Jake Harper." His voice was about half an octave higher than I would have guessed, and I began to wonder if his earlier silence wasn't surliness but rather a habit borne from decades of keeping his high-pitch hidden for as long as possible. He didn't answer my coffee question but took another sip from his mug after we finished shaking hands.

"Well, Marcus, I imagine Wichita's changed a lot since you saw it last. Everything's growing. We're spreading west faster than a prairie fire." Angstrom dropped conversationally into what I figured was an intentional touch of the hick. "When was the last time you were back our way?" It was a slow, easy opening, meant to do nothing but start us on a friendly give-and-take.

I'd already tired of this game. "Cut to the chase, Angstrom. I'm beginning to think your Captain has a sense of humor, pairing you and Harper together. Harper's a dullard, I can tell, and like most dullards he's mean and slow." Coffee sloshed out of Harper's mug as he slammed it on the top of the desk. I added, "And you're all sunshine and grace, avuncular and 'hail fellow, well met.' Let me guess, at interrogation time Harper plays good cop and you're bad cop?" I mimed befuddlement.

Angstrom raised his right arm from his waist, hinging it at the elbow and leaving his palm at a forty-five degree angle in a "settle-down" kind of sign, whether for Harper or me, I wasn't entirely sure. The jolly twinkle in his eyes disappeared. "Can't bullshit a bullshitter, Detective Brace." A statement, not a question. I noticed he was no longer referring to me as "Marcus" in this conversation. "Did some checking on you back in Seattle. A little professional courtesy from the boys out west. I'm charming on the phone too, you see." He winked at me, paused a half-beat, then continued. "Fantastic closure rate you have. Word is, off the record, that you have a bit of a temper and that it's been worse the last few months."

Harper stepped closer to me as Angstrom spoke. Maybe he wasn't as dumb as I thought. Closing off the physical space around a person makes the questions feel more intense, more demanding. Lean in close to someone's face and it pisses them off and makes them uncomfortable. You interrogate not just with questions but also with body language and alterations of space. I didn't like where this was going. I had no idea what they wanted, but it clearly wasn't to invite me to speak at the station about life as a Seattle detective.

"What have you been doing since your flight yesterday morning?"

He paused again. A real pause this time, one pregnant waiting for my response. I figured the odds were pretty good he knew a lot about my day already. He was testing me, waiting for me to trip up on information he already had.

"Is this the part where I say something clever about meeting with Harper's wife?" I asked. I waited my own rhetorical pause, just long enough to watch Harper shuffle forward a bit. "I'm back for a funeral. Or at least I thought there was going to be a funeral. Turns out that it already happened. After my flight I saw an old friend, more like a brother really. It was his dad who died."

"Then what?" Harper questioned, the oddly high-pitched words escaping from a tightly clenched jaw.

"Then I came here and checked in. Crashed on the bed and took a nap. Woke up around 6:00 p.m., grabbed some barbecue, then a cup of coffee from Starbucks. What the hell do you guys want?"

Angstrom took over again. "We know about Mike Brey and his dad's death. So let's get this straight. You had a long flight from Seattle. Then you find out no funeral after all that flying. Then you have to deal with your junkie brother. How long has it been since you've seen him? Did you even know he was cooking meth?" More statements than questions; I knew he was winding up for something bigger. "You see Marcus, death is stressful business. And on top of that, you're dealing with your toothless brother too. Now I bet that made you real angry. Hell, that'd make anyone just a little bit pissed off. Wouldn't you say? And I'm thinking for a guy like you...for a guy like you, who has a temper and is used to getting answers—well, let's just say I don't think a guy like you likes leaving no loose ends. But the thing is, word out there in Seattle is that you've been hitting the old spirits pretty hard lately. Clouds the judgment, them spirits. You see what I see when you put these pieces together? Just how mad were you at the Brey house yesterday?" This last question wasn't rhetorical.

"Why do you ask?" I knew better than to say anything until I was sure what this was about.

Harper piped up again. "Because, asshole, Mike's dead. Beaten to death. And a neighbor heard tires squealing yesterday and saw your rental vehicle leaving in a hurry."

The news jarred me. Though part of me knew Angstrom and Harper would be watching me closely to see how I reacted, another part of me dragged behind and couldn't control anything. I knew what was going on, but from a distance. I blinked a few quick times and my professional brain caught up with my personal brain.

"Angstrom, we both know that if you thought it was me, we wouldn't be doing this in my hotel room."

Angstrom said, "There are certain inconsistencies that make me think it's probably not you. But I wanted to see if it *could* be you, from a temperament standpoint. So I pushed at you. Wouldn't have pushed so hard but you've been a jerk to my partner. Professional courtesy goes both ways, Brace. You have a receipt from the barbecue place?"

I gestured toward a crumpled wad of papers on the desk close to Harper's mug. "Should be over there," I muttered. "Help yourself." Harper turned and started teasing the credit card slips apart and smoothing them out. There was an entire day of receipts to separate, a wrinkled paper trail starting from Seattle and ending at a Wichita Starbucks.

Angstrom nodded. "We already know that the hotel checked you in at 2:24 yesterday afternoon. Estimated time of death is a little after 6:00 p.m., which sounds like around the time you claim to have been eating dinner. Looks like you'll be okay, once we find that receipt and talk to the restaurant."

"And the inconsistencies you mentioned?"

"Well, a smart guy like you, I can't see leaving your own business card behind if you were the one to beat him to a pulp. We found it on the desk in the office."

I nodded and was thankful for the first time that Mike was such a mess. This might have been a whole lot more complicated if I hadn't left him a card and a promise to help him find treatment. I picked up a picture that Angstrom had tossed onto the bed in my direction. I felt my face turn pale and my hand, already weak from the energy used during my run and lack of food afterward, trembled slightly.

I stared at a standard crime scene photograph. Mike was lying on his stomach. Both knees had been broken, his legs twisted outward at almost right angles, like a ragdoll. His fingers, every single one of them, appeared shattered. A few small metacarpals poked through his paper-thin skin. The back of his skull caved inward, leaving a sickening crater where blood had pooled and dried black.

"We found a shard of wood in the head wound. Looks lacquered. We think maybe a baseball bat. Probably used the end cap on the fingers is my guess." Angstrom mimed someone holding a bat vertically and slamming it like a piston toward fingers splayed on the ground.

All of that was terrible but none of that was what had made my hand shake and my face whiten. I handed the picture back to

Angstrom. Harper rejoined him, holding the yellow, "Customer Copy" portion of a credit card receipt in his hand.

"We're not sure what the mess on his back is yet," Angstrom said. "The lines aren't straight at all, so it's not the easiest thing to see. Our best guess is that it's supposed to be a message or sign cut into his skin. From the blood loss and splatter, looks like it had to be done before he died. But what it means, we're not sure."

I lowered my head and shook it slowly side to side. I grabbed a towel and wiped my face, like you do when you wish you could wipe away an entire day or a bad memory. Then I carefully put the towel down on the dresser, on top of the folder Mike had given me yesterday so they wouldn't see it.

"We checked Mike's sheet. He had one, of course. Meth-heads always do. Nothing too serious. We're looking for a dealer he pissed off, or a user friend he stole from. My money is on the latter, someone mad and high or someone needing a fix. Have to be high to do that to your brother." I didn't say anything. Angstrom didn't look like he expected me to say anything. What, after all, do you say in that situation? Angstrom tossed his card onto the bed and he and Harper walked toward the door. "Don't leave town without checking with us first, okay."

"Sorry about earlier, Harper," I said as they passed. He didn't respond or even look at me. I didn't care. I wanted them to think all was kosher and that I was shaken and no longer a worry.

In truth, I thought we were probably just getting started. This was more than a brutal, tortuous killing of Mike, my almost brother. This was related, I knew, to Mr. Brey, my almost father. The unknown symbolic writing found in Mr. Brey's shirt pocket after he died was exactly what the killer had attempted to carve into Mike's flesh.

Chapter Five

As soon as Angstrom and Harper left, I locked the hotel door. I wanted to tear the folder open but I forced myself to walk slowly to the desk at a pace forty times slower than my heartbeat. Methodical plodding, I'm certain, solves more cases than passionate enthusiasm; I was doing my damnedest to force myself toward the former.

I took another deep breath as I reached the folder, ignored the sarcastic "hero" note on the front, and flipped the cover open. On top of the pile of papers that Mr. Brey had arranged were my own additions: the photograph that Mr. Brey had been clutching of the Asian woman, along with the strange symbol that was found both in his pocket and also on Mike's skin.

If Angstrom were right that the carving was done before death, then surely Mike had squirmed violently, wrenching his drug-wasted body for all he was worth in response to the blade digging into his back. No way the killer could have carved the lines perfectly, which meant that the killer had left at least two messages: one was certainly the symbol and whatever it stood for; the second message was the method of delivery—the anger and the desire to inflict pain along with the symbol. All of which raised another issue: assuming that Mr. Brey was indeed murdered, the dramatic change in killing method between Mr. Brey and Mike didn't make sense. They each became carriers of the symbol, but in radically different ways. Why torture and kill Mike with such brutality and leave Mr. Brey relatively untouched, so much so that his death hadn't even been considered a murder?

I leafed through the rest of the folder's contents, but there wasn't much there. Certainly nothing earth-shaking. No keys to the universal meaning of life or missing Zapruder film of the JFK assassination, or really much of anything personal. It looked like several pages of genealogical research that Mr. Brey had undertaken. I stared at hollow names of people long since dead and forgotten, cold cases to which I couldn't attach even the beginnings of a story.

The genealogy research condensed human existence into shorthand and purged lives of all detail. A four digit year tried to stand in for the joy of birth and trauma of death. The form reduced an entire lifetime of hopes and dreams, of failures and faults, into a solitary dash between dates. It transformed the meaningful moments of life into something empty, inscrutable, and lost forever to a casual observer.

The last page of Mr. Brey's genealogical pursuit had an illustration shaped like a tree. It might have been an oak, something meant to denote solidity and virtue and deep roots. I found Mike's name, the last in the line of Breys. Two diagonal branches connected Mike to Mr. Brey and Mrs. Brey, who had died of breast cancer when Mike was in elementary school. Mr. Brey had dutifully recorded the year of her passing after the dash of her lifetime. The diagonal lines continued into the past, a pair shooting out from each of Mike's parents as the trees branches grew bigger, into names that meant nothing to me.

My own family tree, I thought, would have presented a greater challenge for Mr. Brey. I hadn't heard from my mom since she ran out on us. She could have had more children for all I know. I didn't know what kind of lines would connect me to half-siblings never met, names and dates of birth unknown. The genealogical conventions were mysterious to me: could a dashed line, instead of the solid diagonals I saw on the Brey's tree, capture even a portion of the broken relationships between my parents and me?

I turned the pictogram over and noticed a picture at the back of the folder. I didn't know if it was included by accident or was meant as a coda to Mr. Brey's research. Mr. Brey stood in the center of the picture, his right arm around Mike and his left arm around me, the basketball hoop standing tall in the background. I remembered that day. He had set the timer on his old Nikon after an epic game of "21" in the driveway. We hadn't set the camera at quite the proper height, and the framing wasn't especially good. The tip of Mr. Brey's head had been cut off and Mike and I were off-center, with more space to the side of Mike than to the side of me. This made the photograph somehow more endearing to me; it seemed more real than today's digital pictures, where you can delete and retake and polish to no end. The imperfections of this old, pre-digital photograph held a charm for me.

I carried the basketball in the crook of my left elbow with a goofy smile on my face. Mr. Brey was wearing what now looked like a ridiculous sweatsuit combo, though I suppose back then it must not have been unusual. A plain white headband caught the sweat coming from his balding head. Mike was smiling and at least two inches taller than me. Seeing the picture of him young and smiling and happy, full of the promise of youth, jarred me. The contrasts between this picture and the two versions of Mike I had most recently seen—one alive but broken, one dead and brutalized—were absolute. It was as though I had missed an entire lifetime of events and pain and trouble in Mike's life as surely as if I were a stranger left only with a cryptic dash between the year of his birth and that of his death.

I flipped the picture over to see if Mr. Brey, as I knew was his custom, had recorded the date. It was there, neatly inscribed in the bottom right corner in red ink: July 24, 1984. Mr. Brey had left something else as well. Centered on the back of the picture, scrawled in his precise handwriting, was a directive:

Marcus, you're a son to me. This photo is my family. But you need to reconnect with your father. Don't ignore or forget what happened, but don't stop yourself from trying to build beyond it. Don't let it prevent you from making things better. I'm proud of you, Marcus.

Beneath his note was an address in western Kansas. I couldn't be sure, but it looked like the same one my father had moved to years ago when he left me. I read the missive three times. We *never* talked about my father. Probably more my choice than his, but the words waiting for me on the back of this photograph altered our pattern. It rattled me. I assumed Mr. Brey meant this as a note from the dead, as a final request that I wouldn't be able to reject or ignore.

Trying to figure out if the various pieces in front of me fit together left me bewildered. I didn't see how the photo of the Asian woman and the symbol from the murders could fit with the ancestry research and the basketball picture. I didn't know if the basketball picture and the note on the back connected to the genealogical research, or if these were two separate issues that Mr. Brey had left for me.

I returned the pages to the folder and closed the cover, determined to take a closer look at the genealogical information later to see if something fresh would strike my eye. Almost as soon as I had closed it, though, I reopened the folder and looked at the illustration of the oak tree. I grabbed the hotel-provided pen and carefully recorded the year of death for Mike and Mr. Brey. I paused for a moment, trying to make sense of this mess in my hometown. Then I gently tapped each name, grabbed the folder, and headed for the door.

I went straight to the Business Center. It wasn't much. It was the kind of place where upgrading to a quality fax/printer/scanner combo remained a low priority. But they had a fax machine, and that would do just fine. I walked to a desk and set my folder down. I grabbed a fax cover sheet, scribbled my name on the "FROM" line and my partner Ryota's name on the "ATTENTION" line. Then I found a piece of paper and opened Mr. Brey's folder. I removed the bizarre symbol that was found in his shirt pocket. It was on a small piece of paper, like something from a scratch pad one would keep near the phone. I didn't know if the fax machine could handle a piece of paper that small and didn't want it damaged. As carefully as I could, I sketched the marking onto some printer paper. I faxed it to the detective bullpen back in Seattle.

I dialed Ryota's desk to give him a head's up. Ryota had great contacts within the Asian community in Seattle; I figured if he didn't know what the writing meant, he would be able to find someone who could decipher it without much trouble.

"Detective Hisada's desk," a terse female voice answered.

"Ash?" I asked, surprised. "It's Marcus. Where's Ryota? I thought he was due back today." He and I hadn't talked much about why he was taking time off or what he planned to do. It had something to do with his wife; it usually did with cops. Being married to a cop was a test of resolve that most spouses couldn't handle. And I can't say I blame them. Beyond that, I didn't know much, which made me realize yet again what a poor partner I'd been lately. I resolved to get my shit together and be a better partner when I got back to Seattle.

"Nice to hear from you too," she said in a tone of mock hurt. "You should probably thank me, now that Markeze has me covering *both* of your desks. Ryota called in and said something came up but that he should be back tomorrow. Guess 'Right-Way' took a wrong turn somewhere, huh?" She jokingly asked, exploiting the nickname circulating around the department.

"Right-Way Ryota," they called him. He did everything by the book and took hell for it. Divorce and talking shit are two things cops are great at. He wasn't the most popular guy in the department. Most detectives, myself included, believe that life and police work aren't constructed with straight-lines. But Right-Way sees only linear intersections, ninety-degree angles, black and white print. There were rumors he once cooperated with Internal Affairs. He annoyed me at times, but after working with him for the past ten months, I knew that along with his by-the-book approach was a profound respect for words like honor and loyalty. Even Right-Way knew that only the kiss-ass types trying to make Captain talk to IA. Even though we weren't the closest of friends, I figured I could count on him, if not from affection for me, then because that's just what partners do.

"I just sent a fax to Ryota," I replied. "Need a favor. Grab it off the machine and put it on his desk, front and center. It's important, so leave a note saying that I need to know what it means ASAP. Don't let him sit on it."

"No problem. You can pay back the favor by telling Markeze to get me partnered up and into the rotation again." Ash's partner had transferred out several weeks ago and, for some unknown reason, she had been pegged with back-up duty since then.

"I'll do my best," I promised. I didn't get why Markeze had kept her isolated this long and could certainly understand why she was frustrated. "Any other bodies turn up holding my business card?" I asked.

"Nope. Your secret admirer seems to have gotten shy."

"Figures—my admirers rarely stick around. Anything come back from the lab about the woman beneath the Market?" I asked.

"Still no ID. Lab says the spot on her hand was made with a black permanent marker."

I decided that she was right about the mark itself: that it was indeed a cigarette burn—she would have told me if the lab had found something different. I wasn't sure if she didn't give me more details because she didn't want to be an "I told you so" kind of person or because she didn't like how vulnerable I had seen her when she mentioned it at the crime scene. I didn't push.

"So how are you, Marcus?" she asked, her voice completely different from the joking tone that greeted me at the beginning of the conversation. Her tone made me feel like she was as protective of my moment of vulnerability as I was around hers. It was as though she wanted to protect me from something, which was usually my job.

"I'm doing okay," I said. "I'm not sure what to make of the past few days, but I'm hanging in there." I paused, searching for stable footing yet also wanting to push beyond the familiar, move away from the rescuer and protector roles that I had exclusively adopted and failed at so completely with Paige. "I'll tell you more when I get back." It wasn't good, but how could I explain over the phone feelings of loss and anger that I couldn't fully articulate even to myself? Far easier to turn to the job and the case at hand, to contain those feelings. "Anything else need my attention?" I asked.

"Nothing pressing, but you had a visitor. An old Asian woman came in and asked for you. She didn't leave her name and wouldn't leave a message. Looked like she was about a hundred years old. Never seen her before."

"Interesting. Call my cell if she shows up again. I have to check a couple more things out here. I'll be back by tomorrow. I owe you a thank you cup of coffee when I get back," I answered.

"I know," she said. "It'll be the perfect chance for you to tell me why some of the guys call you Melville." She hung up before I could argue. I smiled and turned my phone off.

Angstrom's and Harper's request to stay local notwithstanding, I had somewhere to go. Mike had mentioned my dad to hurt me. Mr. Brey had mentioned him to heal me. After all these years, I needed to see my father again.

Chapter Six

I'd been driving for a little over two hours on my way to Western Kansas. The Kansas winds buffeted my rental back and forth along the highway. The drive from Wichita toward Colorado is mind-numbingly dull. I found it mildly interesting when the highway cut through a few limestone formations and I realized that my tires were moving over vertebrae from sea creatures that had been dead for eons. Both the limestone and the mild sense of wonder, however, soon passed, leaving me to traverse open space and open thoughts.

The western Kansas landscape seems so unchanging, so flat and monotonous, that at times it feels as though you are part of a B-movie, where the "driving" scene consists of a continuous roll of the same shot over and over again. I looked toward the horizon, searching for a hair stuck on the projector and cast onto the clouds or the telltale sign of a bird in the same flight position from frame to frame. If the gas-gauge hadn't been dropping steadily, I would have sworn that I hadn't moved in the last hour.

The confluence of geography and temperament caught my attention. Flat and wide-open, the land left precious few hiding spots. It reminded me of the simplicity bordering on gaucheness that my memories associated with dinnertime on the Plains. A place where desserts consisted largely of instant chocolate pudding in various disguises: "Texas Panhandle Yum-Yum" and "Mud Pie," with their chocolate pudding and Oreo crust. The land of casserole cooking, where tater tots were combined with hamburger or canned tuna and maybe some frozen peas. I remembered kitchens adept at transforming Jell-O into an epicurean amber that trapped slices of apples and oranges and bananas inside its jiggling mass.

There's more, though, to my home ground and its people than what first glance reveals. As with the landscape, so with the people: the repetition and minimalism lull you to sleep until you miss vitally important deviations that don't fit within what you have been conditioned to see. In truth, everywhere I looked I had found complexities beneath the surface, waters roiling below a calm top. Mike was a junkie. Mr. Brey carried a mysterious picture of an Asian woman whom I had never seen and he had never mentioned. My mother had run off with a guy my father had worked with at Boeing. My father had then run off, abandoning me to a family now murdered. I had a killer to get back to in Seattle and had thought Kansas would be simple compared to the chaos back there. It wasn't exactly working out as planned.

I lowered the window to let the wind race across my face and regain a sense of moving forward. The air hung heavy with moisture. The metallic smell of ionization from imminent thunderstorms combined with the odor of farms animals and the fecundity of crops growing and being fertilized. I had forgotten both the smell and feeling of the air just before a Kansas thunderstorm. Seattle receives a lot of moisture but it's gentle and persistent, like a force of erosion. Here the sky bursts open and everything pours out with fury. There's a terrifying, terrible beauty in the force of thunderstorms on the Plains, as lightning jags across the sky and thunder rattles pictures hanging on the walls and gutters overflow with rivers of rain. I could feel and smell all of that hanging in the air, teasing me and throwing me back to childhood storms.

Thirsty for a drink and hungry to see Ashlynn, I wanted something or someone to hide in and ignore how broken I felt. I had given pieces of myself to Paige and when she ran off I lost not only her but also part of who I was. The job and its constancy of death had taken other pieces, slowly and stealthily. At times I felt as though I had more holes than solid matter remaining. And now I was driving to see a man who I hadn't talked to in years. A man who I had pushed down and written out of my life as completely as I could. I was driving forward, full of fissures and doubts, to see a man who had punched one of the largest and earliest holes in me.

My earliest image of my father is of the pores of his skin. Thick pores, like craters to a small child's eyes. Filled with dirt if he'd been working outside. A scarred one on his nose that I remembered with a strange clarity. My image of my father moves outward from these pores. I see the pores before I see him.

When I do picture him, he's always expressionless. Neither a glower of anger nor a smile of delight. Not even a wry grin that could be interpreted either way depending on circumstance. He's completely self-contained in my memories of him. Even after my mom ran away. Maybe that's *why* my mom ran away from him. He had a taciturn approach to life, a Plains stolidity that was more confusing and disturbing to me as a child than if he had been filled with scowls and angry howls.

I had no idea how our conversation would go, though I was close to finding out. Farmland would soon shift to Main Street, which I could see only a few miles away. I tapped my thumbs nervously on the steering wheel. Pulling *any* information or emotional insight from my father would be harder than most of my interrogations. He locked everything inside, so that you could never get an accurate measure of his emotional resources. Truthfully, I wasn't sure if I even wanted to peel back the curtain to discover what lay beneath.

I have my suspicions, but to this day I don't know what my father felt after my mom left, or what he felt as he dropped me on Mr. Brey's doorstep and ran. As a teenager, I decided that my father loved my mother more than he loved me. While I was around, I think, he could never forget her or get over her decision to leave him. Every time he'd look at me, he saw a reminder of his failed past. I became a genetic millstone around his neck. Then again, he never talked to me about anything, including my mom, so this was just speculation to fill in the gaps.

The most painful gaps, I've learned from my job, are those most in need of narrative explanation. Dealing with victims of crime or people who have lost loved ones to it, I have seen how aimless and confused we become when all we have are gaps that leave us unable to resolve WHY? You find an answer, you make up an answer, or you are lost.

Off the shoulder of the highway a beat-up sign warned of a speed zone ahead. The sign's top left edge, the part nearest the road, curled backward where it looked like a baseball bat had smacked it; the bottom right was pocked by a plague of BB-gun fire. Small town youth with nothing to do but take out their angst on innocent highway signs, I decided. I smiled slightly, both at the thought of skinny rural adolescents in Wranglers and cowboy hats beating up on the sign and at the fact that my father had settled in what I fully expected to be a complete backwater town.

I slowed and entered the main drag, with John Cougar Mellencamp (or was he just John Cougar or just John Mellencamp now?) irrepressibly filling my head. My wheels bumped along rhythmically to the beat provided by an honest-to-goodness brick road on what certainly *had* to be named Main Street. Along either side of the brick road, diagonal parking spots spurred out, pointing toward a small-town hodgepodge of businesses: a café, a hardware store, a craft shop full of sewing machines and scrapbooking paraphernalia, and a combination music and bookstore. It was Sunday and all the shops appeared closed for the day. At the end of the strip sat a shiny new McDonald's, out of place and yet somehow more comforting and more "real" to me than any of the other shops I saw.

I found my father's place without difficulty. He lived in a small, one-story house. Not at all what I had expected. It looked tired. It was a yellowish house but I had the impression that once upon a time it had been a cream color and had aged into its current yellowish hue, like a piece of lace long forgotten. The upkeep had been neglected, that much was clear. The brick chimney showed a large, crooked crack and had shifted slightly toward the backyard. Overly worn shingles shimmered smoothly from the roof. Scales of the yellowish paint flecked away from the siding. The grass was thin and patchy.

All of it surprised me. I remembered my father as a quiet, withdrawn man, but I also recalled a man who never let responsibilities slip. "At least until he left you with Mr. Brey and took off," an unbidden voice whispered inside my head. He always kept busy in his workshop. Laconic, he seemed to talk more with his hands than his mouth, constantly building and repairing things. To see his house neglected and in need of upkeep didn't fit within what little understanding I had of him. I shut down the rental, wondering whether my memories, or my father, had slipped over the years.

My palms were sweaty but the backs of my hands, especially my knuckles, dry and itchy. My legs felt heavy from the drive. A million things suddenly demanded my attention and kept me in the car. I gathered myself, then opened the door and paced off the distance to the front door. The entrance was guarded by a screen door, the spring slightly oxidized and the aluminum frame dented down low, where you would try to catch it with your foot to push it open or stop it from closing on you. I pushed the doorbell. And waited.

He opened the door. Slowly, no hurry at all. His face had wizened during the years we'd been apart, so that I could see portions of the man I knew underneath but couldn't quite recognize who he had become.

"Marcus," he said with no inflection, "come on in." His eyes might have sparkled for a millisecond when he saw me on top of his porch but his face gave no other tell and I couldn't even be certain about the eyes. He moved further into the house. He didn't hold the door open for me but somehow it didn't seem like a mark of rudeness. It fit with his flat voice and struck me as the action of a man who didn't expect anything from the universe and therefore didn't give anything back either.

I entered his dilapidated house. "Thanks, Padre," I said as I crossed the threshold. It sounded stupid. I have no idea why I said "Padre" except that I didn't really know what to call him. I had hours during the drive to think about this but somehow it never crossed my mind. "Dad" seemed out of the question—too chummy. "Father" was *too* formal and inaccurate and might make me appear meek, as if he were still in charge. Richard, his given name, seemed out of the question; he'd think I'd come back to be a smartass. So I went with "Padre," and regretted it immediately.

He led me into the living room, a formal space that looked like it had never been used. The coffee table wore a coat of dust, undisturbed by a casual handprint or even the mark of a coaster. Small clods of dirt on the worn carpet highlighted a path from the front door, through the living room, and into what looked like the kitchen. Muddy shoeprints, I thought, that had dried long ago and never been vacuumed.

My dad/father/padre gestured toward a stiff looking chair. "Have a seat." He sat on a gray loveseat, a starburst of dust jumping off of the cushion and into the bright light as his weight came down. He stood up again, before, it seemed, the dust had even resettled. "How about a drink." Statement, not question. He followed the path of the dirt crumbles into the kitchen.

I trailed behind, not comfortable in the stiff chair and not wanting to sit with nothing to do while I waited for him.

The kitchen, obviously more used than the living room, looked even worse in terms of dirt. Used dishes, several days worth for a lone bachelor, sat by the sink. Food had petrified on the forks and spoons and knives resting atop the plates. The cabinets near the stovetop were splattered with cooking grease, which had hardened into translucent droplets.

Yet in the face of this neglect, I noted that he had at some point installed modern under cabinet lighting, a tile backsplash, and elaborate cabinet handles that looked like changes from whatever had been there originally. The room wore the marks of a man who once cared, but no longer did.

He grabbed a bottle of cheap scotch that was already sitting on the counter. Then, without saying a word or even looking at me, he put the bottle back on the counter and reached to the half-sized cabinet above the refrigerator. He pulled down a Balvenie, Twelve-year, which I took must be the scotch he saved for special occasions. After pouring me a generous serving, he handed me my drink. Then he grabbed a glass for himself from the counter, a small amount of amber liquid already in the bottom. I gathered that this wouldn't be his first drink of the morning.

I was mildly surprised that he had already been drinking. Not at all surprised that he typically drank cheap, metal screw-top stuff. The man was tight with his emotions and even tighter with his money. His cheapness, I remembered, had always driven my mom crazy. I don't know exactly why she ran away from my father, but I always picture her seducer waving baubles and expensive gifts that must have seemed even richer for the contrast they made compared to her life with my tightfisted father.

"Thanks," I muttered and raised my glass in a half-salute, something I must have seen on a television show somewhere. It was an unconscious reaction that, once completed, made me feel terribly self-conscious. The Balvenie peat rose into my nostrils as I took a gulp. The smoky charcoal acted like a blast of menthol from Vick's Vaporub at a crime scene. It functioned admirably as an obscurant, but as soon as it faded, I picked up smells I hadn't distinguished or even noticed before.

Dankness curled into my nose, a smell of mildew that matched well with the dirt and dust I had seen everywhere. This was clearly a house where cleaning was beyond a low priority; it wasn't even thought of. Looking at my father, his thin shoulders crouched and almost crab-like, I knew the dirt wasn't simply that of a bachelor who didn't know how to clean or didn't want to be bothered by cleaning. This was the dirt and mildew and mustiness of one who had given up.

Rather than directing us back to the living room, he leaned

against the counter, drink clutched near the center of his chest. He stared at me for a long count, then cleared his phlegmy throat. "Have to admire someone with enough foresight to cask away scotch for twelve years and not touch it," he croaked.

It sounded rehearsed. Not necessarily like something he had practiced in front of a mirror but like something he had once said to someone else and had received a favorable response. A joke he had told before and now told again. Not like a craftsman does, to hone his timing or his delivery, but as a conversational crutch for a man fundamentally handicapped in that area of life. He suddenly seemed like a nervous schoolboy to me. A grown man filled with anxiety upon my visit. A man quiet all these years not necessarily because he didn't want to share, but because he didn't know how. He dropped hackneyed phrases and twice-tested conversational markers like a lost child drops breadcrumbs to help find his way out of the wilderness again.

I didn't answer, reveling in the newfound realization that my father felt even more uncomfortable than I did. Looking at me expectantly, he seemed to be waiting for the next link in the conversational chain he had started with his witty insight about aging scotch. When I didn't play along, he took another large drink, emptying his glass. Turning for a refill, his gaze dropped away from my face.

After refilling, with the cheap stuff this time, he immediately took another drink. The edges of his mouth momentarily curled downward in a tight grimace as the cheaper scotch burned its way down. "What are you doing here, Marcus?" he asked, now stripped of all attempts at conversational banter and moving directly to the point. A man most comfortable when his hands were occupied, he moved his left along the lip of the Formica countertop, as though he were tracing the bevel to verify its consistency. His right hand held his scotch, but his index finger curled upward and tapped incessantly on the lip of the glass. "Must be a good reason you're here."

I really didn't know how to answer his question. What should I say, that I came to fulfill Mr. Brey's last wish, though I didn't fully understand it? That I stood in front of him after all these years because of a murder investigation? That even though I hated dwelling on old pains, a secret part of me inexplicably wanted to take this side trip to the past?

I took a drink and avoided his question. "What have you been doing out here? It's a long way from Wichita." I still couldn't bring myself to add a "Dad" to anything I said.

"I run the hardware store," he answered. Then, almost like an afterthought, he added, "I like that it's not Wichita." He didn't elaborate.

His eyes were shiny from drink. His bony fingers jutted out especially sharply at the knuckles where the skin seemed thinnest. His hair, dark brown in my childhood memories, showed gray tending toward a dirty white. The nose that I remembered first for its dirt-filled pores had been broken at some point since he had left me with Mr. Brey. Given the way he was downing the scotch, I guessed a barroom brawl.

But his voice struck me the most. I remembered it filled with authority. As a child I understood that my father didn't speak much, so when he did start to talk, you had better pay attention. It was always a voice whose words were resolute, planned out and double-checked internally before being spoken aloud. Even his words seemed crafted in his workshop, a conversational corollary to the "measure twice, cut once" advice he followed on all of his home projects.

His current reedy voice struck my ears as an aberration. Each syllable cracked, as though he had just woken up or just had a breathing tube removed from his throat. His vocal cords sounded as neglected as his dirt-filled and mildewed house, as tired as his slouched, thin shoulders looked.

Everything I had seen and heard—his movements, his voice, his face—manifested resignation. He reminded me of someone who had become accustomed to being knocked down and no longer railed against the unfairness of life when the invisible blow cuffed him atop the head, as it had so many times before. I had the impression that he lived and drank under the assumption, or maybe the desire, that he wouldn't make it to old age. Yet somehow, despite years of emotionally wasting away and profound alcohol abuse, his physical body had inexplicably kept chugging along.

"You always were good with projects and building things," I said. "The hardware store sounds like a natural fit." He didn't respond. He seemed to know I had given the near compliment solely to be saying something. I suddenly realized that all of my interrogation tactics could have been absorbed from my days interacting with my father. Holding my tongue to let the suspect fill the empty space was a direct descendent from this taciturn man. His silence always pulled words out of me, as though any lulls were my responsibility to fill, the quiet pauses my fault.

I snapped. Perhaps it was this strange need to speak in the blanks left by my reclusive father, or anger at the realization that I still fell prey to that trap, or repressed frustration at this man being more a stranger than a father to me. Whatever the reason, as the current pause became more oppressive, I let loose with the same accusation that Mike had used to try and hurt me. "But maybe you spent too much time on the projects and not enough on your family. Is that why mom slept with Mr. Brey, because you weren't there?" My accusations came quickly. It was the first time I'd ever yelled at him.

He slammed his glass down on the counter. Hard enough to crack the glass or chip the counter, though I don't think either actually occurred. His eyes bulged and the left side of his top lip curled upward, giving him the look of a mangy, malnourished dog preparing to harness its strength for one final attack. But then the lip lowered and the eyes narrowed to mere slits.

"A lot you don't know, son. A lot you don't understand. Can't understand." Another pause, one that I managed to leave empty this time. "Your mother never slept with Mr. Brey."

Silence again, and again I resisted the urge to speak. This time it was he who filled the awkward nothing that floated like sheet ice on the ocean between us.

"I would never have left you with him if that was true." His reed-thin voice sounded even thinner. Wounded. "A victim of cuckoldry and then a victim of a kidnapping by the same man. That's what you think of me," his voice trailed off.

He seemed more exposed to me over these past few minutes than he ever had before. I started to believe that his quiet exterior hid complexities I had never guessed were there. Maybe my father's emotional landscape, much like the physical landscape I had seen on the long drive out here, wasn't barren but rather an adaptation to survive the dangers of exposure, endure gusts and extremes. I decided that he wasn't so much emotionally destitute as he was an emotional miser, hoarding everything for himself. He languished with emotions and pains that he could never forget but also never share. Like all misers, though, he misunderstood how currency works: financial and emotional resources are only valuable if put in circulation, not when hidden away from everyone else. Rich to himself, bankrupt to all others.

"I respect Mr. Brey," my father continued. "He's a good man. I'm shocked he would poison you against me like this."

My nervousness evaporated. Not because my father and I were at last communicating. Rather, I could feel myself slipping into my detective persona. It felt comfortable, and comforting. I realized that I could play the silences against him. I could counter his emotional miserliness with my own professional detachment. Father and son bonding at its finest. I decided to withhold Mr. Brey's death for now. I would dig out whatever guilt or anger or insecurity lurked like a darkness within his interior depths.

I said, "You have a different story for me? I'm all ears." I tried to sound slightly incredulous. "Some kind of cover-up you can paste on top of everything after all these years?"

He rubbed both palms along the thighs of his worn-out, faded Levis. His hands moved slowly but with a great deal of force, so that his jeans bunched first in ripples and then in denim waves as his hands moved closer and closer to his knees. He repeated the action as he took a few quick breaths.

"I'm sure you remember her as a saint, but like I said, there's a lot you don't get. Your mother cheated on me. You know that. She ran out on me. On us. What you don't know is that the guy was my boss, John Robinson. John. Everyone who worked for him called him John. She called him Jonathan when she told me she was leaving. Took me a second to figure out who the hell she was talking about." He swallowed, lips pursed tightly as the saliva and whatever emotion he was suppressing worked their way back down inside him. "Your mom destroyed me when she cheated. That I could accept. But not what she did to you. That's no kind of payback. But she never slept with Mr. Brey. I'm sure of it."

Done with his confession, he moved back to his glass of scotch, draining what remained and then refilling. I held my glass out also, for a refill, and maybe as a kind of peace sign. He generously poured, perhaps as his own version of a peace sign.

A silence fell again, but neither of us filled this one. We sat with our scotch and our thoughts, recovering from the latest outpouring. Small to other families, I'm sure, but a veritable flood of connection for us.

Sharing drink with my alcoholic father made me wonder about genetics. There's a gene for alcoholism, I know. I wondered if emotional inadequacies could be passed down genetically as well. Was it coded within my genes that I, like my father, would be emotionally handicapped, would cling too tightly to a relationship at the same time that I stayed distanced, doomed to end up crushed when the relationship then failed? I pictured Mendel with his pea plants, charting physical deformities from one generation to the next and wondered if a black heart could be genetically transmitted too.

I took another drink and pulled myself back from such musings. Bullshit excuses for a weak mind, I thought. Eschew the easy answers and work the evidence, locate the patterns and evaluate the soundness of those patterns. That's what my detective work taught me. If this were a case of genetics, I'd need to know what my mom had given me. But I had nothing to go on. She remained even more of an enigma than my father. She was an uncrackable cipher because I didn't even know where she was. I felt drawn to my father and his errors because he represented the last line of defense. Being present the longest and abandoning me last, my father had become the unlucky placeholder for all parental failures.

All of this broke to pieces the simple answer that I was miserable at relationships because of the way a few proteins combined on my double-helix. We're more than a genetic code, more than an automaton engineered to reproduce past mistakes over and over again until the earth collapses. Thinking of what Mr. Brey had given me, I felt guilty for wallowing in self-pity and blaming the past or my genes. Mr. Brey served as more of a father to me than the man now slouched in front of me. I didn't want to erase Mr. Brey by finding a hidden tie to the man who had abandoned me years ago. Irrespective of whatever genetics had given me, Mr. Brey had helped mold and change me into something better.

"You're right," I said, "Mr. Brey was a good man. The only reason I'm here is because of him." I pulled out the note Mr. Brey had left me and handed it to my father. "Any idea what Mr. Brey had in mind with this?" I asked.

My father was slow reading the note. He handed it back. A small, crooked smile was plastered on his face. "Ain't that sweet," he said.

I felt my blood pressure rising. "He's dead," I said. "They both are. Mr. Brey and Mike were murdered. Mr. Brey wanted me to see you again. That's why I'm here. To honor his request. To honor Mr. Brey." My phone vibrated inside my pocket. A few minutes earlier, I would have loved to answer it and have an excuse to extricate myself from the silence and stumbling. Now, however, I let it go to voicemail. "I think a hug between you and I is out of the question. But I can't abandon Mr. Brey's wish. So here I am."

"Murdered? Like a robbery gone bad or something?" He was processing out loud, something I had never seen this reticent man do before.

I really had no idea what Mr. Brey expected when he asked me to come see my father. I didn't believe that our past could be overcome, that we could build upon something so rotten without having it collapse onto itself. A quick visit and several rounds of scotch weren't going to create a new foundation to cover the chasm of all of these years. This was, I figured, as good as it was going to get between the two of us. So I made a silent toast to Mr. Brey and slipped back to where I was most comfortable: I took a swig of my father's scotch and moved effortlessly back to detective mode.

"No, not a robbery gone bad," I answered. "Two separate murders, days apart. Targeted intentionally. For what reason I don't know. Yet."

My father collected himself and, it seemed, slipped back to the persona he felt most comfortable with as well. Quiet, held back, waiting. The difference for me now, though, was that I pictured his silence differently: not as a rock-solid exterior that grew out of an equally tough interior, but more as bait meant to draw you in. He reminded me of an anglerfish in the deep ocean, equipped with its own lure to attract prey close enough so that it could then pounce and devour them in one large gulp. I saw my father as ravenous to consume anything that he could find wandering close to the lonely emotional spaces in which he lived; he waved his silence back and forth, drawing words and emotions out of you so that he could gobble them up and store them in his own interior life.

I added, "How about these? What do they mean to you?" I pulled from my shirt pocket the picture of the Asian woman and the symbol that the killer had left with Mr. Brey and, in a different way, with Mike.

My father took the picture and the symbol from my hand. He looked at the symbol first, then turned to the picture. He took his time with each, particularly with the picture.

"Neither of these looks familiar. Don't know a thing about either of them," he said in a monotone as he handed them back. He stopped, turning inward and looking to the past again. "It's been years since I've seen or talked to Mr. Brey," he eventually continued, "and I never really knew Mike at all."

I wondered whether he felt the same about me as he did about Mike, whether he felt he barely knew me too. Maybe he thought he knew me better than he did, falling prey to that common parental error of seniority: parents delight as their babies learn to walk on their own but have difficulty accepting the cognitive and emotional jumps that children make as they grow into adults more damaged and injury-riddled than they want them to be. It is a peculiar inability to see, a parental myopia that blurs the pictures they have of their children, filing the rough, real-life edges away until they are, once again, baby-smooth.

My father's thin voice creaked forth. "He was the best man I ever knew. The best man, I imagine, you ever knew." The last part was spoken even more emphatically and was, I suspected, as close to an apology as my father would ever get.

He continued, this time with very little pause, either to cover up for the near-apology or to deliver the rest of what sounded very much like a eulogy before he changed his mind and decided to keep it within his internal emotional vault. "He was the best when you were at your worst. He always tried to help out, be there for you."

I found it odd to hear my father speak of Mr. Brey this way. Just by speaking of him, my father tainted my memory of Mr. Brey. Everything was praise, and what he said rang true with what I remembered as well, but I hated that my father knew him the same way. I wanted to believe that my father was so damaged that he couldn't see the world right, that he possessed some enormous internal flaw that skewed his life and therefore partially explained why he could leave me.

"His concern," my father started again after draining the rest of his scotch, "was always about family, roots in the past and growth in the future. Your mom leaving..." His voice broke. "Your mom leaving killed me. I shut down. Had terrible thoughts. I wasn't right for a long time. And he knew it. I think he waited and watched from his window so he could check up on me. Every morning he would ask me, 'How ya doing today, Brace? How's Marcus?'"

My father stopped again. He tried to take a drink from a glass already empty. He gripped the glass with both hands at his sternum and lowered his head, to look for the few drops that remained or for a silent prayer or for shame.

He said, "When it got really bad, when *I* got really bad and really drunk and really approached the edge, he told me, 'Think of Marcus. Think of Marcus.' He, and you, saved my life."

I was stunned silent. I suppose this was exactly the kind of thing that Mr. Brey had hoped I would learn when he directed me here. But I didn't know what to do or how to respond. I wasn't sure I could let go of the disgust I had harbored all these years. I wasn't sure I could revisit a past that I had already closed off, a history that I didn't want to rewrite because doing so would be even more painful than living with the contempt and hurt and hatred that comprised my understanding of the broken-down man standing in front of me.

A fractured laugh escaped from my father's throat as he reached for the bottle to refill his glass. It sounded small and laced with melancholy, the kind of forced laugh that you offer when you've just said something you swore to yourself you would never reveal to anyone.

He was good and loaded now, something that I felt sure happened daily with him.

He said, "I'm ashamed of myself compared to him. You know the best I could do? My way of comforting him when he was falling apart? I brought over a bottle and got him good and drunk." His sad, soft laugh came out again. "This was after Diana, his wife, died. You didn't really know her, did you?" He didn't wait for a response. "I wasn't there for him during the cancer. Thought that was something he would need to figure out privately. Didn't want to intrude. Then the best damn thing I could do when she died was share a bottle with him."

I started to feel claustrophobic around my father. The dankness of the house attacked my nostrils once more. All these years I had cursed him for keeping so much inside himself, for being a closed book to everyone around him. Now I had the impression that I was seeing what he saw every day; it was stifling and choked away my air. Under the quiet surface lurked a man who hoarded everything and forgot nothing. A man who presented silence outside but seethed inside, who constantly relived past mistakes and shortcomings until they became an iron trap that slowly squeezed the life out of him.

"He was a philosophical drunk," my father reported. "Said stuff that night I still think about. Talked about feeling lost and alone. About family ties disappearing—poof—before you." My father threw his hand out as though performing a magic trick, his closed fist opening wide with the word "poof." Then he fell quiet once more. I wasn't sure whether he was recalling more of Mr. Brey that night or thinking more about our own family life disappearing. He weaved to the right and almost fell over.

He caught the thread of his story again. "He said Wichita wouldn't be the same without Diana. Thought about transferring from Boeing in Wichita out to Seattle. Said the dreariness and rain would fit him well. Also a way for him to get back to his roots."

I found myself stuck on the idea that Mr. Brey had considered moving to Seattle. He never mentioned anything of the sort to me. Maybe it was just drunk rambling to my father, who fortunately or unfortunately seemed to keep everything like a court stenographer inside himself, but it didn't make sense to me. Mr. Brey, in fact, seemed to hate Seattle. When I told him I was moving, he said it was an isolated, dreary place at the edge of the country, tailor-made for dreary and depressing people. He had never visited me in Seattle. Not once. Now my father claimed that he had once considered moving there, that Mr. Brey had hidden roots in the Pacific Northwest.

I said, "That can't be true. You said Mr. Brey thought about transferring to Boeing in Seattle, that he had a family history there. I don't understand."

"I don't know," he said. He sounded decidedly drunk. "He hated being in Wichita after Diana died. Made perfect sense to me later, after your mom left," he rambled. "I hated Wichita after that. The whole goddamned place reminded me of her and her leaving. Despised Boeing. Felt like everyone snickered at me behind my back. Laughing at me because your mom took off with my boss."

"But any reason for Mr. Brey to go to Seattle in particular?" I pressed.

"That's where Boeing's main plant was," my father said. He looked at me like I was an idiot.

"I know that," I said. "I live there. But what was that stuff about family in Seattle? He said something about roots, right?" Frustration washed over me as well, but somehow the anger bubbling up between us was comforting.

He was shit-faced. He said, "You live there? Seattle, huh? Dreary and rainy I bet."

"Right, dreary and rainy, rainy and dreary. What about Mr. Brey and Seattle and roots?" I asked again.

"Dreary and rainy," he repeated quietly and I wasn't sure if he was processing what I had said or if he was again remembering Mr. Brey's words about Seattle from all those years ago. Then he picked up the story again. "Boeing was a family tradition for them. He worked there. His dad worked there too. Said his dad got hired on in Boeing in Seattle after the war. He loved family, you know. Loved genealogy," he trailed off again for a few seconds. He took a pull of scotch. "Then his dad volunteered to transfer out to Wichita. Mr. Brey thought about going back. Completing the circle. Never did it, of course."

"What circle? Him and his dad?" If any of this were true, I didn't see why he'd hide it from me. I needed another scotch. Things didn't make any sense and were in fact becoming even more bizarre the more that I uncovered.

He said, "It was just sad drunk talk. Sad and guilty talk. Guilty for being alive when his wife was dead." He cleared his throat. "Talked about wishing he could change the past and erase what had happened. That it had to have been a mistake. Said part of what he had always trusted completely was taken from him. Then I made him go home. I didn't want to hear more of his pain. A man regrets it the next day when he lets too much out like that."

As if to emphasize this belief, he stopped leaning against the counter, staggering to find the vertical. Not looking at me, he swerved out of the room, throwing a slurred, "Be right back," over his shoulder as he left. A few minutes later, he returned with a smile and—of all things—a sword. It was curved and protected by a black leather sheath. Scotch sloshed over the edge of his once more refilled glass as he thrust his arms toward me as if bestowing something of great significance.

"Crazy, crazy shit," he said. "He tried to give this old sword to me that night. We went into his house and he was all slobbery about giving it to me. Some kind of heirloom. A World War II treasure." He smiled again, almost as though he were making fun of Mr. Brey's foolishness. "I didn't take it. He was drunk and I didn't want the damn thing anyway. What am I going to do with a sword, for Christsakes?" That was a question I certainly couldn't answer, though it did raise another one for me.

"So why do you have it, then?"

"Huh?" He was drunk and confused.

"Why are you standing here with a sword from Mr. Brey if you refused it?"

He smiled again. "I took it later. He offered it to me again and I took it. Gave it to me when he took you in. Before I moved out here." We sat in another one of our silences, then he extended his arm, pushing the sword to me at chest level. "You take it," he said, his eyes breaking away from our stare. "Sure he'd rather you have it than me. What was I supposed to do with a damn sword?" he mumbled.

I took the sword from his hand and stepped back. It felt like an apology of sorts from my father, a gift given instead of words spoken. I felt lousy. Mr. Brey had taken me in; in return, my father got a sword that he had never wanted. Was that the best Mr. Brey could offer? Was that all I was worth?

But I took it. Not because my father had offered it, but because it had once been Mr. Brey's. He had evidently treasured it. I still felt lousy. But maybe there would be markings on it that matched up with the Asian symbol I'd found. I'd have to find out why this sword meant so much to Mr. Brey.

My father's eyes looked glassy, from the alcohol and from focusing on the past. He appeared close to passing out. Just as my father had felt after Mr. Brey's outpouring all those years ago, I felt uncomfortable getting so close to the pain and emotional turmoil that were always near my father's side. I saw him stuck in the past, moving again and again from mistake to mistake, pain to pain inside his head, trying to numb himself each day with scotch. Sometimes uncovering what is hidden isn't as rewarding as you hope.

I wanted to leave. I had fulfilled Mr. Brey's last wish for me, but I doubted I would have a talk like this with my father again. He certainly wouldn't track me down; the guy didn't even know that his only son lived in Seattle. And I didn't plan on coming back here for more drunken interactions with the man who had left me years ago but seemed even more damaged than me. I didn't have the strength for it. So I risked one more emotional connection with the man collapsing in front of me.

I asked the questions that had circulated within me over and over all of these years: "Why, Dad, did you never come back for me? How could you just forget about me?"

No pause this time from him. Maybe my questions weren't as difficult for him as they were for me, or maybe he had thought about them many times before and already had an answer. "Can't change what's done, can you?" he answered, simply and with surety.

I didn't reply. I set my glass down on his counter and turned to leave.

I heard my father scuttling his ragged claws behind me. "Marcus, wait," he hollered after me. I thought this would be the moment when he finally apologized to me. "Marcus, have you heard from your mom? Does she ask about me? Tell her I forgive her," he drunkenly implored.

I hauled myself into the rental, bug-spattered and dirty from the long-drive, and slammed the door. My last image was of him in the doorway, leaning against the jamb for support, one hand clutching the glass of scotch as though it were a natural appendage, his thin shoulders slumped in exhaustion, his chest caved inward. I knew I'd never see my dad again.

Chapter Seven

I retreated on autopilot toward the McDonald's I'd seen earlier, not really thinking about or seeing much. The visit with my father had left me both emotionally and physically exhausted. As I had expected, he was a mess. Not, however, for the reasons I had suspected. I had pictured him as an emotional void, a man who didn't give voice to any feelings because he had so few of them. After my visit, though, I decided that instead of being cold, he was in fact burning up inside with all that he could not express. Incapable of moving forward, he stagnated within the trauma of his past errors and past pain, letting them destroy him from the inside out.

I pulled into an empty parking spot beneath an elm tree, remembering the little helicopter-like seed pods that reminded me of my youth in Kansas. I thought through the new information I had garnered. My father's revelation that Mr. Brey's family had roots in Seattle challenged my understanding of the man who had taken me in. The explanation that Mr. Brey's family had moved from Seattle to Wichita because of Boeing certainly made sense logically: the airplane supergiant forged a distinct, viable connection between the two cities. I didn't understand, though, why Mr. Brey hadn't mentioned anything about family connections to me before. I had always taken his decision not to visit me in Seattle as simply a sign that he didn't like to travel; he rarely went on trips anywhere and those vacations that he did take were almost exclusively by car. After my visit with my father, I wondered if some other reason existed, some hidden motivation that compelled him to obscure or ignore a connection to the Pacific Northwest. That bothered me. It felt as though my father had unwittingly attacked the most stable thing, the most dependable person, in my life.

I grabbed Mr. Brey's genealogy folder and turned again to the family tree. I hoped it could offer insight regarding ancestors who had once lived where I now lived. I found, tied to antiquated sounding names, a number of Oklahoma and Kansas references but nothing of Seattle or Washington, no entry point that allowed me to read the stories behind those anonymous people. It was a bit like scanning through the catalogs of tribal names and descendants in the early books of the Old Testament: as a kid I felt as though I *had* to read through each and every single one, without quite knowing why or how they were important.

I pulled the folder closer to my eyes, shifting my weight and scrunching my back slightly as I did so. Then I saw it. Or thought I saw it. I turned the overhead light on to see if that made it clearer. There, on top of the name "Adam Brey," Mike's grandfather, rested the faint tracings of a giant X. It stretched completely across the name, from A to Y. No ink trail showed anywhere along the almost invisible "X." Just a slight indentation in the paper that could very well have simply been grooves made by an imagination addled by a mixture of cheap scotch, coffee, and confusion.

The lines, in fact, were so indistinct that they could have even been transferred from a piece of paper resting on top of the illustrated tree: an old grocery list, for instance, where pen had crossed out "milk." I tried to be objective. I understood that part of me was desperate to see something there. I yearned to find some sort of hidden mystery that would make Mr. Brey's death more significant and grant me a reprieve from letting him go entirely. Even recognizing that desire, the detective in me continued to scream that there was indeed something here, an anomaly that needed explaining, even if it would alter everything I thought I knew about Mr. Brey, maybe about myself.

That sense of personal involvement with the case troubled me the most. The events of the last few days had disturbed my understandings of Mr. Brey and my father. I felt unsettled, unmoored from anchors and stories that I had clung to for years and years. Truth and fiction, the solidity of experience and the slipperiness of narrative, melted into one another. Reflecting on what I had thought of as iron-clad absolutes regarding my two fathers, I realized that we had each been living with our own stories of one another, perhaps never touching, never even coming close to what the other person actually thought or felt.

Even worse, our stories contained flaws from the start, were rotten from the core, and we built outward upon those mistakes until we couldn't even recognize one another. We lived errors of the past: not necessarily or solely mistakes that happened long ago but mistakes borne of an astigmatism that didn't allow us to see history with any kind of clarity or see how past and present cohered.

It all made me feel worse than what I imagined an amnesiac must feel. Amnesia would be terrifying but you would at least know that something existed out there for you, some past that you just needed to recover. I felt, rather, that the past had been slowly, systematically eaten away, with nothing left to salvage. The man I had idolized had a hidden side that made me distrust my unquestioned devotion; the man I despised had an internal depth that I feared but that also gave him a greater humanity than I had suspected. I was free-floating, alone and adrift in what felt like quiet, dark, freezing-cold isolation.

I knew the pattern. Having recently gone through the throes of a dying relationship, I recognized the feelings of slow disintegration: once the worm of doubt crawls inside, it changes everything. It feeds, slowly and patiently, undermining previously stable foundations until they crumble to dust under their own weight. I pictured it clearly, a very small, almost invisible worm crawling inside me and gorging until it grew to enormous proportions and I had nothing left inside, no more stories to believe in.

I retrieved my cell phone from my pocket and checked my voicemail to see what waited for me. "Marcus, it's Ash. Two things I thought you'd be interested in, one small and one maybe big. Small one first," she directed. "That old woman was back in again today looking for you. Didn't leave a name or want anyone else's help. Just you. Now the big one. That thing you faxed in for Ryota, I'm pretty sure we caught a body with that same thing painted on it. Actually that symbol plus another one painted next to it. Victim is male, middle-aged, white. A pretty much nondescript shopkeeper named Jamie Parks. I haven't told anyone beside Ryota about the fax you sent yet. Thought you might want to tell Markeze about the possible connection yourself. You owe me for sitting on this, you know. Call me back."

She was smart, no doubt about that. She knew that if something larger tied the average-Joe shopkeeper to what I was working on, then this was a case you could ride for awhile. Risky for her too, though. Linking herself to me also meant being tied to what the general consensus saw as a fading star, one ready to implode at any moment. If she was as smart as I thought, then she saw that too. And that actually made me feel good, because she was still here. Maybe she simply thought the case was worth the risk, but a part of me wanted to think that she believed I was worth the risk as well.

What dug at me, leaving an opening for yet another worm to crawl inside and eat away, was her reference to Ryota. I gathered from her message that Ryota was back from wherever he had been and had seen my fax. Not hearing from him irritated me. I hadn't been especially forthcoming or remarkably warm to him. But partners are partners. When one of you asks for a favor, the other one helps. That's just how it is. The reluctance with which you do it might increase or decrease depending on how close the two of you are, but you do the damn favor. Especially one as simple as this. So Ryota not calling me back about the symbol was an issue.

He could, I suppose, still be in the middle of tracking down what the symbol meant. Maybe, though, he decided to take the opposite tack of Ash, zigging where she zagged. He was the one sharing cases and space and a car with me these last few months. He knew exactly who he was dealing with. Maybe from what he had seen he, unlike Ash, figured that I wasn't coming back, that I was already in the middle of going supernova and didn't want to be close when the explosion happened. Maybe I wasn't worth the risk, after all.

My cell phone still rested in my hand. I pulled myself away from thoughts of implosion and dialed Ryota to see what he would, and what he wouldn't, say. He picked up on the third ring and must have checked his Caller ID beforehand. "Marcus, how're you doing?" No mention of my fax.

"I'm hanging in there."

"When you coming back?"

"Sooner rather than later. I'm about done here and don't want to extend my time away. Heard you took some extra time off, though. Everything okay, partner?"

He responded quickly, almost cutting me off. "I'm fine. Everything's okay. Just something unexpected at home that needed my attention." There was a brief silence, pushed away quickly as he continued. "Oh shit, got your fax but got bogged down in something and haven't had a chance to call you. It's a *kanji*."

"A what?" I asked.

"A kanji. It's Japanese," he said. "There are about 2,000 kanji. At least 2,000 that are used fairly often. This one means 'Harmony.' Where'd you run across this?"

"Harmony, huh?" I mused out loud, ignoring his last question for the moment. "Looked like a Chinese menu symbol to me," I said, not really joking but making it sound like I was.

"Not quite," Ryota answered. "But the Japanese did take a lot of their writing symbols from Chinese, so not as crazy as you think."

"And that one little symbol is basically an entire word in Japanese?" I asked.

"Yep," Ryota replied. "There isn't really an ABC alphabet in

Japanese writing. You've got kanji, like this one, *hiragana*, and *katakana*. They all work together: kanji stand in for chunks of ideas. Nouns, values like 'harmony,' for instance. Hiragana give you the basic syllabic foundation. Katakana are used for foreign words and names and as emphasis. It's complicated but what you sent is definitely a kanji and definitely means harmony."

"Thanks, Ryota. That helps a lot. Appreciate you digging into this for me."

"It's nothing. Really. I learned most of the kanji when I was young. My dad was big into the respect your Japanese heritage thing. Like I said, I'm absolutely positive that what you sent me is a kanji and just as certain that it means harmony."

I realized I had garnered more personal information about my partner in the last fifteen seconds than I had in the last several months. He wasn't a very open guy with his personal life. I knew he was married. Knew his wife's name was Tracy. Knew they had no kids. Didn't know why. Didn't know if they wanted kids someday or not. Didn't know where he grew up. Didn't know he knew Japanese because of his father's insistence.

"Do me another favor, Ryota. Run all of this by Ashlynn next time you see her. And then have her fill you in on a new murder, last name of Parks."

"Parks? You got it. Anything else?"

"No, that should hold it for now," I answered. I wanted time to process through how a Japanese symbol meaning "harmony" could relate to Mr. Brey and Mike before I shared that part.

"See you soon." He hung up.

The kanji translation was great. The killer almost certainly knew Japanese, so I now had my first fact with which to start building a picture of who murdered Mike and Mr. Brey. "Harmony," however, meant nothing to me in relation to the killings. I couldn't figure out how "harmony" and the brutality of Mike's death fit together; the message and its delivery seemed so at odds with one another.

Mr. Brey, I was sure, had never mentioned anyone named Parks, or Jamie, to me. And I still had no definite link between Mr. Brey and

Seattle. This is how investigations work: they get bigger, more complicated and nebulous before they get smaller. The trick is to not get overwhelmed by the influx of discordant facts.

First order of business was clearly to find out as much as possible about Jamie Parks. Maybe more lines would appear after that. Determining who the woman in the photo was would be a huge step as well, but that would be trickier than learning about Jamie Parks. She was, for the moment, almost as anonymous as the killer.

I fired up my rental, backed up, then pointed the nose back onto Main Street. Rather than retracing my way back to Wichita, I turned west, heading for Denver International. It was marginally closer than going back to Wichita but, more importantly, flights between Denver and Seattle were plentiful.

I felt both the professional and the personal pulling me toward the Pacific Northwest. I needed to get back to Seattle as quickly as possible, to find out about Jamie Parks, to resurrect my reputation with Markeze, to uncover, perhaps, what Mr. Brey thought he needed to hide from me. I needed to rediscover him. And somewhere within all of this violence and confusion, I thought perhaps I could rediscover myself as well. It sounded like a terrible marketing campaign by the Seattle Chamber of Commerce: Find a killer, Find your family, Find yourself.

Chapter Eight

I had arrived at Sea-Tac Airport late last night, still energized by the prospects of regaining my form as a detective and of repaying a portion of my debt to Mr. Brey by tracking down his killer. Somehow that energy evaporated in the middle of the night, disappearing while I slept.

To fight the fatigue, I was working my way through a quadruple tall latte at my favorite local coffee shop while I waited for Ash and Ryota. I wanted to go over my notes with them before talking to Markeze. I sipped my coffee, listened to music from the always terrific KEXP morning show play in the background, and thought about the strange encounter with my father. I didn't have a clue why Mr. Brey had a sword, or why he thought of it as a special possession. I felt like I had misunderstood the very past that I had lived.

I had spent years developing my efforts to wall off the past and live a life in and of the present, but I felt those walls crumbling. Echoes from the past, like ghost music that you can feel vibrate within you but not quite clearly hear, shook the foundations. The murders halted my forward momentum. And that scared me.

I feared that I would no longer be in control if I gave up the present to look at the past. It felt like staring at a lake to locate ripples from a stone tossed into the pool of the past, watching in panic as the circles radiated outward, beyond what I could easily see.

My father had said that the sword was a World War II artifact. I set my mug down and pulled the weapon from its scabbard, the metal glinting as it found the light. The end of the sword curved in a slightly upward arc and the cutting edge looked razor-sharp. Beyond that, I couldn't tell you much about it. Guns I knew. Swords not so much.

I believed my father's report of it being tied somehow to World War II, however. When we were kids, Mr. Brey had been fascinated with World War II, especially the campaign in the Pacific, where he told me his own father had been deployed. He had built, with the same exactness and care that he devoted to everything else in life, scale replicas of the U.S.S. Arizona and Missouri. He studied the Battle of Midway extensively, preaching on the vicissitudes of time and chance and how Yamamoto could have defeated us if he would have pressed ahead and not waited to rest his men. A moment different here or there changes everything. I would need to check more on the sword. Given Mr. Brey's interest in World War II history, I wouldn't be surprised if it once belonged to some famous Japanese Admiral or something.

As a teenager, Mike loved telling me that his grandpa was a war hero, like he had something that I would never have. He deployed his father's interest with, and his family's service in, World War II as a line of demarcation that separated Mr. Brey and him, father and son, from me. It worked. During those moments, I felt my lack of family as an embarrassing inadequacy, with a depth of anxiety that only a high school kid can feel. When they talked about their family, I felt like I had a giant pimple on the very tip of my nose, one that formed every time the star cheerleader looked my way.

The door opened and Ash smiled as she entered; Ryota's facial expression was dead-even, as always. Ryota wore his charcoal suit, the lines immaculately pressed and a pocket square peeking out. He might have purchased it solely for the way it coordinated with his dark black hair. He was dapper, I had to give him that. Routinized too: this was his Monday ensemble. I suspected he kept a spreadsheet at home, laminated and taped to the inside closet-door, showing which suits and shirts and ties were appropriate for which days. He would never need to look at it, of course, but he was the kind of person who nevertheless would. There might even be a grease pencil hanging nearby so that he could inscribe a neat checkmark in the box uniting the column for "Charcoal" with the row for "Monday."

I, having neither a spreadsheet nor a grease pencil handy, had chosen my suit by the "wrinkle method": I never make it to the dry cleaner's as frequently as I should, so I often choose what to wear simply by what has the least amount of creases on it. I might have been slightly wrinkled, but I knew I looked good in today's winning suit—a tasteful midnight blue number with a cerulean blue shirt and an understated, though powerful in its minimalism, black and blue tie. Paige once told me you could tell a lot about men by the ties they wore. She could be right, understated and black and blue didn't strike me as a bad summary.

Ash, like Ryota, wore charcoal, a business suit that made her look professional and proud of where and who she was. I hadn't felt that confident and comfortable in my own skin for a long time. Self-doubt and self-loathing are like tar: they're sticky and the more you pull and try to remove them, the more you just seem to get the rest of you dirty.

Ash had pulled her reddish-brown hair back in a ponytail anchored low by the bottom of her ears. I saw a freckle peering from just below and behind her right ear, my eye catching it as I noted where the ponytail started. Her eyes shone a bright, emerald green. Everything about her seemed full of energy: shiny eyes, lips curled slightly upward in the start of a smile, a ponytail trying to corral auburn ringlets that looked ready to spring into action. Watching her was like catching that moment when potential energy turns to kinetic energy, that first powerful burst of activity that starts everything else moving in response.

As they neared my table, Ash slowed to let Ryota approach first, obeying some unwritten rule that because she was the new one in this setup she should hold back to let the partners greet and bullshit. Except, of course, that Ryota wasn't into the bullshitting part.

"Marcus, good to have you back," he intoned. He pulled back one of the modernist wood chairs from the other side of my table, lifting it slightly so that it moved easily, without scraping the floor or creating any noise.

"Good to see you, partner," I replied, intent on working to create more familiarity and ease between us than I'd let develop before.

Ash moved closer now, reaching for my hand and smiling. "Marcus," she said simply but with more warmth than what I had felt from Ryota.

I looked at both of them and felt a small smile begin to form. This felt good. Like we were in the midst of constituting a team. We would talk about the two cases and strategize. And I knew from past experience that a good case often forged good camaraderie. I could maybe finally get a better handle on Ryota and turn our partnership to the better, and Ash's energy seemed contagious, something that I wanted in contact with me.

"Let's start by you guys telling what you found out about the Parks murder."

Ash waited for Ryota to speak. He didn't. After a long pause developed, she picked up the ball. "Not much. Larsen and Mills have the case. I talked them into letting me take a quick look at the crime scene photos but I haven't seen their case notebook at all."

Ryota still didn't speak. So I did. "How are the photos? You said on your message that there were two symbols on this guy, one similar to what I faxed to Ryota," I said, looking back at my partner, "and another, different one. Anything else?"

She sat silent for a moment, trying to recompose the crime scene photo in her head. While she thought, her eyes moved to her right. That side of her mouth tried to follow the same line of sight, scrunching up while the left side stayed still. I caught myself staring at the freckle I had seen when she walked in.

"The first looked pretty much like your fax. The second kind of resembled a stick figure with a flattened head. Maybe with something like a package or a box down by its feet. But it didn't make any sense to me so I don't remember it all that well. The lines seemed neat. Done with a small brush or something. But I saw spilled ink or paint too. Splotches. So neat, but not neat, you know?"

I opened up the folder to show them the crime scene photos from Mike's murder. I slid one picture toward Ryota and one toward Ash. "This definitely isn't what you would call 'neat.' The killer carved it into his flesh."

Ash's face didn't change when she saw the photo. She was striking but strong, young but maybe not as young or inexperienced as I would have guessed.

"Same symbol," Ash confirmed, "but definitely a different way of marking it. No question. No carving in the pictures Larsen and Mills have."

Ryota finally broke his silence, looking to Ash. "How about the killing itself? Same type of violence?"

"You haven't seen the pictures Ash got from Larsen and Mills?" I asked.

Ryota shook his head, unperturbed and restrained. "Something else came up. Besides, it's not our case."

Ash glanced between us, unsure if she should let us hash it out or ignore it and move back to my question. She chose the latter: "Parks's skull was collapsed. Obvious blunt force trauma. But no sign of torture like with this one."

"What do we know about Parks's background?" I asked. No one answered, which I guess made sense given that Ash hadn't been able to dig into Larsen's and Mills's files and Ryota hadn't done much of anything, even after I had asked him to follow-up on Parks. My frustration made me want to go running. Or smack Ryota.

"Ry, I thought we were on the same page with this one, with you finding out what you could about the Parks case."

Most of his body still looked as unflappable as ever but his left hand made a fist and then released, fingers splayed. His eyes held something feverish. I got the sense that I wasn't the only one who felt his blood pressure rising. "I couldn't do anything. It's not our case. It's theirs."

I realized I had been holding my breath and I now let it escape in a slow hiss through my top lip and down my chin. When my lungs emptied I took a deep inhalation and arched my shoulders up then down to let the tension out. This crafting of a team and building camaraderie sure was a lot of fun.

"Let me lay out for you two what I see. That symbol chain is way too coincidental. These murders *have* to be connected. The pictures I showed you are from a guy I grew up with, basically my brother. His dad was killed too, though not violently like this. I want Markeze to give me this case. I don't know how this is all tied together yet, but it is. It absolutely is. There's also this woman somehow related to it." I tossed the picture found in Mr. Brey's pocket toward Ash and Ryota. "I don't know how on that either. Maybe she's somehow tied to these symbols. But there's something there. Something we need to find."

Ash looked excited; Ryota looked unresponsive. Then he spoke. "It's not our case, Marcus. Plus, the killings don't match right. If you're thinking some kind of serial killer then why so much violence in the murder that *preceded* the Parks one?"

He had a point. These things usually escalate, and what I had was complete calm with Mr. Brey, utter violence with Mike, and, it sounded like, movement back toward a pretty typical murder with the Parks case. But they were connected. Everything told me they were.

"I'm gonna take this to Markeze. I'm putting my chips on the table and calling in every favor I have and mortgaging all the history I have with him. I want this case. I want you two with me. So here's the proverbial line in the sand: what should I tell Markeze when I go see him? We can do this. I need you guys. Markeze won't give it to me alone. I'll work it unofficially even if he doesn't give it to me, but it would be easier, and better, to have you guys with me. They *are* connected."

Ash didn't wait for Ryota this time. She slid the picture back to me and looked me in the eyes. "I'm with you."

Ryota looked pained. I'd put Right-Way in a tough spot: steal a case from another team or let your partner down and, having let him down, know that he would be working the case unofficially anyway. A classic no-win situation for a guy always looking for the right, proper answer. I didn't know how he had survived, or would survive going forward, living the black and white in a cop's world of gray. I kind of admired him for it, but also feared being around when the tension would finally tear him in half someday.

"I don't like it. I don't think the cases are necessarily tied as tightly as you think. And I hate stepping on Larsen and Mills. You convince Markeze to move the case and I'll work it with you. If he doesn't give it to you, keep me out of it. Not a word of it to me."

He moved his chair back, again slightly raising it so it wouldn't scrape the floor. He stood, took one more look at the crime scene photo, closed his eyes briefly, then gave the photo to me and turned to leave. "See you two at the station."

I got the sense he wanted to get there before me so Markeze wouldn't think he had a direct part in any scheming I brought forth to get the case. He'd done a pretty good job of finding the balancing line. He would help if it were official, knowing that Larsen and Mills would be mad at losing control of a case they'd already started working but would respect him more than if the case were transferred and he didn't back his partner. Not helping me if it wasn't official was crap but no one would think it too out of character for Right-Way. I knew Markeze would never give me the case if I came in without my partner backing the play, though, so first hurdle overcome. Shouldn't have been a hurdle at all, but there you go.

I turned my attention to Ash. "You two didn't ride together? I saw you at the door at the same time and thought you must have shared a ride."

"Oh, no. Just saw each other in the parking lot." Then she shifted gears. "We can do it, can't we? We can make this case. I know it's not there yet, maybe not even close. But something is there, waiting for us to find it. Know what I mean?"

"I know exactly what you mean."

"I can feel it. Like it's right there and I can't quite see it but I know it's there. I know it in my gut. I can *feel* it, Marcus" she said as she rose to leave.

Her voice was quiet but you could feel the energy in it, the excitement. The belief. Police Faith, I call it. It's a trust in the chase, in your ability to track the signs and bring to light what others want to hide. It's a faith that *what* you're chasing matters, that because of you and because of the chase you might add a small grain of weight to the "right" side of the balance. Not a Right-Way kind of "right," where everything remains proper and unsullied. But "right" in a broader, more trying and nebulous sense: that the world could be shit and the scales completely tipped against you and against puppies and kittens and sunshine days but that you and your chase don't care and won't give up. Police Faith: you see evil and you see people do things that make you doubt humanity but you do the chase despite all that you see, maybe precisely because of all you see.

Ash's excitement resonated in the air like that of a new acolyte. I, on the other hand, felt more like a weary priest who has tired after never hearing back from God, who has served the faith for a lifetime only to wonder if he had been duped after all. With this case, it wasn't enough for me to push a measly grain of sand onto the other side of the scales. I wasn't interested in that, didn't trust in that right now. I wanted Mr. Brey's killer to die, to suffer.

I was truthful with them: I was prepared to mortgage everything I had left of value to the department and to Markeze to get this case. What I didn't tell them was that I didn't care if I got any of that back. If necessary, I was ready to default on whatever loan Markeze gave me. I feared that if I failed, I would have nothing left to hold onto and would at last complete the cycle of abandonment in my life by giving up on my self.

I gathered up the genealogical file, thinking of last acts of faith: chasing for Mr. Brey, searching for redemption with Ash. I didn't know if I wanted Ash near because I wanted her to help me, because

I wanted her to stop me, or because I craved a witness to my destruction, a scribe to record my final act and decide later if it had been a deed of faith or blasphemy. Watching her leave, though, I knew that whatever the reason, I wanted her around, *needed* her around.

Chapter Nine

I exited the coffee shop, the sound of mellow guitar-strumming following me out and then disappearing as the door closed, like steam off a latte floating away with a gust of wind. The gentlest of rain, only a touch more than mist, fell softly to the street. The tiny, cool drops pricked my skin just enough for the wetness to feel cleansing and invigorating without being sloppy or overwhelming. The silence of this particular version of Seattle precipitation always appeals to me. The moisture hangs in the air and insulates against other sounds, while the drops that do make it to the ground hit so quietly that you never hear them land. Contrasting with the images of murder we had just looked at, the rain seemed tender, almost protective in its feel against my skin and the quiet with which it caressed.

I had been fortunate enough to find on-street parking only a few spots away. I climbed inside my car, a black Subaru WRX that I had spent too much on and gunned the engine to feel the power push my spine into the seat. Slipping silently across my windshield, the wipers created a momentarily dry opening that looked out onto Puget

Sound. Cloud cover blanketed Seattle, filtering all yellow out of the sunlight. It left a murkiness that reminded me of the fluorescent bulbs in a storage unit, the type of cool lighting that never fully illuminates the corners, so that you don't trust that you're truly seeing everything. The water on the Sound appeared a darker hue of gray than the sky, as though the sky and water were coordinating elements within a land colored entirely by concrete blocks. In the summer you can see the Olympic mountains hailing to you from across the Sound; in the winter you would never even know they are there, blocked out by clouds and the concrete gray.

After splashing through a small puddle iridescent with the purples of oil and road grime, I drove up the entrance ramp to the Seattle Homicide Unit parking garage. It felt good to be back to the department and even better to think that I would be helping Mr. Brey if I could convince Markeze to give me the case.

My welcome back was warm, everyone giving me a fist-bump on the shoulder or a smile or the friendly ribbing that camouflages fondness so that it doesn't come across as overly emotional or sappy.

I stopped at my desk, glancing at the notes left for me. On top was Ash's message about the old Asian woman. I had forgotten about her, but she hadn't left any contact information so I'd have to wait for her to return for me. Not much else of import awaiting my return.

I gave Markeze's door two quick raps at each corner of the glass, as though I were testing the soundness of the construction or looking for a secret panel. It started years ago, when we were both much younger. I was less sure of myself as a detective back then and knocked on Markeze's door about fifteen times a day, yearning for an "okay" from a superior that would give official sanction for every step I took. He showed me patience, at first. He finally blew up late one afternoon, telling me that he wasn't there to hold my balls for me and that the next time I needed something to not even enter his space, just knock and shout out "testicle check, Sir" and he would holler okay from the other side and we could both get back to doing some real police work.

Sean loved it, and I found a new pair of golf balls waiting for me on my desk every day for a month. I didn't bother Markeze for the rest of the week. The next week, when I truly did need his help, I tried breaking the ice with one of those secret-club knocks—dum da da-dum dum, dum. It had since evolved into its current manifestation, the way baseball players have high fives at the start of the season that become elaborate rituals by the time October rolls around. It was our own code, telling Markeze before the door even opened who it was and that I needed something from him.

I found him, true to form, already standing in front of his desk by the time I opened the door and entered.

"Marcus," he said with as much warmth and excitement as a ten-year hooker offers to her tenth john of the night.

"Geez, Captain, you could at least fake it, you know, give me something to work with." He smiled, sort of.

"Feelin' better? Ready to get your ass back to work?" He looked straight, unblinking, into my eyes. I held his look, knowing that he wanted to try and read what was going on inside me. Words were surface dressing for him, not as trustworthy as most people foolishly believed.

"I feel like I'm already moving and I don't want to be stopped." He looked at me without speaking, waiting for me to finish. "I heard about the case Mills and Larsen have. I need it, Captain. I know it's theirs but I'm asking you to give it to me and Ryota instead." I decided not to ask about Ash joining us until after I actually had the case secured from him. Baby steps.

He continued staring at me for a few moments longer. I held his look. "Why would I do that, Marcus? There's no shortage of work. It's not like you'll just be sitting around if not for that case. So, why?" He leaned backward against his desk and folded his arms in front of him. Classic pull-back, defensive body language. Not starting out well.

For the last few months I had been treading water, all of my energy expended just to stay above the surface. These murders broke that pattern. I felt this case pulling me toward its center and I hoped that it would, like a planet with an approaching satellite, slingshot me onward with greater momentum as I left its orbit. On the other hand, if my calculations were off, I would burn up and crash. But how to tell this to Markeze?

"I just need this one. I need it and it needs me. And I'll solve it. You know I will. I need you to trust me on this."

Markeze's brow furrowed, his eyebrows darting inward toward the bridge of his nose.

"Captain," I spoke quietly, "I know my work has been shit lately. But I also know that, up until this thing with Paige leaving, I've given this department my best, year after year. I'm not trying to steal headlines. You know me better than that. I'm putting every case I've solved on the table for you, telling you to look at that and look at me and know that I *need* this case. This one case. Then I'll take the shit cases for the rest of the year. But this one I need."

He exhaled through his nose, arms still crossed. His brow remained furrowed while he looked through what I said and, it seemed, looked through me as well. He was a bulldog of a man, short and solid throughout. He had that perfect bodybuilder's frame, with a compact physique and short, powerful arms that moved like pistons firing up and down during bench press sessions.

"Marcus, you have to tell me *why* you need this case in particular. I trust you, you know that, but I need you to trust me and give me more than what you've given me so far."

It was an issue I didn't want to answer. From an ethical point of view, being personally involved with any of the subjects of an investigation or any of the victims was questionable; from a practical standpoint, it provided fertile ground for defense attorney accusations of biased police work. I folded my arms across my chest and looked closely at Markeze while I tried to figure out where to go next. His close-cropped hair looked as gray as the concrete sky outside. His suit appeared neatly pressed, no lint showing. His suits weren't in the same ballpark as Ryota's as far as expense or fashion, but they were immaculately maintained. No stubble showed on his face, never a hint of a five-o'clock shadow with him. Yet I had seen pictures of him from years past with a full beard. I suspected he shaved in the morning and then again after he got done at the gym during his lunch break.

"How's Laura doing, Sir?" I asked, noticing the family pictures on his desk, one fairly recent of him and his wife Laura and a much older photo of his daughter Lisa. "That's a good picture of Lisa," I added.

He uncrossed his arms and moved back around the desk to his chair and sat down, the leather squeaking. "Laura's good." He looked at the picture of the two of them. "Had our twentieth anniversary last month. Twenty years."

"Congratulations." I smiled at him but didn't feel it. Twenty years sounded like an eternity to me. I figured I could probably fuck up a marriage fifteen or thirty times in that length.

His eyes trailed over to the picture of Lisa and stopped. I felt shoddy for bringing up family with him, knowing that I was calling in a marker that I once swore to myself I would never demand payment on. I think Markeze sensed something of the same.

"It's been almost ten years since Lisa was killed." He didn't say anything else, though he turned his eyes toward mine again as he held the picture with his right hand.

Lisa and some friends had been coming home from a high school basketball game when a drunk driver ran a red light and T-boned her car. Lisa died at the scene, the driver's side door pinning her inside and a shard of metal severing her femoral artery. Her two friends were bruised and shaken but otherwise okay. Markeze made it to the scene before the jaws of life arrived but after Lisa was already dead, her blood pooling in the foot well, her face ghostly white.

The drunk driver, also relatively unharmed, fled on foot. I found him only a few blocks away, at a bar. His hands shook but not so much so that he couldn't take one more long pull on his beer when he saw me approach. I called Markeze before I took the driver in to jail, before I even called it in to the station. I walked the guy to the bathroom and waited for Markeze to show up.

He left Laura at the hospital with Lisa's body and I think that in retrospect he felt worse about that than anything that happened afterward. When he arrived, I left him alone with the driver while I stood outside the bathroom door, making sure no one would interrupt. I heard the mirror crash, a toilet stall door bang open with the impact of a body and the dull sound of shoes connecting with soft flesh. When I entered the bathroom, Markeze looked crazed. Blood spatter colored his face near his eyes, which were pulled open unnaturally far. He had reached an animal hatred deep inside of himself. It scared me. He had a deep cut on his knuckles, probably from the driver's incisor, which I saw laying on the floor, strangely alone and out of place. I pulled Markeze away to the sink and turned the water on for him to clean himself off. I checked the driver, who was still breathing but had taken a hell of a beating, one of the worst I had seen.

I pulled the driver up and dragged him to the car, pausing for a moment by the bar to tell the owner that this guy had just killed a girl and it would be a shame if we needed to start keeping a close eye on his bar and clientele to make sure no other drunk killers were around and that I had slipped and broken one of his mirrors and would be happy to pay for it myself. He declined.

I took the driver into the station, writing up his injuries as a result of the car crash impact. He was a three-time loser who had been arrested several previous times for drunk driving and whose word didn't mean shit to anyone else. Internal Affairs took a cursory look at me for excessive violence—I suspected this was one of the incidents that the Wichita detectives had tried to bait me with. I never gave up Markeze for the beating.

At Lisa's funeral, Markeze, with tears in his eyes and his broad shoulders slumped in defeat and pain, patted me on the shoulder and croaked out "thank you." I'm still not sure what part he was thanking me for: calling him when I found the driver, letting him beat the driver senseless, stopping him before he killed the driver, or keeping everything quiet and writing up a false report. Maybe all of it.

It changed him. He became quieter after Lisa's death. Angrier, more efficient in his work but I think with less love for the job or for life in general. I didn't want to make myself part of his pain or his loss. I never spoke to him of that night again. But I know he felt indebted to me. I know that was partly why he had cut me slack with my own marriage crisis and sloppy work and terrible mentoring of Ryota.

"Sir, I need this case. Might be better if you don't know the particulars of why just now."

He took his hand off of the picture of Lisa. "Tell me, Marcus."

I knew what I was asking would be treading somewhere we hadn't gone before. It seemed I had to tell him of my personal involvement and once he heard that, his sense of obligation for what I had done for him would prevent him from denying my request. I wanted, in effect, to trade the breach of investigative and personal conduct in his past for a breach of my own in the present. I felt as though I were using Lisa and I hated that; I only hoped he wouldn't think the same of me.

"I went to Wichita for the funeral of the man who raised me. You know that part. Someone killed his son while I was there. I think it's the same guy from our Jamie Parks case. The same symbol was left at the scene in Wichita and the scene here. I know it sounds far-fetched, but it's the same killer. And I need to catch him. For my family. For me, Sir."

He didn't say anything but I could see him working through the moral and investigative difficulties, as well as the ethical dilemma of his need to fulfill his debt to me now that I finally called it home. He straightened his pictures of Laura and Lisa, turning them away from my line of sight. Then he stood, shooting the cuffs out of his suit sleeves as he rose. He buttoned the top button on his suit coat and came around the desk, standing in front of me once more. I felt shitty for meeting on ground we hadn't walked over in so long and maybe I imagined it, but his eyes seemed suddenly duller.

"Marcus," he began, "this is trouble. I know you realize that." He sighed before continuing. "I still think of Lisa every day, wondering about where her life would have taken her. Where her life might have taken me and Laura. Where we'd be different." He looked at me closely before starting again. "We live our past daily, I think. Or our past lives us. I'm not sure which. Deeds done are redone every day for me. It's hard to atone for the past, Marcus. Maybe impossible. I hope this isn't about atonement for you. I hope even more that this won't be something you feel the need to atone for later."

I held his gaze. "I just know that this is a case I have to have."

He frowned, crossing his arms again. "It's yours then. I'll have Mills and Larsen give you and Ryota everything they have. Don't fuck this one up, Marcus. You need to be righter than Right-Way on everything you do so this doesn't get bounced in trial. Listen when Ryota objects to something. This time he might be a better judge than you."

"I'd like Ashlynn on this with us too, Sir. She's sharp. She first saw the similarity of the symbols and alerted me to it. She deserves a piece of this too."

Markeze shook his head. "Work it with Ryota. You've been ditching him every chance you get. I'll make sure Ashlynn hears from me that you fought to have her on this with you and I'll make sure it doesn't get forgotten that she saw something on this first. But she's not on this case with you. We clear on that?"

I didn't answer.

"You don't have to be happy with it, but you do have to be clear on it. You clear on this?"

"Yes."

As I turned to leave, his voice, quiet but absolute, caught me and made me misstep on my way out the door. "And Marcus, don't bring up Lisa to me again."

Chapter Ten

I left Markeze's office conflicted. I was glad to be working the case, but I felt bad that Ash wasn't, and I felt downright lousy that Lisa had played any part whatsoever in this. I had told myself that I would never trade on that night. Another promise broken.

Ryota and Ash looked in my direction as I exited Markeze's office, Ash peering toward me expectantly, Ryota wearing a mask of reserve and wariness. For the moment, I ignored them both. Weaving between desks stacked front-end to front-end so that partners could communicate easier with one another, I made my way straight to Mills and Larsen. Having a case poached from you was on par with someone stealing your significant other: even if you didn't like what you had, you didn't necessarily want anyone else going behind your back to take it away from you. I wanted a face-to-face moment to talk to them before Markeze did.

I had always gotten along fine with both Mills and Larsen. Mills was a short brunette in her forties, divorced with two teenage boys at home. Most days she went without makeup, wearing instead the fatigue of a single parent. I don't know which made her tougher: her time as a detective or having raised her boys alone after their father took off before the youngest even had his first birthday. I always felt a kinship of family pain and abandonment with her, though we never talked about it.

Larsen was a few years younger in age and a lifetime younger in other ways. Never married, he had a new girlfriend every other week. He and I occasionally played pickup basketball at the department's fitness center. He was slow of feet and fleet of mouth: he couldn't beat you off the drive but could trash talk you into submission or fits of laughter after a particularly good verbal jab. We called him "mouth" during our games.

"How you feeling, Marcus?" Mills asked, looking at me with a depth that manifested genuine concern, not just casual chit-chat. I guess everyone had noticed that lately I'd been off my game, whether we were talking about basketball or my work as a detective.

"Listen guys. Any second now Markeze is gonna emerge from his cave. He's going to tell you that I'm taking over the Parks case. I want you to know, from me, that I begged and cajoled him into this decision. He's not kicking you off for any reason that has anything to do with you. It's me driving this."

Larsen smiled. Mills spoke. "It's a dead end case right now. No leads. You want it, be our guest. Saving us from a dog of a case."

When I approached Ash, she greeted me with an uncertain smile, the corners of her mouth not curling as high as they had earlier this morning. She shuffled some papers absentmindedly, her thin fingers curling and uncurling as they searched mechanically through the paperwork.

"What's the story? What'd Markeze say?"

"He gave me the case." She perked up. "But he doesn't want you on it. His line in the sand on this one, I guess." She looked down at the papers, the cheap fluorescent lighting casting shadows from the wisps of curly auburn hair that had escaped her ponytail. The lighting and the loose hair made her look more vulnerable than I had anticipated; she had sounded so strong and self-confident on the phone and at coffee this morning. The moment of fragility passed quickly, however, and as she looked back up and caught my eyes again, I wasn't even sure it had been there at all.

"Well shit, Marcus, that's not what I expected to hear." She said it without any trace of acrimony, like we were talking about a movie that we had both enjoyed but that had inexplicably received poor reviews from everyone else. Her voice carried surprise and disbelief, but something else too, a durability that didn't match her lean frame or ringlets or thin fingers but that I nonetheless felt emanating like heat from her every time I came near.

She was only four years younger than me. Maybe, though, she had managed to hold onto what I had already let go and had retained that residual tension of youth in which strength and fragility are never so close together again, when hurts are felt easily but injuries can also heal quickly. My wounds, on the other hand, had grown gangrenous and the pain had petrified deep within the bones, turning me brittle and ready to crack apart. The contrast I perceived in Ash as she bounced between vulnerability and rubber-band resiliency drew me in irresistibly. I saw the freckle on her neck again, saw her eyes look at me without guile or expectation, saw her mouth smile once more and suddenly I was already disregarding what I had just agreed to with Markeze.

"Listen, Ash. You deserve to be on this. I want you to work this with me, with me and Ryota. Markeze said no and you should probably follow that. But I remember what you said at the coffee shop, about feeling something in the pit of your stomach about this case and knowing we could solve it. I know that feeling. If you want a spot on this, it's all yours."

"I appreciate that. I do. But I don't have a history with Markeze and doing a run around on him could kill me here. I want this case but I'm in no position to demand I be put on it or ignore what Markeze says. You know that." She was doing the right thing, I knew, but I was hoping for the wrong thing. "Don't look so worried. You seem allergic to smiling, you know that?" she asked, her mouth turning up as though to show me how it worked.

"Not much to smile about right now. But I'll work on it in front of the mirror, along with some self-affirmation exercises, and be the cheeriest detective in the station before you know it," I joked. I wasn't ready to let her leave that easily, though. "Tell you what, just come look through the murder book photos with me and Ryota. You've seen them once already and you've seen the ones I brought back with me. You were the first to notice the connection and I could use your eyes on this one more time. I'm not asking you to work the whole thing, just come have a look and let me know what you see, what stands out to you."

"I'll make you a deal," she replied. "Try sneaking out one itsy smile so we both know that there isn't some neurological problem with your face. Then we'll go see what we see."

Everybody's a comedian. But I smiled. "See," I said. "No nerve damage. Your turn: let's go take a look at the murder book."

She took off in the lead, heading toward Ryota. I hurried to catch up and when I did I gripped her shoulder, near the freckle, to slow her down. "One more thing. Ryota doesn't like any of this and I know is going to pin my ass to the wall any time I don't do things exactly, and I mean exactly, the right-way. We don't need a scene just because you're going to look over our shoulders for five minutes and then go back to your life as a desk warmer until Markeze figures out where to put you. So let's not mention that Markeze doesn't want you on this. I want him focused on the pictures and the case, not blubbering about you taking a quick peek. Okay?"

Either the file exerted an irresistible pull on her now that we were physically close to it, or she had already made peace with the idea that looking through the book wasn't the same as working the case, or she knew that Ryota was over the top with his worries. Whatever the reason, she didn't seem troubled.

"Sure, Marcus. No sweat."

We neared Ryota just as Larsen and Mills exited Markeze's office. Larsen handed me the case notebook, another slight smile on his lips. "All yours, buddy."

"I take it you convinced Markeze to give us the case," Ryota said, then took a sip of his tea. He drank about twenty cups of green tea a day. He'd brought me a cup instead of my customary coffee soon after we were paired up. I had to admit, it did taste good, but it didn't have enough caffeine kick for me.

"Let's take a look," I replied, and tossed the notebook on the desk in front of the three of us. I skipped the handwritten notes and the typed reports, figuring there would be time later to peruse those. I wanted to see the crime scene photos.

The symbolic chains immediately drew my eyes. Ash was right: part of the marking on Jamie Parks's body showed eerie similarity to that discovered on Mike. The other portion of the chain, however, revealed something new.

"Ryota, what do you think? Can you read this symbol also?" I asked.

"Another kanji," he replied. "Both of these are much clearer, better delineated than what was on the body in the pictures you showed us this morning. No trouble reading this one."

"Okay. So what does the new symbol mean?"

"Truth," Ryota answered. "It means 'Truth.'"

"So he gave us 'Harmony' first and now 'Truth,'" Ash mused. "And even on the body we get 'Harmony' before 'Truth.' See how the 'Harmony' symbol is higher on the body and 'Truth' inscribed below it?" she pointed out.

I picked up the thread. "So what's it mean? From harmony comes truth? First find harmony and then you find truth?" I was thinking out loud but not gaining any clarity from the process. It sounded like the core of a bad poem, or a cheesy refrigerator magnet, or some kind of bumper sticker you'd find on a Volkswagen Bug. Not something carved or painted on a body.

"The neatness of this one compared to the one you showed us earlier stays with me," Ryota said. He flipped away from the pictures, looking for something in the written reports. "Maybe he switched from cutting into the flesh to using paint or a marker so that what he wrote would be clearer. Maybe he wasn't pleased with the mess last time. And by mess I mean the mess related to the symbols, not to the killing itself." He took another sip from his green tea before returning to the pictures.

"But see what I was talking about this morning?" Ash asked. "If it's so important that the killer be clear with his message and he was so careful this time, then why this mess over here?" She pointed to a few drops of paint on an otherwise clean body. "This is what I meant at the coffee shop when I said there were stray drops of splatter or something from the paint."

I leaned down to study the picture closer. "I see it. It's definitely not like the castoff from the head wound," I said, pointing at irregularly shaped droplets splashed on candy bars near the register, on the register itself, and on the floor near the body. "These on the body are too uniform. And darker in color. I agree—paint and not blood. But even so it doesn't seem like splatter from a paintbrush."

"What do you mean?" asked Ryota.

"Think Jackson Pollock. You can see velocity in his paintings. The movement and speed of the paint hitting the canvas. These from the crime scene are almost perfect circles, no movement to them at all. More like the killer stood still and intentionally waited for the paint to drip on an otherwise clean body. I think he wanted us to see these drops. They're part of the message."

"Could they be ellipses?" Ash thought, "like a message to us that there will be more to come?"

"Ellipses are three dots. There are only two here," Ryota said. "Not ellipses."

We sat in silence as we looked over the rest of the scene. There didn't seem to be much else of importance. The photographs showed a small, cramped, hole-in-the-wall convenience store. The aisles looked narrow, as did the entire store, with the floor plan laid out inside a skinny rectangular space instead of a more conventional square. It appeared as though a giant vice had squished the store, elongating the frame of the building and pushing displays closer together than they should have been. The store sold about what you'd expect for that type of downtown stop-and-shop: candy bars and other hydrogenated snacks, a few books and magazines, condoms and cigarettes, beef jerky and downtown maps near the register, a line of coolers in the back offering soda and beer, and a tub-like display up front holding energy drinks. It was the kind of place that probably made most of its money off of beer and cigarette sales and would have bred wariness in anyone who worked there: employees would automatically assess customers for the amount of danger they posed.

"How the hell did our killer walk in holding a baseball bat, or something similar, and convince Parks to walk out from behind the counter and then turn his back so that he could be bludgeoned to death from behind?" I asked. "It doesn't make sense."

"We need to see this place in person," Ryota agreed, almost eagerly.

I smiled to myself, thinking that the smell of the hunt had gotten to Ryota too. Ash continued to peer at the photos, absorbed trying to memorize all the details. I pulled the file away, slowly and delicately. Her emerald eyes followed the movement.

"Be right back," I said, taking the notebook with me. "Have a question for Mills and Larsen," I explained as I left Ryota and Ash alone.

When I got to Mills and Larsen, I opened the notebook to the pictures and pointed at the two anomalous dots.

"You two have anything running around your head that you hadn't put down on paper yet about these dots? Also, did you run across any references to Parks being linked to other states, places of residence or work outside of Washington? For him or for his family?" I wanted to ask directly about Kansas but they were good detectives and I might just as well put out a breadcrumb trail that led right to my ass crack if I mentioned Kansas to them.

Larsen turned his head in my direction, but it was Mills who spoke.

"We didn't have much time to work this. The dots are most likely a latex paint, the kind you could get at a million Home Depots."

Larsen then spoke. "Just brainstorming, but I kicked around the idea of the dots as periods. Like a punctuation for the end of a life. But two dots instead of one doesn't really fit with that idea."

"Nothing on anything out of state. When we canvassed, one business a few doors down was closed. The drycleaners. A few neighbors weren't at home and need to be tracked down still too," Mills recapped.

I mumbled thanks and then, instead of heading directly toward my desk, made a detour to the Xerox machine. I made two copies of the crime scene photos and of the interview notes for both Parks's business and residential neighbors. I also Xeroxed the picture, found first in Mr. Brey's pocket and now carried in my own pocket, of the mysterious Asian woman.

Back at my desk, the previously upbeat and confident Ash remained strangely quiet. Ryota has that effect on people: small-talk isn't an art form he has perfected to the same degree as folding his pocket squares. Ash was, however, finishing her own cup of green tea. My eyes crinkled slightly, amused at the thought of Ash searching for a way to connect with Ryota and finding, I was sure, only about twenty seconds of discussion about green tea.

"Good tea, isn't it?" I asked innocently. Ash stared at me with a look of coy anger, the kind you give when someone is teasing you and you want them to know that there will be payback at some point down the line.

"Mills and Larsen didn't run across anything linking Parks to Kansas or anywhere else outside of Washington," I reported. "I know the Breys had a tie to the Seattle area, though, so we need to push more to see how in the world they might be connected to Parks. We need to dig through histories on these people. We also don't know who this woman is," I said, pulling the picture of the Asian woman from my pocket. "I haven't been able to figure out how she is tied to Mr. Brey. Let's push and see if she's tied to Parks in any way."

"I need to get back to my desk," Ash replied, reluctance in her voice. Answering the phone and covering for other detectives certainly wasn't much of a pull next to a case file open directly in front of you. It didn't make sense to me why Markeze hadn't given her more to do. "Thanks for the tea, Ryota. Marcus is right, it really is good," she finished kindly and genuinely.

She still hadn't moved, caught between knowing she should get away from the case but not quite being able to drop it. Markeze opened his door, coffee mug in hand, then paused when he saw the three of us.

"Ashlynn, in here." I heard his coffee mug slam to his desk. For the first time I could remember, she looked worried, the corners of her lips turning down fractionally. Once she was inside, Markeze's voice erupted again. "Close the door." She did, gently and in diametric contrast to the power and chaos riding the sound waves of Markeze's exhortations.

I felt lousy, thinking that I had pushed Markeze to a spot he didn't want to be and that he took out that frustration, not on me, but on Ash. Ryota gave me a look of curiosity, one of the few moments of connection I had felt with him as a partner.

"You look like he's raking you across the coals, not Ashlynn," Ryota noted. "Wonder what she did to get Markeze so riled up?" he wondered.

Ash emerged from Markeze's, her concern replaced by anger. Whatever he had said to her, it hadn't been accompanied by a lot of small talk. Her complexion made me think of a chameleon. Her face had turned red, as though it were trying to blend in with hair. I dashed after her, the murder notebook pumping up and down in my left hand as I skipped around the desks standing in between the two of us.

"Hey, hold up," I called as I reached her. I caught her shoulder with my right hand but she shrugged it off. The cosmic balance of the universe: I piss of Markeze and he takes it out on Ash; Markeze pisses off Ash and she takes it out on me. If only the rest of life made such nice, neat circles. I tried again.

"Wait a sec, would you? Please." She slowed, then turned. "Markeze's not mad at you," I continued. "He's mad at me. Just blow it off and know it has nothing to do with you." She didn't look convinced. She opened her mouth to speak but then changed her mind.

Silence squatted uneasily between us. I was beginning to think my life was defined not only by what I had done and whom I had hurt but also by the awkward and painful silences that seemed to follow me around like ghosts refusing to leave.

Then she erupted, her anger breaking the silence like glass crinkling to the ground. "I've been doing this shitty desk work, waiting as patiently as I can until they feel comfortable enough to give me some real cases again. And nothing. Not a damn thing." Her anger flushed the nape of her neck.

She began again, calmer this time. "I just don't know how to prove to them that they should trust me with the big stuff. Why keep me here if I'm not going to work? Why accept my transfer in and then make me sit. I'm a good detective. A *damn* good detective. And they're wasting that, wasting me."

I opened the notebook I had been carrying. I removed the Xerox copies I had made of the crime scene photos, the interview notes, and the unknown Asian woman.

"Tell you what, why don't you keep these. If you're comfortable with it, look them over tonight and tell me what else you see, what strikes you as an anomaly, anything we should follow up." She didn't hesitate, took them right from my hand and flipped through them to see exactly what I had given her. Her left hand pushed a few wisps of hair that had escaped her ponytail back behind her ear.

"I'll tell *you* what," she replied, resolution in her voice. "I'll do better than that. Let me look through these interview notes in more detail and then I'll go re-canvas, or at least try to track down the people Mills and Larsen missed the first time around." The red of anger drained away from her face and neck as she spoke. I looked at her closely, examining her gray-green eyes for any hint that she was speaking in anger or haste. All I saw, or maybe all I wanted to see, was determination, finality, that strength of hers.

"You're sure?"

"Yes."

"Okay," I agreed. "Start with the neighboring businesses. Ryota and I will go over the residence. Divide and conquer, okay? Ask about the symbols, if anyone recognizes them, knows what they mean. Ask about Parks and any ties to Kansas. Show them the picture I brought back of the Asian woman. See if anyone recognizes her, either from that picture or if they imagine her older." I spoke in a rush.

"Marcus," Ash spoke in reply, slowly and with the hint of a slight pause between each word, "I am a damn good detective. I know what I am doing. Don't fall away like Markeze and the others did."

I pulled the Xeroxed picture of the Asian woman back from her, our fingers brushing momentarily. I turned the photo over, pulled a pen from my pocket, and scribbled my phone number on the back. It felt vaguely like a cheesy pickup move at a cop bar, where instead of a matchbook we would use a crime scene photo to exchange our phone numbers.

"Call me later tonight to update me." I handed the picture back to her. "You know how Ryota is, so let's keep this between us. If any trouble comes up for you, tell everyone that I lied to you and told you Markeze had changed his mind about your role. I'll take the blame for any fallout."

She smiled again. Different this time, with less innocence and more pity.

"That's sweet," she said, softly. "Not exactly tenable. But sweet." Then she turned, heading for the door and, I assumed, toward the interviews that would be going directly against what Markeze had told her. I felt like I should be wearing a fedora and admiring the spunk and moxie of the "little lady." But I figured if she knew that I was thinking in those terms she would slap the fedora off my head, maybe even demonstrate just how spunky she was by shooting me in the kneecaps.

So I turned instead toward Ryota, who I knew would never shoot me because there was no way to justify it in his inner book of right and wrong, no matter how much he might wish at times to fire a slug into me. When I reached our desk, however, I decided that I might have been wrong about the not shooting me part. He wasn't red in the face like Ash had been, but his eyes were colder than hers were. They showed a pool of anger that ran much deeper, with more violence attached to it, than anything I had seen in Ash. Cold and deep, like currents at the bottom of the ocean where sunlight never reached and oxygen remained scarce.

"Captain Markeze stopped by while you were with Ashlynn," he reported, no emotion coming through in his voice. I found the flatness more disturbing than any anger that might instead have been attached to it. "He told me that Ashlynn isn't to be involved in this case at all. He said, in fact, that you already knew that." He stared at me, coldly and angrily, then continued. "Don't put me on the bad side of this, Marcus. Don't put me in a spot where I have to choose between lying to Markeze or hurting you." He blinked and it all disappeared and he was a different person again. His eyes lost the icy coldness, as though some translucent outer layer had moved down to protect and hide everything underneath it. Pictures of snakes and nictitating membranes slipping over reptilian eyes filled my mind.

"No worries, Ryota," I replied, staring back at him. I thought again of cosmic circles: Ash would lie and hide the truth from Markeze; I would in turn lie and hide the truth from Ryota, who would then unknowingly hide the truth from Markeze.

As I walked away I realized that I had put myself in a familiar, uncomfortable space. I had lied in relationships before and had been on both sides of one partner cheating on another. I felt some of that taint now with Markeze and Ryota. Never before, however, had I felt like so much of a snake.

Chapter Eleven

Lake Washington roiled dark and choppy as Ryota and I drove over the I-90 floating bridge toward Renton, a Seattle suburb on the eastside of the water. I drove, while Ryota stared out the passenger window. Quiet tension filled the car, like the expandable foam that you use to fill cracks in the exterior of your home. It took all the air away as it expanded, until there was nothing in the car except a feeling of pressure. It reminded me of the last month Paige and I had shared together. Such good times.

"Not exactly a Rainier day, is it?" I asked.

"A what?"

"A Rainier day, that's what I used to call it with Paige. One of those gorgeous days we get where you can see Mt. Rainier out the window while you're crossing the water." I pointed to where Mt. Rainier hid behind the gray cloud cover. "Paige always said Seattle was schizophrenic that way: you get postcard views of Rainier in the summer; in the winter it's a completely different space around here."

"No, not exactly a Rainier day." He paused, looking out the window as he looked for the right words. "What went wrong with you and Paige? What is it that lets someone watch their marriage unravel as they cheat?"

They weren't questions I anticipated from a partner who never got personal. I feared he was going to offer me some dumb-ass self-improvement book. Maybe he'd even written one, I mused, imagining something entitled *The Right-Way to Live Your Marriage and Save Your Soul*.

"Shit, Ryota," I said. "You don't talk for half the ride, I chit-chat with you about Mt. Rainier, and now you turn into a therapist? Listen, if you want to bust my balls, forget it, I got enough of that from Paige." I shook my head as I turned toward him, but he seemed serious, like he truly wanted to know, to understand a depravity that his world couldn't encompass.

He looked ready to ask me something else, his eyes questioning or confused and his dark eyebrows lowering as he debated with himself whether or not to ask it. Then his face cleared, everything proper and back in exactly the right place, as neatly put together as his immaculately folded pocket square.

"Marcus," he started, his voice a flat-line this time, "I was serious when I told you not to put me in a bad spot with Markeze. I don't do well with deception. It eats me up. Don't force me into it."

I didn't say anything. Ryota was a pain in the ass but there was a part of him that I admired. I envied his ability to always do the right-thing, seemingly without any effort. He emanated an air that said he knew, and had always known, exactly who he was and where he was going. I lacked that kind of inner stability. Something inside me prevented complete connection with another and sabotaged things precisely when they were going "right." I could hold aloft the ideal but I also knew that I possessed some hidden, ineluctable weakness that barred me from getting there, keeping me mired in the mud of compromise and stuck with self-loathing for not reaching it.

I exited the freeway into Renton. Not your idyllic, get-away-from-it-all type of suburb, downtown Renton greeted us with a rundown Burger King and several overcrowded car lots. Rain-slicked pavement dominated the view, establishing a dreary symbiosis with the charcoal sky. A few turns later, however, and we moved away from the asphalt aesthetic. The dreariness proved harder to lose, the sun still coming through only as a translucent gray.

Jamie Parks's neighborhood wasn't anything special, but it did offer a view of some strikingly tall conifers that must have been marked as a Natural Growth preserve area to have survived the demands of suburban housing. Mostly bare at the bottom before sprouting into a pyramid of limbs and needles at the top third, they reminded me of giant pipe cleaners or those brushes used for cleaning baby bottles. They swayed slowly in the wind, in time to their own waltz, the tops bent crookedly.

The houses down Parks's street were small, architecturally dull units made even drabber by the weather. They were all at least thirty years old. Most looked worn down for lack of upkeep. A handful of homes, however, sparkled in comparison, the paint new, small yards well maintained, some with flower boxes holding the decorative cabbages and kales used for winter color.

We wheeled slowly down the residential street, turning right at a three-way stop that brought us across an invisible line demarcating single from multi-unit housing. Town homes and condos and apartments littered the area. Here too most were old and in need of some type of repair.

Jamie Parks's small apartment complex crouched low, close to the ground. The building struck me as utilitarian, post-WWII construction. L-shaped, it was only two stories, constructed out of painted cinder blocks that had aged into a dirty cream color.

I pulled close to a green Corolla covered in dirt from winter road spray. The street was largely empty, most cars resting for the day at business parks. The rain kept pedestrian traffic minimal, the sidewalks empty except for a group of three gangly teenagers, two Asian and one white, who joked raucously with one another as they walked by, each with a backpack lazily slung off of a single shoulder.

The manager, a balding man who might have been selected because he looked as short and squat as the apartment complex itself, let us in to Parks's unit without any trouble. He left to make it back to the end of the *Magnum P.I.* rerun we had interrupted.

"Not much to look at," Ryota noted, "but he kept it clean." The latter point garnered a point of appreciation from my partner.

"You start in here and I'll take the back room."

"Sure thing."

The bedroom appeared tidy as well: the bed made, no clothes strewn about on the floor, everything dusted fairly recently. No guns or illegal drugs or human body parts hiding in any of the drawers in the bureau. Just clothes, neatly folded and well organized. The furniture, though well cared for, was poor quality—particle board with flimsy joints and a thin, plastic veneer on top. In the closet, the right-side of the clothes bar had been devoted to long-sleeved shirts and the left-side had been segregated for short-sleeved ones. The walls were typical apartment complex "eggshell" white. No posters, pictures, or paintings anywhere in the room. On the whole, it was one of the most boring bedrooms I had ever seen.

The bathroom looked similarly unremarkable, though I was happy to note that the toilet had the start of an orange stain in the bowl. It helped me believe that Jamie Parks wasn't a robotic life form, interested only in cleanliness and order. All the bathroom accessories and accouterments looked discount-store cheap. The beige vinyl shower curtain hung by itself, no decorative cover on the outside. He brushed his teeth with a generic knock-off of one of the big-brand toothbrushes.

The small medicine cabinet held a mirror bordered by a narrow strip of white plastic, chipped in a few spots. A spider-web crack in the upper right corner fractured the mirror. The interior of the medicine cabinet, however, offered more evidence of human, rather than robotic, life: Zoloft and some prescribed sleeping pills. Nothing else of note.

"Anything here?" I hollered as I made my way back toward the kitchenette.

"I kind of like this guy," Ryota replied over the noise of a kitchen cabinet squeaking shut. "He keeps things clean, ordered. 'Good planning shows good sense,' that's what my father told me and this guy lived it. Besides," he finished as I entered the kitchenette, "the guy liked my brand of tea." Ryota smiled as he held out a tea bag, evidently of the same green tea that he and Ash had enjoyed earlier. Then he showed me a bamboo whisk with his other hand. "Looks like he mixed matcha tea as well. It's better than anything in a tea bag. I do the same when I have the time and space for it."

"That's great, Ry. I'll check the bedroom again to see if he has a secret stash of pocket squares too. Maybe he's a long-lost relative," I joked.

"He couldn't afford my kind of pocket squares." I think it was wry humor but maybe not. Hard to tell with him.

"Nothing good in the living area?" I asked, glancing at the small television, the worn out sofa, and the coffee table that reminded me of something you'd find in a college apartment.

"Not a thing," he answered.

"Strike one," I concluded, gesturing toward the door with reluctance. "Let's check the neighbors." My grand hope of finding the twin of the samurai sword or a folder of genealogical information revealing a hidden tie to the Breys had died a quiet death, suffocated by the ordinariness and cleanliness of Jamie Parks's apartment.

No one answered the door to the left of his place, so we moved to the other side of his apartment. As I knocked, I heard both a television and a radio on, the sounds colliding in chaos.

"Help you?" asked a heavy woman in her thirties, her limp hair hanging down to her jowls.

"We'd like to ask you some questions about your neighbor, Jamie Parks," I said as Ryota and I both badged her. She opened the door wider and invited us in. I found the sound level from the radio and television deafening, confusing.

"Jack, turn the damn television off. And turn down my radio," she commanded. Jack sat still on the couch for a long moment, as if to either register disapproval or prove to himself that he didn't have to do anything he didn't want to. After rising, he first turned the radio down to a low hum, then waited another long pause before flipping off his television program. I exchanged a glance with Ryota, feeling we had walked into passive-aggressive hell, where radios and televisions became weapons in a subtle, childish war for power. Ryota looked disturbed, maybe disgusted, by what he saw.

"Smells good, Mrs . . ." I left off with a questioning tone so she would offer her name. The odor of chili, cooking all day long in a crockpot, surrounded us as we waited for her answer.

"Shannon Sullivan. That lump over there is my husband, Jack Sullivan," she pointed to the couch. The lump didn't look back or even offer a polite nod in our direction. Guess I might not either if my wife introduced me as a lump.

The apartment had a similar layout to Parks's, though it was as filthy as his was clean, the dishes and dirty clothes probably doubling as props for whatever dysfunctional drama we had walked in on. Like his wife, Jack too was fat. His thin brown hair had started to recede at the temples. Unfashionable round, gold glasses highlighted his face. He fiddled with the remote control absentmindedly, embarrassed for us to see his life or anxious to get back to his show or angry at the strategic blunder of turning his television show off but leaving his wife's radio on and only turned low. He was probably planning some sort of nefarious revenge plot that involved hoarding the oyster crackers for tonight's chili dinner.

A closer look at Mrs. Lump convinced me that she would be big even if she lost the fat. She looked physical, carrying the sort of frame that on a man would lend itself to football or weight-lifting but for a woman had probably made it difficult to find a flattering prom dress. She gestured us toward the sofa. Seemingly unaware of our presence, the lump still watched the empty television screen, searching for patterns in the black. She stepped in front of the blank screen so that the lump couldn't miss her, then opened her eyelids wide as she moved her pupils to the left. She did this two or three times, marking an invisible path for the lump to follow. He stood up and moved to the smaller loveseat. Mrs. Lump chose not to sit next to him and remained standing in front of the television.

"What can I help you with?" she asked as Ryota and I sat on the sofa warmed up by the lump. "You said something about Jamie."

"Were you contacted yesterday by other detectives?" I asked.

"No, yesterday we were at work. We're only home today because it's our therapy day." She looked pleased, glad to tell us about it. "We each take a half day off for therapy. I like to go. He doesn't."

Given what we'd seen so far, the therapy part wasn't a shocker, though they might want to ask for their money back. Her tone and her eyes convinced me that she enjoyed bragging about the therapy, that talking about it to total strangers proved to her that she was damaged but on the road to recovery, while her husband was, well, a lump. I figured her for a drama queen, someone who would insert herself into any stressful situation, even if it didn't really have anything to do with her. Good news for us in that regard: hearing about Jamie Parks would make her feel part of something larger than the squat surroundings of her everyday life. She might be more than willing to spill anything she thought about him or the company he kept.

"He's dead. He was murdered. Bludgeoned to death," I said. The more drama the better for this one. Her eyes opened wide again, this time with excitement. Something new to talk about in therapy—yippee!

"That's terrible!" she gasped. Lump, shoulders slumped, still didn't move or show any awareness that we had spoken. Sitting mute and motionless on the loveseat, he became a part of the room, trying his best to blend into the background and melt into the furniture. He complemented her perfectly.

I had the feeling that she would relish Jamie Parks's death for the way in which it would allow her a momentary freedom to think that others had it worse than she did. I saw her as a vulture with a nose for carrion, rooting for the smell of a rotten marriage or a wayward child or, jackpot, a murder. This tragedy presented a perfect contrast for her: she could relish the idea that her neighbor experienced more pain than what she had to put up with, then congratulate herself on her own strength to trudge on tied to a lump. I wanted to leave as quickly as possible, leaving Lump to fend for himself with his oyster cracker defense.

"Yes, atrocious," Ryota agreed, having picked up on how to play this one. He had erased the look of disgust from his face, replacing it with what almost looked like a cold sparkle of enjoyment in his eyes. "Probably a baseball bat. Back of the head. Skull crushed."

Lump examined his fingernails. I pulled out a crime scene photo of Jamie Parks's body that clearly showed the Japanese kanji. I covered his head with my hand so that she would only be able to see the symbols. I didn't want her feasting on the carcass of Jamie Parks.

"Does this lettering mean anything to you?" I asked.

"Heavens no," she exclaimed. "Who is that? Is that," hand to her mouth, "Jamie?"

Ryota looked angry again. Lump remained lost to another realm of existence.

"The lettering doesn't ring any bells at all?" I asked again. "Nothing you've seen before? Nothing anyone else has ever shown you? Nothing Jamie mentioned or showed you?"

"Absolutely not," she answered, probably more affronted that I would doubt her than anything specific I had said. "I've never seen those before. Ever."

"How about this woman?" I asked, showing her the photo from Mr. Brey's pocket.

"No, I've never seen her either. Who is she?"

I turned to Lump.

"Sir, have you seen these symbols or this woman before?" He looked up briefly, then shook his head in the negative. A very quiet "no" escaped from his lips, proving he could, in fact, speak. He was beaten and damaged, but it was emotional and psychological damage, nothing to his voice box.

Turning back to Mrs. Lump I saw a dull gleam in her eyes as she spoke. "Terrible, isn't it? That poor family has already had so much to deal with. Now this. I mean, we all have a lot to deal with, don't we?" She cast a quick glance in the direction of the lump. "But this is more than a family should have to bear."

"What do you mean?" Ryota asked, his voice as innocent and as pleading as he could make it.

"Oh, you haven't heard?" she asked, delighting in having information that we didn't, in being able to offer something special. Another gold star for the upcoming therapy session. "His mother was killed too. Last week." Ryota and I both pulled out notebooks, as though we were synchronized swimmers trying to earn a medal from Mrs. Lump.

"I felt so sorry for him," she continued. "I knocked on his door several times and tried calling him over and over again to let him know I was there for him if he needed me. We had each other's phone numbers for emergencies. My idea. When I finally saw the poor man I told him how bad it was for me when my own mother died. Natural causes, of course. Not murder like his. But I wanted him to know, to really know, that I was there for support."

As strong as balsa wood for him, I was sure. The kind of support that gets buildings condemned and lives lost. Lump looked down at his shoes and then bit his nails. He had seen this all before, I suppose. The rest of us formed a triangle, Ryota and I on the couch and Mrs. Lump still in front of the television. Lump sat outside our boundaries, yet somehow couldn't leave. Rooted to the loveseat, silent once more, he reminded me of a worn out decoration, an old, ugly throw pillow, one you'd find at a thrift store, with stuffing creeping out of loose and broken seams.

"My goodness," Ryota said, "how was his mother killed?"

"You know, that man wouldn't talk to me hardly at all. I offered and offered and he just pushed me away." She had a look of amazement on her face. I had the feeling she could fund her therapist's vacation home all by herself.

"A pity," I said. Ryota nodded his head in agreement.

"I brought him a lasagna right after I heard. You shouldn't feel alone when you're at your weakest."

Prime feeding time for parasites, I thought.

"He thanked me for being there, you know," she said with barely suppressed pride. "I don't know why he got so cold toward me later," she mused.

"What did he say when you brought the lasagna? So nice of you, by the way," Ryota said.

"Oh, he was sad but happy to see me. He looked pale and seemed about to cry."

"I can only imagine," Ryota confirmed. "But what did he say about his mother?"

"He wouldn't tell me much about it. I finally convinced him that he had to let some of it go. I learned that in therapy." She looked smug. "That's when he told me that the poor woman was beaten to death. Can you believe it?" The last seemed less a query about how tragic it was and more a question about the level of titillation it offered. She shook her head from side to side, lips pressed thin at what the world had come to, but her breath came quick with the excitement of living on someone else's suffering instead of her own for a few minutes. I wondered if perhaps she weren't big-boned but instead bloated with a dark, sad place inside of her that she would unleash on others like a cancer, gorging on their pain before it returned inside of her. I shivered slightly.

"I don't think he told me all of the details." She pursed her lips and angled them to the side, considering that there was more that she hadn't dragged out of the man. "But who I feel so terribly sorry for," she mused, "is his poor son. You know, for the longest time I didn't even know Jamie had a son." Ryota and I both scribbled away in our notebooks. I made a note to see if we could find any more information regarding Jamie Parks's son.

"Can you believe that he never mentioned he had a son before? There must be something wrong there, don't you think?" she asked, her query a camouflage for judgment. "Around the time of his mother's funeral I saw someone going in and out of his apartment with him and, you understand, he didn't get visitors often. So I asked him if everything was all right and who the young man was that I kept seeing. I didn't want anyone to take advantage of him while he was in such a state of mourning." She paused to look at us. "He said it was his son. His son. I could hardly believe it. And now that poor boy has lost a grandmother *and* a father. Even if he hadn't really been there much for him, Jamie was still the boy's father." She shook her head slowly.

"What was his son's name?" I asked. "You wouldn't happen to have any contact information for him, would you?"

"I don't know his name. Jamie wasn't very talkative about him. I know it was a hard time for him. But really, he could have introduced us. You two probably get it all the time so you'll know what I'm talking about. It's hard when you're trying and trying to help someone and they just push you away."

I removed a business card from my wallet as Ryota and I stood. My instinct was to hand it to Lump, give him some ammunition in the slow-spiral toward mutually-assured-destruction that constituted the marriage he and his wife lived. But I knew he would never contact us, and giving him the card might assure that Mrs. Lump would, out of spite, never call us if she happened to remember something else. She needed to think of herself as special, that we had made her privy to something no one else was. So I gave her the card, with as much formality as I could muster.

"Ma'am, this is my business card. If you think of anything else of importance, regarding either the late Jamie Parks or his deceased mother or his estranged son, please get in touch. You've been a big help," I finished, a taste like alum puckering my mouth.

"I will detectives. I most certainly will," she said, a glimmer of pride and self-importance overtaking her shock at the murders. Lump remained seated while his wife led us to the door, which now felt more like an escape hatch.

Chapter Twelve

Outside the apartment, a look of disgust overtook Ryota, as though he were afraid that their sad life could somehow infect him.

"Marital bliss," I joked. He started to answer but stopped, instead nudging me in the ribs and pointing to the formerly empty apartment on the other side of Jamie Parks's place.

A man appeared to be just locking up to leave, a backpack, not unlike what I had seen earlier on the kids outside on the sidewalk, hanging from his shoulder. He started to turn toward the stairs to exit, his keys jangling as he moved to put them in his pocket.

"Sir, could you hold on a minute, please?" Ryota asked in a very official sounding voice.

The man turned, quizzical and harried at the same time.

"What do you need? I have an appointment and need to jet." He wore dark, expensive-looking jeans and a black leather jacket—the kind popular in the 70s and making a comeback today. He must be doing better financially than most of the people in this rundown complex, or had different priorities. He started toward us.

He had black hair with blonde strands, the hair covering about half of his ears and also hanging partly in front of his eyes. A closer look showed a short man, older than I thought at first. Certainly older than I imagined the age range for blonde streaks and a backpack.

"Thanks for stopping, Mr. . . . ?" I again let the intonation hang in the air, demanding to be answered.

"Stimson. Hank Stimson. Friends call me Stimmy."

"Do you know your neighbor, Mr. Jamie Parks, very well?" questioned Ryota.

"Yeah, I know Jamie. What's up?" he asked.

"What can you tell us about him?" Ryota continued.

"I dunno. Guy's quiet. We're not drinkin' buddies or anything. Different priorities." He paused, deliberating. He looked only at me, even when Ryota directed the questions. "Guy's kind of an asshole. Ignorant."

"How so?" I asked.

He sucked his lips toward his teeth as he heard my question, then answered. "Just an asshole." An undercurrent of venom traveled with his words but he smiled at me like we were making fun of Jamie Parks together.

"When did you last see him?" I asked, refusing to let my stare break from his eyes.

"I dunno. He's not high on my list of priorities. Maybe four or five days ago. Why?" he asked but didn't really seem to care.

"He was killed. Murdered," Ryota replied. Stimmy still didn't say anything. Just looked at me, indifferent.

"Where were you yesterday morning?" I asked.

"At work, dude," he said, offended. "Bellevue Best Buy, speaker department. Check it. Then you can come apologize to me, man." Ryota jotted down the information while I stared back, feeling my anger rise while at the same time knowing better.

Ryota's cell rang, no special music or anything, just a normal ring, which sounded abnormal in comparison to the crap everyone else used. He glanced my way. I nodded to let him know he could take it. I didn't see Johnny Cool making a mad dash to get away. Ryota answered, then stepped away.

"Did you know Jamie's mother was murdered too? Does that mean anything to you?" I asked, glaring at him.

"Wiping out the whole clan, huh?" he answered. His eyes had lost some of their coldness, filled now with glitter and amusement at how he was getting under my skin.

"Not exactly. He has a son."

"I didn't know that," he answered, quieter this time, almost silent. "That's not good."

"Does this woman look familiar to you? Or did Jamie ever mention Kansas to you?" I asked, showing him the picture from Mr. Brey's pocket and trying to seize the momentum I had gained. He didn't answer right away.

"No. And no," he finally said. "I have to jet. You know where to find me." He stood for a few long seconds, then turned, pushed open the scarred metal door to the stairwell and left.

Ryota finished his phone call as I finished the conversation with the charming Stimmy.

"Everything all right?" I asked.

"Everything's fine." He left me standing while he headed down the stairs.

The drive back across the water was even quieter than the drive over, with Ryota consumed once more with thoughts that didn't include me. The water on Lake Washington still churned, though the north side of the bridge appeared perfectly calm while the south side was choppy. I suppose the floating bridge itself arrested the movement of the waves, forcing a false calm where there otherwise wouldn't be one. It made me think of split personalities, of seeing one thing and missing something else entirely.

Once across the water, we left I-90 for the bumpy concrete of I-5. Rainwater bejeweled the glass, steel, and concrete of downtown Seattle. The moisture clung to the buildings like a protective layer, sheathing the skin beneath.

We parked along the curb in front of Parks's convenience store. We were south and east of Pioneer Square, an area filled with bars, clubs, and late night violence that often spilled out at closing time. We were a bit north of the International district, a spot bustling with Uwajimaya, the great Asian grocery store, and myriad Asian food spots. Jamie Parks's store sat between these two downtown areas. Not fitting neatly into either category, this in between area had grown neglected, overlooked by those in search of either Pioneer Square or Asian food and culture.

I exited the car before Ryota. It might have been the first time that had ever happened. He usually had the handle of his door in his hand while I was still moving the gear selector to "P." I usually figured his eagerness grew from an inner impulsion to always be ready, never let the job or anyone else down. Or maybe I smelled. That's the danger with a quiet partner: you can fill in the silent blanks however you want.

We approached Parks's convenience store, which had crime scene tape festooned across the doorway. From the outside, it seemed an unremarkable space: a single glass door, one big metal handle on the outside for customers to pull and one skinny bar on the inside to push the door open. Smudges all over the door, with black fingerprint powder clinging to many of them. Both the door and the small rectangular store window had been updated with black bars to discourage would-be intruders from shattering the glass. A cardboard sign advertising Powerball lottery tickets in crooked handwriting stood askew in the bottom right corner of the window.

The neighboring shops presented a downtown potpourri determined by rental rates and the age of businesses. It looked like an area dominated by businesses either very young or very old. The upwardly mobile, middle-aged businesses had departed for better real estate, leaving those just starting out and desperate for lower rent and those that had been here forever and whose outlooks for growing into something more prosperous had died a long time ago.

Ryota looked surprised, then furious as he glimpsed Ash inside Parks's store. "Just think of her as an advance scout, Ry. Let's see what she has." I moved toward the door. He didn't follow. I turned back toward him as I reached the yellow crime scene tape. "She's been helpful. She deserves this and it's all on me. You're clean."

This time I didn't wait for him. The shrill tinkle of a bell, a real bell and not the electronic ding that you often hear now, accompanied me as I entered the store. Ash looked up from behind the counter. No smile this time, just a look of concentration.

"Find anything at the residence?" she asked and turned back toward her survey of what Parks had stashed behind the counter. The bell chimed again, briskly, as Ryota pulled angrily at the door and entered.

"Ryota," Ash said simply. This time she didn't return to her study of the counter and its contents. Ryota didn't answer. If this were a cartoon, his face would have been bright red with steam jetting from his ears and puffing from his nostrils. Since I didn't have a bottle of seltzer water to spray on him, I chose to ignore him and let him cool down on his own.

"His apartment wasn't much to see—clean and boring. His neighbors were interesting. So interesting that we might want to look into suicide," I joked. "What do you have for us?"

"The guy next door on the left—the marble and tile dealer—wants to be helpful but doesn't have much to offer. He closes his shop at five every evening and hadn't noticed anything unusual during the day. Says he had talked to Parks a few times when he popped in here to buy a bottle of water or a snack. Didn't really know him very well. Said Parks was quiet. Unreadable and quiet, with a cup of tea always at hand. The drycleaner on the other side," Ash concluded, "wasn't there when I stopped by. The marble guy said the drycleaner has been closed for about a week now. No idea why. Nothing of interest from any of the other neighboring tenants."

Ryota continued to glare, his eyes shuttling his anger back and forth from Ash to me. The store smelled stale, the air resonant with the dried sugary odor of spilled soda and a heavy quality that made me think of hydrogenated snacks: powdered sugar donuts, fruit pies, Doritos, and the like. Tension, or maybe it was the trans-fats, pulsed through the air, settling like invisible dust motes on the pores of my skin and leaving me uncomfortable and vaguely itchy.

"I found this tucked on the shelf below the register, covered with this handkerchief," Ash said. Her gloved hands held a rectangular white cloth and a slender book detailing *The Art of Tea*. Ryota's eyes relented a bit and he approached Ash to take a closer look.

"I know this book," Ryota started. "It's about the Japanese tea ceremony. And that," he said, pointing at the white cloth, "isn't a handkerchief. It's a *chakin*. A cloth used in the tea ceremony to wipe the tea bowl, or *matchawan*."

"That fits," I said. "You found the business neighbor who didn't know much about Parks except that he always had a cup of tea. And at his home he had a cabinet stocked with tea, greens and matcha. Remember Ry?" I asked, trying to draw him further away from his anger and closer to the case.

"Of course I remember," he answered. His eyes were hard and cold again. "You shouldn't be here, Ashlynn. This shouldn't involve you. This is the last thing I need right now. You shouldn't be part of this. I like you." He spoke slowly, his words measured and hard, each syllable like iron. His eyelids dropped almost mechanically. I could see his eyes moving behind them, scanning from side to side as though he were in the midst of a nightmare. He opened his eyes and shook his head wearily back and forth at me, the movement small but firm. Then he turned and left the store, the bell's brittle chime hanging in the air.

It wasn't much, but it was as mad as I had ever seen Ryota. He likes to stay in control, of himself and any situation in which he finds himself. I had the sense that I had pushed the latter beyond his grasp, and his grip on the former had almost unraveled as well. One look at Ash told me I had more than Ryota to worry about and that my damage control was going to be more complicated.

"What happened to me giving you a call later to update you?" she asked. "You showing up here feels like you're double-checking on me and don't trust me. And worse, now I've got Ryota tangled in knots and yelling at me too."

"Shit, Ash. It has nothing to do with trust. We finished up quicker at Parks's place than I would have guessed. What do you want me to do, tell Ryota that we should just pack it in for the day? You know he'd never go for that. Plus, I need this case done quick: it's personal for me, remember? We can't sit around and wait, even if that means we have to step on toes." I looked her in the eyes. "I need you with me."

She took a deep breath, her nose quivering slightly on the exhale, her anger draining out of her green eyes.

"I have to run and grab Ryota before he tries to leave me without a car or something. He is, you know, the type to hotwire a department ride and go nuts." I winked at her. "Finish up here. I trust you, that's why I wanted you on this with me. You know Spitfire, in Belltown?" I asked. She shook her head no. "You can't beat their guacamole and margaritas. I'll meet you there at 7:00 and we'll plan our next steps."

Another deep breath from her. "This isn't going to end well, is it, Marcus?" She didn't wait for an answer. "See you at 7:00."

I stepped from the convenience store's fusty air to the smell of rain on asphalt outside. Ryota sat in the passenger seat, staring straight-ahead, no sign that anything of interest to him might be taking place at Parks's store. His kept his back so ramrod straight that my own spine began to ache.

The ride back to the department was a silent one. Ryota never turned his eyes and his back never broke from its vertical plane.

Chapter Thirteen

I beat Ash to Spitfire, which gave me time to drink a couple of margaritas and catch, on flatscreens hanging at every possible eye angle, the last half of the Kansas Jayhawks battling the Texas Longhorns. I had found a spot where I could also keep an eye on the door, watching for Ash. KU moved into their high-low set and, just as Ash entered, found room off of a backdoor cut for a monster alleyoop. The Jayhawk fans scattered throughout the bar erupted with cheers and high-fives.

"All for me," she mouthed from across the room, gesturing toward the applause and putting her hands to her cheeks in mock astonishment.

She looked spectacular. I had only interacted with her on the job. The bottom of her naturally curly hair had an extra spring to it, caressing her neck, waving at me as she walked closer. She wore a flowered shirt, like something from the 60s, that was cut loose and tight all at the same time: it clung to her chest then opened just below, ruffling at the hem that sat even with her hips.

"Marcus," she said simply as she neared my table, her eyes

crinkling into a smile as her mouth worked to stay even. A drunken shout of "ROCK, CHALK, JAYHAWK" made her turn toward the bar. The double belt loop below the small of her back formed an "X," as though it had been sewn especially for me to hook my finger into and draw her closer to me, until I could feel her pressed against my own jeans. The margaritas on an empty stomach might not have been the smartest move.

Ash turned back from the disturbance at the bar and sat down across the table.

"You didn't order one for me?" She pointed at my near-empty glass and feigned hurt.

"Didn't know if you preferred blended or on the rocks," I answered, smiling. "I would guess on the rocks," I added.

"Of course," she replied. "Blended reminds me of a slushee from 7-11. Not *muy auténtico*," she smiled back.

I momentarily delighted in the warmth of the tequila and Ash's smile, until the thought of Mr. Brey pulled my attention back to the murders.

"Listen, Ash," I began, "sorry about today with Ryota. Not fair of me to put you, or Ryota, in that position. It was selfish of me."

She didn't respond right away, looking instead for our server, a mid-twenties guy with messy, spiky hair and a nose ring. When she saw him, she pointed at my margarita then held up two fingers and mouthed "*dos*" at him.

"I hope you realize that you're playing right into my nefarious plot: to woo you with margaritas and warm tortilla chips until you can't imagine anything other than staying on the case." I gave her my best smile.

"No hard feelings," she said, ignoring my plottings and responding to my earlier apology. "I'm on edge right now too." She looked away as if she had shared more than she had intended. Our nose-ringed server brought the two margaritas and took my empty away. A lone half-melted ice cube clanged, like a soggy bell, against the side as he picked it up. Ash brushed away her moment of openness with a smile. "Relax, Marcus," she replied, "you had me at hell-of-a-murder case." She grinned.

I laughed. "That's why I took up this career: the endless opportunities to court women on the job. I wear crime scene odor like cologne, peddle murder as an aphrodisiac, wrap small romantic presents with crime scene tape, that type of thing." She smiled again, eyes sparking, and took another drink of her margarita. A speckle of salt clung momentarily to her full top lip.

She stopped smiling. "You owe me an explanation." Thinking I had ridden the tequila too far and had become too forward too fast, I silently cursed. She laughed again and pretended to throw a chip at me. "Is it really that bad? You're supposed to tell me why some of the old hands call you Melville, remember?"

I relaxed. "You're right, you're right." I turned serious. "You'll also now be one of the privileged few who get to hear the real story. I usually just tell everyone that it's one of those nicknames borne out of locker room humor and has something to do with Moby Dick," I joked.

"You mean like when everyone calls a really fat person 'Slim?' That type of thing?" she asked, eyelashes fluttering.

I smiled in spite of myself, liking that she could keep me off balance. Not sure how to respond to her joke, I moved back to the promised explanation. "I spent a few years in college as an English major. Sean, that's my former partner, took me out shortly after we got paired up. For a get to you know drunk session. It worked. I got drunk. He got to know about my brief time as a lit major—I spouted something stupid about how I thought a good detective had to be willing to chase the white whale no matter the cost. Sean thought that was hilarious. And voila," I said, opening my hands wide, "I became Melville around the department."

"So why'd you leave life as an English major?" she asked. "Too much time in coffee shops instead of bars?"

"Not real enough to me. That's all. I loved it, loved the words and the stories and how it all fit together. But there were times I'd be sitting at my desk and it all hit me that it was plastic and pointless and not important. It left me feeling too alone and isolated doing it."

She looked at me quizzically. "Words weren't enough. I wanted to feel part of something bigger than just me."

"And the department gives you that," Ash finished, understanding. "Police family." I didn't answer, instead jiggling my ice, watching the trail of water that the half-melted cubes left on the interior of my margarita glass. "Do they still call you Melville?" she asked.

"No, not so much anymore."

"Because?"

"Of a case a few years back. A difficult and messy case." I paused, trying to find a path out of where this was going. "It damaged a lot of people, including my partner."

"And you?" Another question I didn't want to answer.

"I was the one who finally caught the white whale. At least that's what Sean told everybody else."

"And the nickname evaporated after that, huh?"

I nodded.

"Police family," she said once more.

I didn't say anything. Picking up on my discomfort, Ash steered us back to the current case. "I didn't find anything else noteworthy in Parks's store."

"Not much to report from his apartment either," I returned, happy to be on safe ground in the present once more. "It's a pretty bare place. A guy with a pretty bare life, I think. He did have more stuff related to tea at his apartment. But no severed heads in the freezer or meth lab hidden in his bedroom or counterfeiting equipment in the bathroom." This time she didn't smile, eyes directed at me but looking elsewhere, remembering something.

"I've been thinking about what Ryota said," she started, "about that cloth being something that's sole purpose is to wipe out a tea bowl. Assuming he's right, and I don't recall hearing any stories about him *ever* being wrong, what's it doing there all by itself? We find a special cloth but don't find the special bowl that goes with it anywhere." She waited a half-second, then continued. "And Marcus, I checked that place good. There's no bowl."

I nodded as I followed her line of thinking. "Doesn't make sense for Parks to take a chakin to work but not the tea bowl itself." We were both quiet for a moment, considering this path. As I thought through the details, I ate the warm tortilla chips, the salt and slightly viscous grease fueling my detective brain and soaking up the tequila that I could feel happily swimming around in my stomach.

"We need to ask Ryota more about what a chakin is and what else goes along with it," Ash concluded. "That's the link to follow."

"I agree," I said, but my mind moved back to Mr. Brey and my father as I spoke. I took another, generous drink of my margarita, negating all the chips I had just eaten. "Do you remember how I mentioned that the man who basically was my father was tied into this, that he might have been murdered by the same guy?"

"Of course." Her eyes narrowed slightly, either from hurt that I would doubt her or from confusion about where I was going with this.

"Good," I said absentmindedly, softly. "Before I returned from the funeral in Kansas, I went to see my real father. My genetic father. Mr. Brey had given him something and he then passed it on to me." I felt my own eyes narrow as I spoke. "It's this samurai sword. I have no idea why Mr. Brey had it or why he gave it to my father. But now I have it and it makes me wonder why we keep coming back to all of these Japanese things: the chakin, the kanji symbols for 'harmony' and 'truth' and, maybe, this sword. I don't yet understand it, but the pattern is pretty clear."

"You're right. You *have* to be right." Ash turned to search for our server.

"No more for me. I had a bit before you got here."

This time she held up only one finger, mouthing "*uno*" to nose-ring guy.

As she turned to the side to order, her profile opened to me. Her tight curls hung just below her shoulders. Her shirt molded tight against her slender arm, until the fabric flared out at the wrist to also cover the bottom third of her milky hand, making her thin fingers look even more delicate and giving her that element of the fragile that mixed so potently for me with her intensity and resolve. The light of ESPN highlights from the flatscreens cast a warm, electronic glow over her hair and her freckles and her shirt that covered just enough of her hands. I ate a few more chips and pulled my attention back to the case and away from the vulnerability that I cast upon her in the midst of all the violence that we dealt with.

"Okay, so what's the plan?" she asked.

I ate one more chip as I thought through her question. "We need to look at Jamie Parks's mom. A neighbor told me and Ryota that she was murdered last week. We need to go back through the case files to find whatever is available on Mrs. Parks and what her story is. See if there's anything unusual or anything we can link to Jamie or Mr. Brey or Mike."

"I didn't know about his mom." Her voice was difficult to hear above the din of the suddenly loud sports bar as a highlight drew shouts and clapping. "But that should be pretty easy to track down. What else are you thinking, Marcus? You look worried."

My answer filled me with more anxiety and tension than I wanted to admit. "We turn to the past. I need to look back more at Mr. Brey. More at his dad. His dad was some kind of WWII hero." I heard myself speaking much faster than I normally did. "I need to figure out how his family is tied to Seattle, why and when they moved to Kansas, what kind of war hero he was." I stopped, reluctant to say more, do more with this.

"How do you do that?"

"I'll start with Mr. Brey's dad," I answered, forcing my attention to stay here and not try to escape to ESPN highlights or toward nose-ring boy and the ease with which I could order another margarita. I could almost taste the salt on my tongue, feel the alcohol sliding down my throat. "I'll put in a call to St. Louis tomorrow morning. The military maintains all personnel records there, so if Mr. Brey's dad earned a Medal of Honor or something, they'll know. To go forward, we go back," I concluded, thinking to myself how odd that sounded to someone who hated to look backward. It scared me, in ways that death or mutilated bodies rarely did.

"Come back to me, Marcus."

"What do you mean?" I tried not to sound defensive. I don't think I succeeded.

"You know how they say that the eyes are the window to the soul?" she questioned, holding my gaze and somehow overpowering my instinct to turn away. "Your eyes say too much, Marcus. They scare me. They shout pain. Like you've walled away all of your hurt but forgot to shut out the eyes." She faltered for a moment while looking for the right words. "It's like you're on fire inside but only your eyes give hint that something is burning down."

She seemed embarrassed for saying so much. Yet she never let her eyes off of my own and I wanted to believe that she was trying to say silently what she couldn't quite voice. I wanted to believe that she could see my damage, had already intuited my limitations, but had also decided that my wounds wouldn't drive her away. In the smoky depths of her eyes, I found more forgiveness of my faults and insecurities than I ever granted myself. Holding my gaze, she gave me back to myself, bolstered, patched over through some kind of magic floating within those gray-green irises.

It was something I had never seen before, either in the mirror or in the eyes of another woman. I continued to hold her eyes, transfixed, while I grabbed instinctively for my margarita, only to find nothing there. I felt naked, exposed.

Then something more flashed in her eyes and an uncanny hunger stared at me, transmitting naked, raw desire plus something else less familiar. I felt from her an intense sexual longing, a yearning for my skin on her skin, mixed with an almost desperate craving that I see and protect the pain and loneliness that she normally kept hidden. It made me feel that she would shelter me but also insisted that I move toward and safeguard her. That was what did it for me, this magnetic sense I saw in her eyes of being simultaneously strong and scared, a demand that I open myself to her but only if I also provide harbor for her when she opened herself to me.

I broke her gaze, not confident at all that I could fulfill either of the demands I saw in her eyes, scared to give my self fully to her and maybe even more scared to open my arms to hold the pain I saw returned. I felt emotionally infantile, as though she had asked me to do something I had never before been able to do. I glanced quickly down and to the left, my eyes and my embarrassment doing a synchronized dance to avoid Ash seeing more of my selfishness and insufficiencies.

I tried to swallow the dryness out of my throat. This time I was the one looking around anxiously for nose-ring guy. I couldn't find him anywhere. Ash didn't say anything. I stopped my searching and caught, once again, her gaze. Her eyes seemed unbelievably large to me, open to everything, filters removed. Her slate irises shimmered from the heat of the emotional fire I saw within her. The outer part of her eyes glistened from tears held back. She seemed so open, so unprotected, as though the tears that I could see rimming were all that were left to shield her. It seemed like such a puny defense, the salt-water of crying an armor so woefully lacking.

I felt, deeply, that showing me this hidden vein of pain was a profound gift. It was my decision what to do with it, how to hold it. It felt disorienting, yet also exhilarating, as though greater textures were there to be discovered.

"Ash," I started, then stopped. I felt my eyes cycling back and forth, left and right in small, rapid movements as we sat on the conversational precipice I had just constructed. I felt an overpowering sense that the next moment was important, as much for me as it was for Ash or for any crazy, delirious chance for an "us." I found myself in a spot oddly lighted, a space that was either the dawn of dusk or the dusk of dawn. What happened next could be the beginning of the end, in which case we had already experienced the best of it and only more darkness awaited. Or, my words might push us beyond the starting line, transform tonight into the end of the beginning phase and open us toward future forward movement.

"Your eyes, Ash, frighten me too. They frighten me for you—for the hint of what I see in them about your own pain. And they frighten me for me—for the sense that you see and accept in me things that I don't even fully see or understand in myself. I somehow have the sense that you look at me and read everything about me, and I don't understand." I faltered again. "I don't understand how if you do see me so clearly you're still sitting across from me. Shit," I said, "this doesn't make sense when I say it out loud. It's what I see in your eyes. It feels like you know me in ways I don't even know myself and accept things in me that I can't accept in myself." I glanced down, searching for better words, finding only chip crumbs and dirt. "And I don't even understand what hurt you have."

When I looked back, her eyes appeared hesitant. Not closed completely, but wary, waiting. I read a cautious desire to speak to me of her own pain, of this part of her that must have been sitting on her shoulder as a third-party to all of the other conversations we had, but I hadn't seen it clear enough.

It seemed that she *wanted* me to see those intimations of her pain and insecurities, somehow trusted me to see them. That openness unsettled me more than seeing the pain itself. I always guarded, jealously, my own hurt, clenched my fist as tightly as I could to keep the pain squeezed inside. I worried that I wouldn't know what to do if I let it out and shared it fully with someone else. I feared that in sharing the hurt I would make it even worse, would by the very act of giving words to the pain, make those pus-filled wounds cut deeper and longer. I wasn't sure how or where to move with what she had given me.

"Why are you with me on this?" I asked. "I know the case grabbed you. I saw that excitement. But I don't get why you're going against Markeze. I don't get why you're here, why you're pushing your chips to the center of the table with me. Everyone else wants to fold and you're still here." Her eyes lost some of the wariness.

A tiny, tired laugh escaped from between her lips. She tilted her head down toward the table as she raised her hands from her lap, capturing waterfalls of her auburn hair between her palms and smoothing it behind her ears. It was a nervous gesture, one probably meant to give her distance and protect her. For me, though, it only highlighted yet again her vulnerability, her neck and the freckles resting there fully exposed. She saw me watching, became aware of what she was doing, and smiled guiltily as she dropped her hands back to her lap and her hair fell back to her neck. Her left index finger pushed a tortilla chip crumb across and around our table, doodling with it on the tabletop like one would with a pen on paper.

"You don't know?" she finally asked.

"Know what?"

"Markeze might be more standup than I thought," she cryptically answered. She caught her breath and continued. "I'm not just caught in some departmental scheduling snafu, Marcus. I'm relegated to desk duty to keep me out of trouble. It's a way to keep me safe from myself. At least I think that's what Markeze has in mind—career suicide watch to keep me from destroying myself. And here I am," she chuckled again, this time with more humor and less resignation, "consorting with the *enemy*," the last word spoken in mock horror, her slate-green eyes opened wide.

"I do have a tendency to burn those closest to me," I warned her.

"I thought you would have heard by now," she responded. "I've been my own fire bug. I can set myself afire, no help from you required." We sat silently, absorbed in our own thoughts, our own past failures.

Chapter Fourteen

I finally broke the silence, not wanting to lose her to it. "We make quite a pair, then. I'm self-destructive enough that I could douse myself in gasoline and then immediately find a fire juggler to date."

She dismissed my half-joke. "Marcus, I painted myself into a corner through some dumb mistakes. A long time ago, tied to my first big arrest. My partner Rod and I got a disturbing the peace call at an off-campus apartment in the university district. We arrive and there's music blaring, so it all seems pretty clear. We knock on the door and, no shit, the guy answers with a roach in his hand, marijuana smoke cocooning around him." While she talked, she grabbed for one of the few remaining broken chip pieces in the basket, her hands in the present but her mind in the past.

"Rod moves into the place ahead of me while I'm putting the bracelets on this guy. He's stoned and slow of speech and won't shut up about 'Jenny Baby' this and 'Jenny Baby' that and 'Jenny Baby' being a bitch and cheating on him. I'm stuck taking care of him and thinking I need to hurry so I can catch up with Rod." She stopped, some mental shortcut operating that truncated everything that was left. "The details don't matter much, Marcus. Upshot is that I forgot to Mirandize the son-of-a-bitch. He told me how much he loved 'Jenny Baby' and laughed to me about how he smoked the dude she was cheating with and then smoked the guy's weed. He walked because of me."

I didn't say anything, giving her space to move around the past. My silence brought her eyes back from the past and up from the table toward mine, searching for my response. Maybe testing my reaction.

"I think you should cut yourself a little slack and find a little space to breathe. You were a rookie. Part of your mind had to be thinking about where your partner was, what stuff he might be walking into."

Ash looked back down at the table again, the top of her head pointed at my left shoulder.

"It gets worse," she said, her voice muffled as her words hit the surface of the black table before bouncing up toward me. She didn't wait for me to ask how. "Rod and I started sleeping together about a week later." Her hands bunched into fists, then her fingers curled down to the base of her palms, her nails scraping against her skin throughout the motion. She repeated this over and over as she talked. "His wife had died a few months earlier of bone cancer. Our thing only lasted a couple of confusing weeks. I think he felt responsible for my mistake. I felt sorry for him. After our few weeks together, we both realized it was nothing more than his pain getting mixed up with my pain, his pity for me with my pity for him. It never became anything that the department had to step in with, nothing more than a word of gossip that I don't think anyone really believed."

"I don't get why that's keeping you from catching active cases. Markeze's a stand-up guy, someone who's been around long enough to know black and white is made up of shades of gray. Hell, he understands that even the shades of gray hold shadows and shallows."

"This seems to be a shadow that I can't get rid of. Rod and I worked it out. No problems. Mutual embarrassment, but no bad feelings. He went on with his career and I went on with mine. I've busted my ass to get here, to get into the squad with you guys." She rubbed her hand vigorously over the top of her head, her curls cascading up and down, left and right, in an explosion of reddish-brown hair. A deep breath in and the hiss of an exhalation later she continued. "You know Walter Harvey, right? I figure you must because he told me to stay away from you. You were, he said, a royal prick who would rather piss on you when you're down than help you up." She allowed herself a small smile and the twinkle was back in her eyes for a quick moment. "That's how I knew you must be okay. If he thinks you're bad, that's good."

Walter Harvey was a piece of work. I'd been told that once upon a time he had been solid. I'd only known him as a total shitball who undertook the least amount of work possible on the easiest cases possible. He was a lazy, hypertensive drunk. His face was always red, his breath labored, sweat mixed with last night's alcohol beading on his forehead every time I saw him. He'd cashed in any pretense at dedication to the job or belief in justice a long time ago and was only hanging on by his yellowed nails to make it to full pension.

Rumors circulated that he cooped it, sleeping in his car while he should have been chasing leads or going home to his wife. He was a sad shell of a man, withdrawn into the bottle and into his odd little hobby—radio-controlled airplanes. He kept R/C airplane magazines around all the time and flew every chance he got. I always imagined that if he really did sleep in his car, he probably used old hobby magazines as his blanket and pillows.

"Yeah, I know Walt," I answered. "He's a vindictive shitball." I left it at that, though could have said more. We'd had our run-ins, including a time when I saw him lean on and then beat a teenager for no other reason than to enjoy the fear in the kid's eyes.

I decided we could both use a drink and signaled to our nose-ringed server for two more margaritas. As the next set of commercials took over the televisions, the rapidly changing images flickered bright and dark off of Ash's hair in an almost strobe-like pattern. The sizzle of fajitas danced past our ears while the scent of lime and perfectly charred steak wafted past and lingered longer than the steam on which it traveled.

"I guess this is one of those 'the more things change, the more they stay the same' deals," Ash said. "Shitball? I worked in the same division as him for three years and, yeah, that about sums up my feelings." She paused while our waiter set down the new round of margaritas. Ash looked a little dazed. As our server walked away, her eyes cleared and I realized it wasn't the margaritas that had left her cloudy but rather whatever imprint Walt had made.

"So what did the dishonorable Walter Harvey do to land in such esteem with you?"

She didn't hesitate with her answer. No moment of silence to ponder how to best construct her response. It came out of her mouth deliberately and angrily, something that she had thought over so many times that it could now be spoken of without thinking at all.

"He ran across someone who knew the rumors about my past. I guess Walter figured I would be willing to have sex with any guy I worked with. Just before I made transfer over here, he came up to me with a sloppy, drunk smile on his face. He mentioned Rod and grabbed at my ass. I dislocated his finger. Just a gut reaction mixed with my anger at him and my surprise at hearing Rod's name and my anger at myself for believing my mistakes were history and could be forgotten."

She took a sip of her margarita, moved her glass halfway back to the table, then changed her mind and returned it to her lips for another, larger drink. Her bottom lip brushed a small, half-oval area clear of salt. A burgundy lipstick imprint of the lines and cracks of her lip clung to the rim.

"I regret my relationship with Rod," she said, looking me squarely in the eyes. "Not because of departmental regulations. That made it worse but that's not what I regret. I regret it because it happened for the wrong reasons, at the wrong time." She paused. "With the wrong guy."

I felt heat move through me, pushing out from a spot near my stomach, radiating through my veins. I wanted to believe she felt the same unspoken heat that I did, but I still feared that maybe it was all in my imagination, alone with me.

"So you turned Walt down. Big deal. I imagine every time he looks for internet porn his own computer turns him down." With the noise of the bar, I saw, more than heard, Ash emit a small laugh.

"Yeah, you'd think that it couldn't have been a new experience for the guy," she said. Her laughter vanished. "He's a mean drunk. He turned like a light switch on me. His sloppy smile disappeared. Cursed me out and told me that I thought too much of myself, that I was nothing more than a dirty whore on too high of a pedestal." She sighed to herself. "This was right around the same time that I helped with a big drug bust. That was really the arrest that gave me enough juice to leverage a transfer over here."

"I don't follow you. Did Walt think you took the case from him?"

"No, not that. Even he knows that he's shit with police work these days." Spitfire's giant door opened and a blast of cool, wet winter air momentarily cleaned away the sticky sweet scent of tequila that hung in the bar. "He knows all of the gossip pathways. Probably tracked them all of these years while everyone spread the word about his drinking and sloppy work. The son-of-a-bitch really tapped into them good with me." Her cheeks flared pink with her anger. "He passed the word that I dropped excessive violence on an arrest. Then he spread the rumor that I was a lesbian. And neither of those do much to ruffle me. I can handle those. He sounds like a whiny kid when he says stuff like that about me, and I think everyone gets that about him."

"If anyone would toss stuff like that to the side, it's Markeze."

Ash rubbed her hand over her face, her eyes squinting in disgust or discomfort at where this was going.

"Yeah, all of that was before I transferred and Markeze has never mentioned any of it. No, what's sticking is that now the bastard says I dipped into the money from the big drug bust—meaning at worst I stole and at best I, again, screwed the chain of evidence for the biggest case of my career. That's why I've been relegated to backup duty and not chasing cases. I'm stuck treading water while they investigate me." Any softness I thought I had seen earlier disappeared. Her lips were a tight line, cheeks flushed with anger, so that they made me think her reddish hair held highlights of flames.

"There's not much Markeze can do. I know it sucks, but he can't just put you out there if IAD is running behind you."

"Damn it, Marcus, I get that," she hollered at me. After a pause she turned toward humor to show me we were okay. "In the best scenario, we'll get lucky and the serial killer we're chasing will turn out to be Walter." Our eyes met as I laughed and then we both reached to finish our drinks.

"Walt, I think, lacks the inner passion for these murders. He's just too damn lazy to bludgeon someone more than once," I joked.

This time she didn't return a laugh or smile. She'd lost herself, returning to that pool of anger that bubbled inside her.

"Those pricks at IAD said that my problem is that I don't know how to wait, that I 'manifest a problematic lack of patience coupled with a troubling bias against authority.'" Here she laughed again, a sad laugh this time. "You don't get to where I'm at, as a woman, by being patient and demure."

I stayed quiet, hoping that she would let me into this part of her, a part I liked to imagine she kept hidden from most people.

"Well screw them," she spat. Our server approached with fresh, warm tortilla chips but must have heard her last words because he turned back at the last second, making the move of a seasoned, veteran server to give us more privacy and detour toward another, less inflammatory table. "This is supposed to be the high point of my career, the moment where I finally get to work the cases I've always wanted to. Somehow that drunk, incompetent bastard managed to strip aside all the layers of success I built to get to this spot. Everything I've done, everything I am, feels in question now." The leading edge of her right hand slowly pushed her glass to the side with a slow, methodical karate-chop movement. Not violent or sudden, but definitive.

"Give Markeze some time on this, let him prove that he'll go to bat for you."

"IAD was right," she responded. "They usually have their heads up their asses but they were on the mark about me not having any patience. It's driving me insane to twiddle my thumbs and wait. I can't sit still, Marcus. It makes my skin crawl. I have this crazy idea that I'll help you solve this case and it will be so impressive that there's no way the department can ignore me or put me on a shelf. The idea of treading water and trusting someone else for help doesn't work for me. I'd like to but I can't get myself to do it. I just don't have the trust that I see you have, Marcus," she confided, which caught me entirely off guard, since trust was one thing I always felt I had in woefully short supply.

"You've misread me. Badly." I felt and heard air hiss out from my nose in a blast of disgust that I didn't see coming and couldn't control. "I feel like I've been treading water too, but my movements have gotten slower and slower. I'm barely staying above water. But I also can't get myself to thrash out much in protest or desperation." I wanted something in my hands to distract me but only had an empty glass or an empty basket to fiddle with—melted ice cubes or salt crumbs to try and escape into. I looked back up to catch her eyes. "I like the struggle you have. I feel beat up enough to almost be in awe of it, Ash. You're still kicking out at everything, and I like that." She smiled at me again, filling me with warmth in the spots where I only felt cold toward myself.

"You're sweet, Marcus. You see me flailing but somehow miss the drowning part. You know what pisses me off the most about all of this?" she continued. "Not that Walter is such a pathetic jerk, or even that he would say these things about me. The worst of all of this is that I'm trapped by something I thought I had moved beyond. If I didn't screw up that first case with Rod, what Walter says now doesn't reverberate with the same strength. If I don't have a relationship with Rod, then Walter never hears rumors and never approaches me in the first place." She paused again, picked up her margarita glass and let a cube of ice fall into her mouth, her teeth crushing it while she thought. "I feel as though years ago, when everything happened with Rod and the case, a scream of weakness rushed out of my lungs. I thought I outran it, but that scream hit off of some distant wall. The echo finally caught up with me."

"Ghost music," I replied, quietly.

"Hmmm?" she asked, puzzled.

"Nothing. Forget it."

"No, tell me. You can't quit there."

I liked that she had called me out for not following through with what I had started. She didn't want any facades or pretending. I realized I *wanted* her to see what was beneath. I felt she was somehow helping give me the strength to show what I would have kept hidden with anyone else. Damn good tequila they had here. Damn good.

"I don't know exactly how to say it," I began, my voice scuffling for traction. "Sometimes there are things, or people, who hit things within me that I didn't even know were there. Things I can't quite grasp. Things I want to clutch and embrace and look at but can't find my way to yet. I can tell they're important, powerfully part of me even though I can't see them or hear them clearly. I feel them resonate inside me but I'm not sure why."

I stopped again, but this time it wasn't a silent imploring for Ash to ask for more; it was a quiet gathering of things I had never allowed myself to collect before, and I loved both myself and Ash for that sense of space and acceptance.

"I think of it as ghost music," I continued. "Something that vibrates inside of me, hollowly, the notes making their unique sound but the vibrating string absent, so that it sounds eerie and uncanny, like a ghost teasing me with something that is there yet not there at the same time." My explanation seemed inadequate for the depth of the experience. "It's like a moment of déjà vu wrapped together with an epiphany. It's unsettling but powerfully felt. It hits your spine like ghost music: hidden but hauntingly present, just out of reach. Something you can't quite explain to anyone else or even to yourself." I stopped to look at her. "Echoes from the past are like that too, I think. They tap on your shoulder and you know you have to turn around or they'll just keep tapping at you. And maybe it hasn't been behind you, but next to you or even in front of you the entire time and you just hadn't heard it or felt it as clearly as you needed to."

I felt emotionally naked when I had finished and wanted to cover up again. I wanted to move Ash's beautiful, piercing eyes toward something else. "I'm thinking about turning my talents as a detective to the private sector." I turned my voice mock serious. "Marcus Brace, detective of demons, police for poltergeists, gumshoe specializing in ghosts and ghouls."

I smiled and she smiled back and everything felt comfortable, restful, like she was okay with what we had each shared, that I could trust her and she could trust me. I had this sudden, pulsating desire that we could rescue each other. I wanted to hold and embrace her, and feel her holding and embracing me.

Our eyes met again. Hers seemed full of questions she wanted to ask and things she wanted to say, full of that openness that I found intoxicating by itself, nearly irresistible when paired with the strength she had as well. I wished I could make my eyes feel as powerful to her as her eyes were to me. Maybe I did, because she suddenly broke contact, tilting her head down with an unexpected shyness.

"I need to get home, Marcus. Last thing I need is to show up late to work tomorrow." Then she gave me another smile, this one fuller, more genuine, somehow filled with much of what her eyes had given me before. It told me that while the earlier moment I had felt, we had felt, might have floated away, it was neither forgotten nor unwelcome.

We each reached for the check. Our fingers brushed for a long instant, forming one of those moments that slows down and you wish could last longer than it does. I pulled my arm back, reluctantly, and as I did so, the hairs on my arm stood on end, as though an electrical current had united them with Ash's arm. I imagined ions of attraction dancing between the two of us, jumping from arm to arm in an invisible circuit that sent a small shiver through my spine. Our invisible chemistry bounced around the room, and I wondered how no one else could detect it. I pictured everyone wearing special glasses, like you do at 3-D movies, so that they could bear witness to the molecular sparks bounding and somersaulting between the two of us.

I paid the bill, leaving a healthy tip for nose-ring boy, both because he knew when to stay away and also in case he was saving up for an eyebrow ring or something through his cheek to finish his look.

Outside, she turned to go left and I was to the right. An awkward pause held us together as we realized we were in two different places.

"I'm parked this way," I noted, curling my right arm across my body to point behind me, over my left shoulder.

She swayed slightly back and forth, not from drink but more from nervous uncertainty, her balance shifting in small degrees toward and away from me. It was drizzling again, small gentle drops that caught and glistened in the curls of her hair.

"Good night, Marcus. Thanks for the drinks," she replied, still swaying. "And the conversation," she added as she caught my eyes one final time before hastily turning and walking toward her car, her shoes leaving a muffled click with each step on the rain-blanketed sidewalk.

"Good night, Ashlynn," I whispered as she left. I spent a long moment watching her fade away while I pushed down the adrenaline I felt coursing through me, until I could imagine it corralled in a glowing ball right behind my solar plexus, powerful yet restrained.

The rain had cleared the air of particulates from exhaust pipes and cooking grease and the chemicals that rise in a haze in any big city. It smelled cleaner, purer than earlier in the day. The rain continued to fall gently, leaving moisture hanging to my every inhalation and exhalation. I drew in a big, slow breath of the rain-cleansed air, the coolness moving into my nose and through my body, further calming that sphere of adrenaline that had gathered.

A kiss would have been nice, wonderful, I thought, but the timing was wrong. I didn't want it to feel as though I were traipsing on, or trying to reenact, that relationship with her former partner. I smiled, thinking to myself that the last thing I needed was for her to dislocate my finger like she did to good ol' Walt when he had trespassed onto that ground. Tonight I would be satisfied to sit and soak in the luxuriousness of the words we had shared. That conversation, that same thing Ash had gestured toward when leaving, felt so open to me, so risky and safe all at the same time.

I pulled into traffic, the drops of rain seeming to fall faster as my headlights caught them, then slower again as they slipped past the light and were released to finish their journey to the ground. I tried to get a grip on myself, recognizing that Ash might be thinking something entirely different about me, about the chance of an "us." More words remained unspoken than had been voiced at this point. Yet what pulled me in was precisely the unknowing, that delicious sense of hoping I had correctly identified where I stood, mixed with the terrible anxiety of realizing I could be entirely wrong.

I let my tongue dance around her name, over and over, in all variations, finding a seductive silkiness to the way I could stretch out the end of her name into a sultry hiss: Ashhhh. Or create completely different rhythms with the two syllables together: Ash-lllyynn, Ashhhhh-lynn. Or draw each and every sound out to slow everything down, to wring every drop out of it: Aaaasssshhh.

Chapter Fifteen

I arrived home last night drunk on the idea of Ashlynn. Her glow still danced in my head when I woke, but as I moved through my morning routine, the drunk started to fade to a more manageable level. I replayed last night's conversations as I moved toward the kitchen for coffee.

I reached the kitchen and stopped. Something didn't feel right. I wasn't quite sure what it was, what had been altered or taken away, but a gnawing feeling lodged inside my stomach that someone else had been here.

I hadn't noticed anything amiss last night, but I was still binging on thoughts of Ash at that point. With the smell of her perfume fading and the sun burning away the night, I tried looking over everything with a fresh eye. It's a tough thing to do, to examine details that your mind has seen so many times that it no longer really sees them at all. The comfort of routine can blind you.

I felt emotionally upended every time Ash and I were together. I was probably just transferring my uncertainty about that emotional movement onto an irrational anxiety about packs of ninjas sneaking into my apartment to surreptitiously move things around. Probably some kind of psychological mumbo-jumbo where rather than look closely at the ramifications of losing control of my emotions, I could focus instead on what I might have lost within my apartment. I don't get why so many women love Dr. Phil—this stuff is easy.

That's when I realized that the cabinet door had been left opened, just a crack. It's easy to do. I'm not exactly staying at the Ritz-Carlton of apartments. This particular cabinet door doesn't fit quite as closely as it should, as though the wood has swollen since installation. You have to give it an extra little push, the wood on wood contact emitting a small squeak that I've grown accustomed to as my own little "good morning" sound. I close that squeaky, swollen-wood cabinet every single day. Today it wasn't shut all the way.

I couldn't remember with exact clarity that I had in fact shut the door completely last time. It's that mental shorthand part of habit again: I would bet you that I did, but it's so routine that I don't really pay attention to it. If I had to stake my life on whether I shut it all the way or not, I would say yes, then immediately squint my eyes shut and cringe while I waited to see if I would continue living.

My cell phone buzzed, alerting me that I had missed a call while focusing on the cabinet door. I checked the voicemail.

"Marcus. It's Paige," the message began, anger bubbling beneath her words and cooking into them a smoky curtness. "Have you been back to the house? I can't find Molly. If you took her to spite me, you're an even bigger shit than I would have thought possible. And I thought big, Marcus, really big." Her tone changed, turning almost desperate in its pleading as she finished. "If you have any idea where Molly is, help me get her back home."

Molly is a fantastic Springer Spaniel that I got Paige from a rescue society about four years ago. Best dog I've ever been around. She could be completely asleep on the couch, yet the moment you left the room, she'd hop up to follow, shaking her floppy ears as she hit the ground. I missed having Molly around. I had, however, absolutely no clue what Paige was talking about.

Nothing else seemed amiss in my apartment and I decided I was being paranoid. I stepped outside and found one of those doubly rare days for Seattle winter: bright sunlight that deepened the wrinkles around the corners of my squinting eyes, and a lazy, slow snow that substituted for rain. The large, soggy flakes hit my windshield and burst apart in a spray of water droplets, as if I were driving through a swarm of white locusts that exploded on the glass as my car crawled ahead.

The entry area to the SPD building squeaked as feet slid through the kind of dirty puddles that only form in winter, when clumps of dirty snow peel off the bottom of shoes and boots. The heat of the building started melting the clumps as soon as they dislodged from the footwear, leaving an irregular trail of puddles to the elevator located only a few yards from the door.

Ryota, of course, was already there when I arrived. Rather than a "good morning," he offered me the ambiguous male greeting of a quick jut of the chin. For Ryota, I suspect, it was the closest he could get to ignoring me entirely, an informal and silent greeting manifesting how near he was to forsaking socially accepted behavior altogether. In his own way, it was a shout, an angry curse at me.

Not bound as tightly to social norms as he was, I ignored him and his quasi-insult completely. Partly it was my disappointment at not finding Ash and flowers and angels singing to me, partly it was irritation with Ryota being "angry" in such a rather polite way. I smiled wanly, transposing Ryota into my memory of a Bugs Bunny episode involving insults, a white glove slapped across the face, and a sunset duel meant to reclaim lost honor.

I sat down and once more opened Mr. Brey's genealogical folder. I held a secret hope that two sheets of paper had somehow remained stuck together all of this time, that they would now miraculously peel apart and one would slowly float down to reveal the killer's signed confession. No such luck.

Flipping to the family tree, I traced my index finger along the line from Mike to Mr. Brey and on back to unknown names and inaccessible histories, people never known to me even before Mr. Brey died and now even more lost. I bit my tongue to keep down my emotions, an odd amalgam of sadness that I wouldn't see Mr. Brey again and anger that I couldn't just ask him about this and that he hadn't bothered to tell me about any of this before he died.

I moved my finger back to Mr. Brey's father, the war hero he had praised so often when Mike and I were young. I lost my staring contest with the name as I turned my eyes toward my iPhone. Scrolling through my contacts, I found who I was looking for: Chief Warrant Officer Gary Tibbs, National Personnel Records Center—Military Personnel Records, St. Louis, Missouri. The NPRC serves as the national repository for any records relating to former military personnel. I hoped that I could find something there that would begin to fill in the gaping historical blanks that punctuated my understanding of both the murders and Mr. Brey's family.

To request a set of military records, you have to submit a Standard Form 180. I had already printed off the required paperwork but wasn't keen on sending it in to get lost in the pile of other requests. Processing a Standard Form 180 and locating the records and getting back in touch with you wasn't an overnight process. Usually. I hoped, however, that it might be that quick for me, courtesy of Chief Tibbs.

Contacting Chief Tibbs required calling in another marker. Unlike with Markeze, though, this one had been spoken of before, with Chief Tibbs openly offering to help at any time and in any way he could. The first time Sean and I met Chief Tibbs, he had tears in his eyes, from the pepper spray we had to use to keep him away from our handcuffed suspect. We'd gotten along swimmingly ever since.

Chief Tibbs was part of a military family, a lineage of soldiers starting with his grandfather, moving through his father, then passed along to him and his brother. Duty, honor, and obligation weren't abstract terms for the Tibbs family.

Chief Tibbs's brother, Michael, had been stationed about an hour south of Seattle at Fort Lewis. He died serving in Afghanistan in 2002. Tibbs's understanding of family and duty to his dead brother coalesced in his suggestion that Lena and Melissa, his brother's wife and eight year-old daughter, move to St. Louis. He wanted to help out and be there as Melissa grew up. Lena declined, moving instead to South Seattle to try and find a new life away from the military.

Their new neighbor was a forty-something white guy, friendly, always offering his help. Within a month of their arrival, he molested Melissa. Lena went to the police. She also told Chief Tibbs. Sean and I got the call because it looked like the suspect fit within a broader case we were already working on.

We went to the suspect's apartment to look around and discovered the guy hiding in the pantry. We left with him in cuffs and found a man in military dress waiting outside. Chief Tibbs's eyes were cold and on fire all at once and I have no doubt that he had every intention of hurting, then killing the man who had molested his niece. He burst toward us, trying to paw his way to the handcuffed man. Sean had to pepper spray him to stop him.

I took the molester to the car while Sean checked on Tibbs. When he returned to the car, Sean was red in the face, his eyes bloodshot with rage. He told me about Michael and the story behind Lena and Melissa arriving in Seattle. This was relatively shortly after the 9/11 attacks and that made the already terrible seem even worse. We drove to the station, sickened that the guy in the back of our car had molested a girl whose father had just died fighting in Afghanistan. The world seemed doubly shitty. Sean related the story, loudly, as he personally walked the guy to a cell. Pedophiles are not popular in prison. Even worse for the man we locked up, post 9/11 patriotism ran high for prisoners too.

Sean knew the implication of what he was doing. I knew it. The other prisoners knew it. The pedophile we escorted knew it. They found him in the shower the next day, alive but with both eyes purpled and swollen shut, with three broken ribs, with one partially collapsed lung, with severe anal tearing.

We made a return trip to the apartment complex to follow-up on the investigation and, more important to both of us, to check on Lena, Melissa, and Chief Tibbs. Sean pulled Tibbs aside and told him what had happened. I suspect our role in passively encouraging inmates to sodomize another human would normally have broken some kind of code of honor for Chief Tibbs, but whatever transgression we carried out must have been overridden by something stronger, a sense of love and obligation to his brother and niece more powerful. He gave us each a card with his name and direct number and told us not just that he owed us one, but that he would help us anytime he could, for as long as he were alive. I believed him.

Remembering that day, I decided that he would probably welcome my call and be thankful for the opportunity to repay part of what he alone had written into an obligation. Honoring your debts and helping those who helped you seemed like the everyday furniture of Tibbs's well-ordered, admirably constructed house. They were the part of the world that was easiest for him to understand and most comfortable to live in.

I dialed the number Chief Tibbs gave us and he answered before the first ring had finished.

"Chief Warrant Officer Tibbs, NPRC-MPR." He offered nothing more. I guess he thought whoever had his direct number must have a good reason for calling and not be in need of prompting.

"Chief Tibbs," I returned, "this is Marcus Brace, Seattle PD." He cut me off before I could insert any further conversational reminder of who I was and how we had met.

"Detective Brace. Tell me what I can do to help you." He left me with the impression that he had been waiting, every day since Sean and I last saw him, for a phone call from us, as though it were part of his morning routine: brush teeth, shave, leave time on the calendar in case those Seattle detectives call.

"Chief Tibbs, I need to track down any information on file for a man named Adam Brey—B, R, E, Y."

"I need the information put on Standard Form 180. Fax it to my assistant. I'll have everything on file returned to you by start of day tomorrow. And Detective Brace, this is an easy one. I owe you more than this. Don't throw away my number." He didn't ask what I needed this information for, whether it was official or unofficial, personal or professional. Whatever I said would have been okay, part of the obligation he was carrying, willingly.

"Why don't you just tell me how Melissa and Lena are doing and we'll call it all even."

A warmer tone entered his voice. "Lena and Melissa moved out here to St. Louis. Melissa is in her junior year of high school now. She's a star on the volleyball team. Diligent with her schoolwork, just like her dad was. Lena went back to school and got her teaching certificate." They're doing great. But that doesn't erase what I owe you or your partner. Don't forget me." He stopped for a moment, searching for the best way to end the call. "I'll tell Lena and Melissa you asked after them, Detective Brace."

I started to fill out the Standard Form 180 and quickly realized that I didn't have a lot of the information it asked for: social security number, service number, dates of entrance and departure from the service. Where possible, I included estimates, noting in the margins that they were the best approximations I could offer. This was going to be more difficult for Chief Tibbs than he had imagined, but I knew that if any way existed to track down the files with the limited information I had, he would do it, and never mention anything about difficulties.

I finished the form under the heavy gaze of Ryota, who I figured wanted to know what in the hell I was doing talking to someone named Chief Warrant Officer Tibbs. I continued to ignore him and walked to the fax machine, feeling his eyes boring a hole into my back with each step.

Chapter Sixteen

I returned to find Ash and Ryota locked in a comical détente: Ash would try to make small talk; Ryota would respond with only the briefest of answers; Ash would try again. It reminded me of my drive across the water with Ryota yesterday. A look of relief crossed Ash's face as she saw me approaching. I couldn't help smiling, both from the pleasure of seeing her and from the shared experience of dealing with Ryota.

Giving up on Ryota, Ash turned toward me. "Glad you're back. So here's what I found. Except for Jamie, no one named Parks has been murdered in the Seattle area in the last two months."

Ryota looked puzzled.

"I told Ash about our visit with Parks's neighbor. Mrs. Lump told us that Jamie's mom had been killed, remember?" His puzzlement and the crinkles around his eyes dissipated. His mouth, however, squirmed, as though whatever had infected the skin around the eyes had simply moved a few inches lower on his face.

Ash continued. "I figure either the neighbor was wrong about his mom being murdered, or his mom had a different last name through divorce or remarriage or maybe even because Jamie was adopted. I've put in a call to track down his birth certificate to see if we can find his mother's name. I'll work from there."

"Nice work. I just faxed in a request for any military files on Mr. Brey's father, so that avenue is being worked now too." Ryota again looked disturbed.

"Did you and Ryota talk about the sword and the chakin yet?" Ash asked.

Ryota's face turned blank with Ash's last question, befuddlement giving way to a cold, impassive stare. I tried to smooth things out.

"Let me catch you up a bit, Ry. Ash was thinking that where's there's a chakin there should be a tea bowl too. We're wondering if the killer took the bowl with him but left or forgot the chakin." I pulled open the genealogical file and turned to the family tree. I pointed toward Mr. Brey's name as I spoke. "We're also thinking about the chakin in relation to a samurai sword that Mr. Brey gave to my dad. I think it must have been one of Mr. Brey's most treasured possessions. And we have the kanji to consider." I stopped to see if I could read Ryota's thoughts. I found only a steely gaze.

"Sounds like you and Ashlynn have been doing plenty of thinking and planning on this." He carried a false calm, presenting a stillness that I read as rage waiting to erupt. "Excuse us for a moment, Ashlynn," he said and pulled me to the side.

"Damn you, Marcus. This is exactly what I didn't want: you've cut me out and pulled Ashlynn in. Both of those," he hissed at me, the muscles on the side of his neck taut, "are *completely* out of line."

"Hey, hold on. *You* were the one who stormed off yesterday. *You* decided to not be involved. Ash can make her own decisions about what to get involved with or not get involved with. We did some brainstorming last night. That's all." I believed it about Ash: she could join or not, but Ryota had a point about cutting him out. That was poor on my part. Yet I still wouldn't have traded last night with Ash to do things in a more professional, steadfast way, especially with a partner who I barely got along with.

"Damn it," Ryota swore at me. He shook his head in disgust,

fatigue cracking through his voice. He stopped looking at me, turning his face toward the ground as he spoke, so that it felt as though he had disconnected from me. "This isn't right. This isn't how it's supposed to be." He looked up and came back. "She's just going to get hurt from this, Marcus."

"That's not your call. I need her help, and she wants to help. It's that simple." I stopped and waited.

Ryota waited too. He looked as though he were going to explode. Not from anger this time, though. His eyes appeared filled with pain rather than rage. His mouth opened but no words came out. He closed it again. He swallowed—a big, dry gulp that brought his Adam's apple up and down in slow motion. He reminded me of a blackout drunk I once brought in on a murder charge: there was a moment of disbelief when everything that the drunk had forgotten came rushing back, followed immediately by a crushing need to tell me about the memories that had returned in an overwhelming rush.

"We cool on this, Ryota? You don't look so hot."

His voice was a mumble. "It's wearing me out." His arms hung like dead weights at his sides, pulling his shoulders into a slouch. "I'm always the one who ends up responsible for everyone else, the one who makes the sacrifices and picks up the pieces from what everyone else breaks. It's too much to carry."

"What're you talking about?"

"I'm tired. Tired of being ignored. Tired of putting what *I* want second to everyone else. I've done this my entire life: suffer and sacrifice and give things up for things to be *right*. There should be more than this for me. I'm always taking care of someone else, never myself—my parents, my wife, now you're forcing me to cover up for you."

Whatever he had simmering beneath the surface didn't fit within the picture I had of the guy at all. I had always thought Ryota derived not just a sense of peace but energy from sacrificing, from being responsible, from doing things properly. Part of me had always been jealous of it. I looked at him again, trying to see him anew, looking for pain where I had only seen contentment and self-worth before.

"What do you do, Marcus, when your sense of how the world works, or how you work in the world, is forced to change?" he mused. "I feel lost right now. Once all that changes, how do you make sense of what you've done or look without disgust at yourself for how you've lived your life?"

He'd pushed us into uncharted territory. I didn't know what had sparked this for him. I certainly didn't know how to respond. I realized that it had been all too easy for me to deride and dismiss what I hadn't seen correctly. There's a comfort in walling it off and pushing it away. His strange confession, though, cracked the veneer and made me see the ways in which I'd turned him into an icon of spotlessness, something unreal that I could simultaneously ridicule and respect, using him as a punching bag for both extremes. I didn't like seeing the rough spots, pits on what I had cast as a pristinely smooth surface. Better to think of him as superhuman, not filled with damages and contradictions. Otherwise, I risked facing the possibility that he might be equally flawed, yet somehow more successful in the struggle against the messiness of life than I was. With everything else going on, I just didn't have the emotional room for him right now.

"Ry, I'm not sure what's going on with you. This sounds like something your wife might be a bigger help with." He closed his eyes and a quiet hiss escaped from his nose.

"Some things you can't talk to your wife about."

"Probably right about that," I answered. "But shake off the martyr complex. You're not responsible for me; you're not responsible for Ash. I'm not asking you to carry my weight for me. Whatever happens, Markeze won't burn you on this. Everyone knows you aren't a rule-breaker, and no one will blame anything on you if this goes bad. Hell, you might even get some points from some of the others for sticking by your partner's side. So don't sweat it." I clapped him on the shoulder. "Let's get back to Ash."

He looked conflicted, but he relented, simultaneously pulling his shoulders up from the slouch of defeat and taking a step forward. It seemed a remarkable transformation. I had the sense that the Ryota

I had seen all of this time was nothing more than a worn-out carapace, fractured from the pressure of trying to hold tight to everything that needed to get out but hadn't quite made it yet.

"Everything okay?" Ash asked once we arrived back at our desks.

I nodded but declined to elaborate. I wanted to involve Ryota immediately, pull him away from whatever bubbled inside him and root him again with the case to cement his participation.

"Ry, what else should we know about a chakin and what it's used for? Anything especially noteworthy about the one Ash discovered?" I asked.

"Nothing much special about this one," Ryota began, pulling himself together as he spoke. "I don't know how much Jamie Parks knew about the intricacies of the tea ceremony, but there could actually be a lot more than just a tea bowl missing. It depends on how involved he was, but there's an entire culture and ritual of accouterments for the ceremony." He seemed in an element second nature to him, something he had learned long ago and knew backward and forward. Yet he also seemed stiff with it, as though it had been inculcated in him but he hadn't really been interested in it and never developed a love for it. "At the basic level, you'd have a chakin, a tea bowl (or *matchawan*), a tea container (*chaire*), a tea scoop (*chashaku*), and a tea whisk (*chasen*). Some of these would then have their own subgroups. For instance, you'd have a different type of tea bowl and whisk depending on whether you were serving thin or thick tea. This is all a gross simplification, but you get the idea."

"Okay, so another area for us to consider," I suggested, "is whether there were other parts of the tea ceremony that were stolen, or whether they were never there at all. If we are looking at least partly at a robbery here, which I still think is a good idea, why not take the chakin too?"

"I don't know. All of the tea ceremony elements would be treated, by the owner at least, as family treasures. The bowls, especially, could be generations old. They're not something you would replace because you want a new style, or even if they became damaged somehow. You wouldn't trash them. Chips or cracks would be repaired. Any anomalies on the bowl would be marks of its unique production, birthmarks of its own history. It would be valued for precisely those things that would be seen as reason to throw it out here in America. There could conceivably be a great deal of value, both financial and familial, at play here," he finished.

"So if anything were stolen, it could have been taken for its historic and emotional, not just economic, value?"

"Exactly."

"How do you know all of this?" Ash asked.

"My grandfather," he quietly answered. "He started a tea company in Seattle after World War II. He made me learn everything he could think of about Japan and tea." He didn't say more about it and it grew quiet around the table. I saw the corners of Ryota's mouth move back momentarily, once more breaking his usually implacable exterior. He looked as though he had swallowed something foul but didn't want anyone to know, like a stoic at a dinner party with spoiled meat. This was the second time within the hour that I had seen his façade crack.

He turned toward me and for a moment I felt as though he were going to tell me about whatever was roiling inside. His eyes were open, pleading or apologetic. But that passed too, flashing at me and then departing as he turned his gaze away, toward the corner of the room and Markeze's office.

"I'm sorry. I'm not feeling well. Excuse me."

I tracked him with my eyes, looking to see if anything else out of character worked its way to the surface. Ash's elbow dug into my side and I dropped my gaze from Ryota.

"That's the old Asian woman who came in asking about you while you were in Kansas," she said, removing her elbow from my ribs and pointing toward the door.

"I'm going to see if anything's back yet about Jamie's birth certificate. I'll leave you two alone," Ash said, and winked at me playfully.

I moved toward the front to intercept my mystery caller. Her spine drooped with age, curving like the top of a question mark, the scapula ready to burst through her skin. She reminded me of an aged bird of prey, wings folded back in rest.

"I'm Detective Marcus Brace," I said, offering my hand and my school-boy charm. I moved my other hand to my brow and tried to look like Johnny Carson in those old reruns where he holds an envelope to his temple: "I have the sense that you are looking for me." She must have been too tired to smile.

"I've been looking for you for days. Why didn't you detect that?" she snapped, though I thought I caught a faint glimpse of mirth in her milky eyes.

"My skills are in high demand," I countered. Any trace of a smile left her eyes.

"Detective Brace, I'm old." Her voice creaked yet carried an overlay of strength and directness, a tone that I imagined once had been primary and had only reluctantly given ground to the quavering of age. "I could die on you right here while you waste our time with chit-chat."

She wore her thin, stringy hair longer than you see on most elderly women. Lacking even a hint of cream or a yellow tinge anywhere, it shone so purely white that it struck me as an eerie removal of color, as an absence more than a presence.

She eased herself down into the chair across from me, her movements slow and shaky. Her arthritic hands curled into claw shapes, which she used to brace her downward momentum. Coated with cataracts, her translucent eyes seemed to look through me rather than at me. She was so small and light that she appeared ethereal, so old and gnarled that she seemed more wraith than woman.

"I didn't get your name," I noted.

Her response was slow in coming. "My name is Sumi Yoshinaga, Detective Brace," she finally began. "I don't know what to say to you, now that I'm here." The earlier strength and certainty dissipated with each syllable. "I came in a few days ago ready to yell at you. I wanted you to tell me what trouble you've put him in." She again paused, gathering both her thoughts and her breath. "He mumbles your name in his sleep. I came to find out why." She again stopped talking, staring past me, searching for something. "He has paper with your name on it. A star next to it." Spittle, white and bubbly, clung to the corner of her mouth.

What she said made no sense. "What are you talking about?" She remained silent. I decided to start at the most basic level and work my way up. "Can I get you a cup of coffee?" I asked, trying a different tack, a way to build camaraderie. Besides, don't all old people like coffee? They drink it with lunch, with dinner, with sandwiches and with sinewy sirloin steaks. She didn't answer. If nothing else, I decided, a cup of coffee might wash away the spittle that continued to stare at me.

"I'll be right back," I said. As I neared the community coffeepot, the smell of stale coffee hit my nostrils, laced with the even stronger stench of overpour that had dripped down the carafe to be scorched by the burner. I poured Mrs. Yoshinaga a cup of detective-grade sludge.

I made it about halfway back to my desk, then had my movement arrested by the postman, Matt. He knew each of us by name, often trying to strike up a conversation about police work as he handed off the mail. He liked to feel involved, united with us as fellow public servants serving the common good or something. "Got some for ya, Brace. Catch," he hollered as he tossed me a rectangular Priority Mail box that had several envelopes rubber-banded to the top of it. The mud-like coffee sloshed as I struggled to hold onto the cup with one hand and catch the mail call with the other. Caffeinated sludge splashed onto both my shirt and the Priority Mail box.

I cursed Matt to myself. He was a strange fellow, one of those people who derives a rush from being around figures of authority but also exhibits a disdain for that authority, as though he didn't like to be the junior member of the brotherhood of the uniform that he had created for us. I thought I saw a smirk move across his lips as he passed.

Back at my desk, I set the mail down and offered the cup of coffee to my visitor. She took it, both hands clasping it in a vice-like grip.

"I have trouble straightening my fingers," she said, answering a question that I hadn't asked.

"Let's move back to what you said earlier. I don't know who you were talking about and I'm still not really clear why you're here." She set the cup of coffee on the table without taking a drink. Her milky eyes scanned my face.

"I'm not clear about that either," she said at last. "I wanted to see you in person, understand why you'd be bothering my boy." She sighed almost imperceptibly, the movement, slight though it was, enough to force her shoulders into an even greater slouch. "I have a bad feeling, Detective Brace. In the bones. Maybe deeper than the bones. Someone's in trouble. I see you and now I'm not sure it's who I thought it was. That scares me even more." Her eyes moved away from me and back to the coffee cup and my desk. "Your package is wet," she added, and I realized that she could see better than I had at first thought.

The sound of a door pulled open hard enough to rattle its glass shifted my attention away from the old woman's cryptic ramblings.

"BRACE, in here now." I turned and saw Markeze within his office doorway, arms akimbo. Ryota's head appeared behind Markeze's right shoulder, reminding me of a child who wants to get by but doesn't have the courage to ask to be excused. My partner gently tapped Markeze on the shoulder, then slinked sideways through the space created for him. He moved straight toward our desk, at least brave enough not to hide from me or look away in shame for whatever he had said to Markeze.

I turned back to Mrs. Yoshinaga. Her cloudy eyes pulled open in fright or surprise. She moved back involuntarily, the hunch of her back getting in her way. The curvature of her spine arrested her movement and kept her head about a foot in front of the rest of her body. Her head didn't like the extra exposure and struggled to continue the movement backward that the rest of her body had managed to carry out successfully: she tilted her head up and back, pulling it as far away as possible, leaving only her chin, simultaneously wrinkled and showing the sharp bone beneath, facing me. Her ghost-like eyes pointed emptily at the ceiling. Her clawed hands scrambled to find a hold on the arms of the chair. She finally clambered halfway up, terrified.

"NOW, BRACE." Markeze's voice boomeranged across the room before pulling my eyes once more toward his. He stomped through the space of the detective bullpen, my lack of movement propelling him forward.

Ryota's face showed confusion, surrounded by a false corona of surety, as though he knew he had made a poor choice but desperately wanted to believe he had done right.

I twisted back to the old woman to excuse myself and ask her to stay put and enjoy the marvelous coffee I had delivered. She wasn't there. I caught sight of her warped body shuffling, faster than I would have imagined possible, toward the exit. I rose from my seat to call after her and chase her down, only to feel a hand block my progress.

"Marcus, I'm sorry." It was Ryota. "I thought I was doing right. Maybe I was doing what was easy. I just don't," he began softly and then trailed off before starting over. "I just don't know what I'm doing anymore." He shook his head slowly back and forth.

I didn't reply, instead bounding toward the door and the old woman. Markeze's anger boomed toward me and wrapped me within his rage as I moved. I reached the doorway only to see the elevator close, carrying the mysterious woman away.

I didn't have time to dwell on her departure. I felt a hand on my shoulder again and turned to tell Ryota to give it a rest. I found not Ryota, however, but Markeze, his body pulling me back where his voice had failed.

"Forget the old woman." He pinched my shoulder with his hand and torqued his wrist to turn me toward his office. With the old woman gone, he marched ahead, once more sure in his authority, knowing that he could turn his back to me and I would go where he had directed.

The collective gaze of the detective bullpen met me as we re-entered, but I dismissed all eyes except those of Ashlynn. I gave her my best smile, hoping she derived half as much encouragement from it as I always found within her green eyes, rimmed this time with concern and confusion. "I need to talk to you. Right away," she mouthed as I passed.

I entered Markeze's office and found him already seated. "Close the door, Marcus," he said, quietly this time, no trace of bellowing. I obliged.

As soon as the door clicked shut, he stood, shaking his head while looking at the ground and waving his right hand back and forth. He turned around, so his back faced me. I saw his shoulders take one giant shrug up and then relax downward, letting the tension roll off like rainwater streaming away from the crown in a road. He faced me again, his face impassive, his brown eyes dull, no longer shiny with fury.

He remained standing, looking down at me, seated. "Ryota came to me. Told me how you've frozen him out of part of the investigation while cozying up to Ashlynn. Pretty much exactly what I asked you *not* to do."

He leaned against his desk, arms crossed in front of his chest. "I can't tell if I'm more angry at you for personal or professional reasons. And I have to tell you, that pisses me off too. You've asked me to help you out, and I don't get to tell you when you can call in your debt. But it pisses me off that you've pushed at my obligation so far that it seems you think you can do any damn thing you want on this case. You've managed to get the personal crawling up our professional asses and it fucks everything up. Maybe I don't get to dictate the terms of my debt from a personal level but I damn well do on a professional level. Get your fuckin' act together and fix the shit relationship you have with Ryota. Do not fuck with me on this. For Chrissake, Marcus, you guys are partners."

I didn't like this. I didn't like that Markeze was right about me going against his wishes to bring in Ash. I didn't like that I felt small for stomping on the delicate ground of Markeze's debt to me. I didn't like that Ryota was cowardly and unpredictable, helping me one second and running to tattle on me the next.

Markeze interlaced his fingers, his thumbs rotating one over the other in a continuous loop. "Maybe I was overly angry because I felt what you did as a slap in the face personally, taking advantage of my debt. Maybe now I'm being too easy because of that same debt. I'm not sure. But here it is: you pull Ash into this at all, even a pinkie toe of involvement, and you're suspended, indefinitely." He moved toward the door to dismiss me.

Blood pounded through my ears in a steady rhythm as neurons in my brain shifted into different pathways, shutting down reason, begging for an emotional explosion. I got out of Markeze's office before I said anything, my neck muscles so taut that I could feel my scalp pulled downward. Once outside, though, I felt worse for leaving without speaking or yelling, the anger a poison expanding in my veins, threatening to burst and destroy me.

I discovered Ryota lurking directly outside Markeze's office. He stood rigid, his bearing speaking of formality and exactness, returning to a behavior pattern that gave him comfort and a sense of order in the universe. It added to my irritation.

I watched Markeze call Ash in. He didn't ask her to close the door. It happened quickly. He suspended her, made her hand in her shield and gun—precisely what he had threatened to do to me. Leaving the door open made me feel as though he had turned Ash into a pawn, an object lesson meant for me. I didn't think my blood could boil hotter but I now felt it vaporizing inside me. Ryota had betrayed me, the old woman had gone, Markeze had treated me like a recalcitrant child, and now Ash had been suspended.

Ryota didn't seem to notice Ash's trouble or that I was in no mood to mend bridges with him at the moment. I needed space to cool down and instead felt smothered by him. "I'm torn apart by pressure inside me, Marcus. Maybe you are too, what with family being involved in this. But you *have* to do this the right way. Don't you see?" he pleaded. "Follow the rules with me on this. It has to be that way, okay?"

Ash walked out of Markeze's office. She didn't stop or look at me this time and that cut at me.

"Got it, Marcus?" Ryota asked. Maybe he had said something leading up to that question that didn't register with me as my anger pounded in waves inside my skull. All I heard, though, even more than the question itself, was smugness, a certainty, the same preachiness that I had felt from Markeze.

I punched Ryota in the face, square on the chin. His neck snapped back, the weight of his head following the force of my blow. His arms flailed upward, grasping emptily, and he landed on the floor, ass-first. He looked confused, shocked that I would have done that, perhaps hurt even more for the way in which I had broken the order of his neat universe than from any physical sensations shooting through his nerve endings. Blood trickled down his chin from a spot where my punch had pushed his teeth into his bottom lip.

Markeze saw the entire thing. "Get the fuck in here. Now, Marcus." Once I entered, he asked, "That's not exactly kissing to make up, is it?" He didn't say anything else about it. The anger continued to pulse through me, slower now, with less force. I felt shame mixing with it, anger directed at myself instead of the world. "Your weapon and shield," he said.

I handed them over, at a loss. I left to find Ryota still sitting on the ground, his knees pulled up close and his arms wrapped around them. A small smile played on his lips, almost like the one I remembered on Mike after I punched him and answered his need for penance.

I walked toward my desk, angered that I had hurt Ash. A few steps farther and I felt punched down by the realization that there was even more at stake, that I had damaged more than just me and Ash. I feared that, without departmental resources to help me with the case, I had let Mr. Brey down as well, that I would never be able to find the man who murdered him.

I pictured the killer as a vulture circling overhead, laughing and smiling at me, his beak ready to peck at the growing trail of carrion that I pulled behind me. A brief image of my father drinking alone in his home flickered through my mind, as I wondered if we all carried within us a hidden timer of ruin, the sands counting down from the day we are born on a self-destruct sequence wired into our DNA, waiting to explode until the moment when we can least afford it.

Chapter Seventeen

I reached my desk, my fingers tight and knuckles throbbing from the impact with Ryota's jaw. The chair Mrs. Yoshinaga had sat in carried the marks of her hasty exit. One arm of the chair was touching my desk and the other was pointing at a forty-five degree angle to the door. I didn't bother pushing it back to its proper spot.

A rivulet of blood ran from the corner of Ryota's mouth down to his chin. I thought he would walk a path back to our desks, where he would offer some platitude and forgive me and make me feel worse because of his ability to do the "proper" thing even after I had slugged him. Instead, he flashed me another wry smile, blood mixing with saliva to leave a pink trail on his teeth. His eyes gleamed, from embarrassment or anger or holding down tears of frustration. They looked as though a film of shiny plastic had been pulled over them. He didn't break pace or offer any word as he passed our desks. He pushed the elevator button, grew impatient waiting, and turned to the stairs.

I sat down in my own chair and rubbed my face in my hands, the pads in my palms working upward against the grain of stubble that fought a daily battle with my razor. It was one of those moments when self-judgment is the most critical, when the sharpest edge drawn across your skin is your own criticism. I wondered what Ash was doing, where she had gone after Markeze dismissed her. I wondered if I could convince her ever again to join me for a drink.

Exasperation bowed my head downward. While rubbing the back of my neck, I noticed a line of thick, dark liquid that curled across my desk. I rose to grab a paper towel, figuring the old woman had bumped her coffee cup as she dashed away, spilling sludge onto the desk. The liquid formed a trail all the way to the mail that Matt the postman had tossed to me earlier. The package looked soggy in the corner, soft from moisture eating away the inner cells of the cardboard. An irregular, wet stain worked its way up from the point of contact with my desk. The shape made me think of a geography quiz of some isolated, island country that I had never heard of and about which I knew nothing.

When I lifted the package to clean the viscous mess, liquid clung to the bottom of the cardboard and stretched away from the desk, like cotton candy being pulled apart but not quite giving. With the tendrils finally separated from the top of the desk, I saw that they were colored a dark, purple-red, not the brackish brown of our department coffee.

I had seen incorrectly and in so doing had reversed cause and effect. I now realized that the liquid had emanated from the corner of the box and moved *toward* the coffee cup, not the other way around. I looked carefully at the address label. The writing was messy, angular. No return address provided.

The center of my chest, behind my solar plexus, felt tight. My lungs constricted so that my breath became shallow. I recalled the old woman's frightened eyes, feeling something similar move from neuron to neuron within my own body. I pictured nerve cells recoiling in fear, squealing in a high-pitch as they transmitted a warning from end to end of my body. I forced a deep inhalation, oxygen rushing in to cool my throat and extinguish the spark of anxiety that built simultaneously in my racing brain and my clenching gut.

I retrieved a pair of latex gloves so that I could handle everything from the package without fear of compromising whatever awaited inside. My prints would already be all over the exterior. I tilted the box so that I could open the end opposite the wet side. Droplets, slow and large at first and then smaller and quicker as gravity took over, fell from the soggy corner as I worked the adhesive loose at the opposite end. Angling the package up further, so that the fluorescent lighting cast its eerie hue inside the recesses of the box, I saw something golden-brown encased in plastic. I set the package down. So that my glove-covered hands wouldn't disturb any trace evidence, I grabbed a couple of pencils from my desk drawer and used them as tongs to pinch and then pull out the plastic-sheathed content.

Once I had removed it from the box, I knew exactly what it was: a Seattle Mariners mini-bat, one of those small souvenir items that possesses enough heft and solidity that you can never be sure if it is intended for kids or for adults. I had one at home that I had purchased on the spur of the moment at the Mariners Team Store in the Bellevue Mall, when I had seen Edgar Martinez wandering around with his wife. He signed it for me as I effused about how I fully expected him to be the first designated hitter to reach the Hall of Fame.

My gut told me, echoing the feeling that I had experienced earlier in my apartment, that something wasn't right. I knew, even before I turned the mini-bat over to inspect the other side, that I would find Edgar's autograph on this bat. This was the bat from my apartment.

I wanted to yell for Ash to come and see, but she was gone and I was alone. The plastic bag that had kept the bat sealed showed smears of blood near the handle. My pencil-tongs couldn't reach to the end of the box to see what else remained, so I slowly tipped the box to let the contents slide closer to the opening. I heard a sickening slurp of something pulling away from a puddle of blood that had collected at the other end of the box. Another, smaller plastic bag slipped out of the box. An envelope had been taped to this bag.

The content inside the bag, however, stopped me from opening the envelope. Bile churned through my stomach. The bag held a bloody dog's paw. The toenails from the paw must have punctured the plastic bag, perhaps even when Matt tossed me the package, allowing the blood to leak through. My abdominals clenched, forcing the bile partway up my throat. The paw held a desiccated and deformed dewclaw, exactly what Paige's dog Molly had.

Panic ratcheted up a level as I swallowed and dialed Paige's cell. One ring, two rings, then to her voicemail. I told her to call me right away, that it was about Molly. I dialed her office number.

She picked up. "What do you want, Marcus? I have a meeting in five minutes."

"Has Molly come home yet?" I asked, hoping like hell I was wrong about the paw in the bag.

"No. You don't have her, do you, Marcus? I'm sorry I yelled at you last time. I just want Molly back and this is all too much." Her voice was a mix of anger and fear and regret.

"No, I don't. Has anyone been bothering you? Anyone around who shouldn't be around?" I tried to keep my voice level and calm.

"Nothing. You're scaring me." Her voice turned accusatory again. "Are you *trying* to scare me? Trying to make me feel like I need you? I don't need you, Marcus."

I took a deep breath through my nose and tried again. "Someone might be threatening me," I explained, "and I want to make sure that whatever is going on doesn't spill over onto anyone associated with me. I'm going to arrange to have a patrol unit at your office at 5:30. I'll tell them to walk up and introduce themselves to you at that time. When you're ready to leave work, call down to them and let them walk you to your car and escort you home." She remained quiet throughout my explanation. She hung up without directing any more snide comments to me.

Knowing that worry could eat me away from the inside out, I tried to shut down that part of my brain by turning my attention to the envelope that I had earlier ignored. The envelope had been taped to the top of the bag and had been largely spared the blood inside. The blood that leaked out had marred part of the envelope, but it could have been worse. As carefully as I could, I cut open the envelope, the knife slicing through not just envelope-adhesive but a splotch of blood that acted as an unintentional secondary seal.

I gently pulled on the letter within the envelope. The bottom of the envelope, wetted with blood, had sucked onto it. The letter didn't budge at first, then broke free suddenly, the paper almost tearing as it jerked out. I unfolded the letter to find the same angular handwriting that marked the address label. The words themselves were clear, unsullied by the leaking blood. Bloodstain, however, obliterated what looked like a symbol, or maybe a postscript.

The message was eerie and cryptic, though I wasn't sure if it was intentionally obscure or if the sender believed it to be as clear to others as perhaps it was to himself:

Dear Marcus,
I have watched you, watch you still. I know you. We are kindred spirits, you and I. You are a brother to me. And I to you. I know you better than you know yourself. I know what you need. I have seen the truth that you have yet to witness clearly. I will help you, Marcus. Free you. I will let you see yourself by cutting away those who keep you prisoner.
You must become an orphan, lose yourself from those who will otherwise stop what is inside you. Alone, you can see yourself for who you are, who we both are. This is my present to you, brother. I will help you become an orphan again.
But what is a present without something to open? So I give you this package as well: a token wrapped for you to help you on your journey. I leave you my mark, as I have been marked by others.

No signature. I held the letter up to the light, looking first at the front, then turning it around to analyze the back to see if the symbol at the bottom could be made out from that angle. No luck. It looked vaguely circular but I wasn't sure.

I felt as though I had moved close enough to an electrified fence so that, while I didn't yet experience any pain, I could already feel the hairs on my arm tingle and wave back and forth; any move that brought me closer to the fence would transform the merely disconcerting into electrical burning.

It felt profoundly unsettling to see into the mind of a killer who had evidently chosen to adopt me, who felt a spark of kinship with me. Thinking about him walking through my apartment, watching me, touching objects in the space of my home, made my breath come fast. My body became a playground for an anxiety that quickly transmogrified into deep, purple rage.

This was the man who killed Mike, who murdered Mr. Brey. He had been inside my home. His fingers, the same fingers that had curled around a bat to beat Mike to death, had touched items in my personal space. He breathed the air that I too breathed; he expelled his sick, polluted breath into my apartment and I had unknowingly sucked it in. This man, who called me his brother, killed those who were family to me. I desperately hoped he would be back at my apartment again when I arrived home. I wanted to beat him to death like he had beaten the only brother I had ever had, wanted to purge myself and my apartment of him by cracking his skull and witnessing the flowing of his blood.

My thoughts of violent revenge returned me to the mini-bat. As I focused again on the evidence, the adrenaline began to drain from my veins and my mind decelerated. I made myself turn all of my attention to my breathing. I concentrated on the coolness of it entering my body and the warmth of it exiting. I imagined the exhalations carrying away any traces of pollution that I had ingested from the killer's breath inside my apartment.

I cut a slit in the plastic and removed the bat, the physical manifestation of the misbegotten link the killer had forged with me. I saw Edgar Martinez's signature on the sweet spot of the bat. I rotated the bat, slowly spinning Edgar's name toward the floor. Three pieces of scotch-tape curled toward the autograph. Encased underneath the tape, reminding me of museum specimens sealed within glass cases, were hairs. The first two scotch-taped display cases each contained two hairs; the last example included only one hair. I had no idea why, what the difference might signify.

The bat also had been marked with another symbol chain, though this one didn't look at all like the other kanjis left by the killer. Next to the samples with two hairs, pyramids of small circles had been burned into the wood: on each pyramid, one dot made the pinnacle, below which were burned two additional dots that formed the base. I didn't know what the dots represented to the killer. We had four possible victims so far: Mr. Brey, Mike, Jamie Parks, and perhaps Parks's mother. The dots didn't make sense with that. Six dots, two pyramids, and four victims was strange math.

Even odder, the lone hair did not rate its own pyramid. Instead, two letters had been branded into the wood next to it: MB. A shiver ran up my spine, in lockstep with the thought that the killer had found one of my hairs in my apartment and had included it in this macabre display. If the killer used a baseball bat to bludgeon his victims, then perhaps he intended this as a miniaturized copy, even including hairs that he had taken from his victim's skulls. The burned MB initials made me consider the possibility that, despite the words in his letter, the killer had me more in mind for victim than "brother."

Chapter Eighteen

I took a closer look at the lone, last hair. Though it had been taped next to my initials, it wasn't my hair color. It showed white against the honey-colored baseball bat, while my own hair was brown. I was getting some gray hairs, maybe even a few white ones, but if the killer really had been watching me, if he knew me, then I doubted he would select a hair different from my primary color. He seemed too methodical, too much of a grand planner to compromise cryptic messages with imprecise details.

I collected the package contents. Mirroring Ryota, I punched the elevator button only to give up a few seconds later and opt for the stairs. Markeze had kicked me off the case, but no one in the crime lab would know that yet. I felt like a cork bobbing in the ocean, pushed and twirled by forces over which I had no control. I hoped going to the lab would help me shift the flow, uncover something that would allow me to stop reacting to events and start directing and shaping them.

The crime lab was located three floors down. Everything looked brighter here and the whites of the walls shone whiter than anywhere else in the building. Chemical smells singed the hairs of my nostrils. It seemed as though the entire floor had been through a bleach drip.

I walked about halfway down the hall, heading toward Nyssa Jurgensen's space in the lab. She didn't owe me anything, but I felt sure she would not only be willing to help, but also put a rush on my request. She would probably even continue to run the tests once word trickled down that Markeze had suspended me.

Nyssa was obsessive, in a good way, in a way that made her a perfect lab tech. Once she found a case in front of her, she committed to it fully. Exhaustive in her attention to detail, she abhorred loose ends. She stayed more interested in the science and in following all possibilities to their conclusions than in departmental fiat. If I could get her started with this, she would resent any call to stop while evidence remained only partially analyzed.

I also liked to think that she had a schoolgirl crush on me. Her brown eyes offered a softness and warmth that seemed to curl around and caress every word out of my mouth. Part of me understood that Nyssa's eyes held that wide-open, full-of-wonder quality for everyone she talked to. Yet when you saw it and felt it, it became intensely personal and made you think she directed it toward you alone. She's one of those people whom everyone thinks of as welcoming and good, full of an openness and innocence that even the detritus of murder and depravity analyzed inside a crime lab couldn't tarnish.

"Hi, Nyssa. You have a minute?"

"Heya, Marcus. What brings you down to see the crazy chemists and mad scientists?" She pulled off a passable Mr. Spock impersonation as she raised one eyebrow toward the top of her head while the other remained rooted in place.

Without saying anything, I pushed a large beaker out of the way to make room and removed the mini-bat and the dog's paw and spread them out carefully on her desk. I kept the letter to myself. I didn't want to lose touch with it if Markeze caught up with the evidence and still refused to put me back on the case.

"You've got a sick one, huh?" Nyssa mused. Yet her eyes never lost that look of unsullied wonder. I had no idea how she could see the stuff she had seen and still keep a cloudiness or jaded wariness out of her eyes.

"Yeah, but it gets better," I told her. "He's made it personal. Sent this stuff directly to me and is threatening me or maybe those close to me." I pointed at the paw. "I think that's from my ex-wife's dog. I need a rush on this and would appreciate a direct call to me with whatever you get."

"You've got it. I'll push all of this to the front of the line for you. 'Detective in danger' does that without any trouble." She rotated the mini-bat to get a better look.

"Check the hairs for matches against any of these names," I suggested, grabbing a piece of paper and writing down the names we thought were linked to the killer. "Jamie Parks should be easy for you: it's a murder case we have in-house. The Breys are out of state cases but Mike, at least, is also considered a murder, so you should be able to liaise with the Wichita Police Department." I reached up and plucked a hair from my own head and handed it to her. "Check the last hair on the bat against my own. I don't think it looks much like a match but the killer was in my apartment. Also," I added, "let me know if you can determine what he used to burn the dots on the bat or if there is anything helpful about how he cut off the dog's paw."

"I'll also look for fingerprints, of course," Nyssa replied.

"You'll find mine all over the bat," I said. "Before you ask, no, I didn't handle it when I pulled it out of the package. I think the bat is mine, stolen from my apartment."

She shook her head, lips pursed. "I don't know how you do it, Marcus. I really don't."

"I've had the same thought about you and what you see in here," I responded. "Can you get me some pictures of all of this to take with me?" I asked, pointing toward a digital camera on a nearby table. I wanted them for my own record if my suspicion held, and I also wanted to show them to Ash and see what she thought about all of this.

"No problem." She retrieved the camera and took photos from several angles of the paw, then photographed the bat in several different positions. She included a few close-ups of the burn marks on the bat and the cut lines on the paw. She connected the camera via a USB cable directly to a very expensive printer, designed exclusively for photography. Glossy prints began emerging about a minute later, the detail on the close-ups remarkable, and chilling.

"I'll call you first thing when I find something. Marcus, watch yourself," she added. I thought the shininess of her eyes momentarily clouded as she spoke but I wasn't sure.

I left, feeling calmer and more in control now that I had the lab working on something for me. As I waited for the elevator, I pulled my phone from my pocket, preparing to give Ash a call to see if she was doing okay and tell her about the package. Something inside the lab must have blocked my reception while I was with Nyssa: I had missed three calls, all from Paige, only one minute spanning the time from the first to the last. I punched in the code to retrieve my voicemail.

"Marcus, where the hell are you? You had me all spooked and now you won't even answer my calls? Someone just called with a tip about Molly. Where are you?"

I dialed her cell but got no response. I tried her office number as I stepped into the empty elevator.

"The office of Paige Hersey. How may I help you?" It was the effervescent voice of Paige's assistant, Liza.

"Liza, it's Marcus. I need to speak to Paige right away."

Her effervescence evaporated. She had never cared for me. With Paige and I divorced, she finally had free rein to express her distaste. "She's not in," she said.

"Tell her to call me *immediately* if you hear from her. It's not a personal matter. It's professional, a police matter and she might be in danger. Do not let her ignore the message."

She faltered after I mentioned Paige might be in trouble. "She left the office. She was happy, excited. She said someone had found Molly and wanted to give her back. She went home to meet them."

Chapter Nineteen

I exited the elevator and tried Paige's cell again as I raced to my car. No answer. Inside the parking garage, my running created a lonely, staccato echo. The harsh reverberations moved from the concrete into my heart, the beat amplifying inside my body as it caught a ride on the locomotive of panic and anger I felt charging through me.

I cursed myself for not immediately sending a unit to Paige's work. I cursed cell technology for dropping calls that I desperately needed to have heard. I cursed Paige for leaving her office, for ignoring my warning to her. I cursed myself for not pressing the danger more clearly to her. It was our relationship in miniature: realizing too late how broken our interactions actually were.

Paige's house, my old house, was about ten minutes away in the Phinney Ridge neighborhood. It was a 1920s Craftsman, with old and troublesome plumbing and a small, mildew-smelling basement that accumulated traces of groundwater every rainy winter. The rooms were small but I had always loved the way it looked and felt. We had repainted every wall, installed a few new light fixtures, and sanded and resealed the hardwood floors.

I left traces of rubber as I cornered one of the roundabouts installed in Seattle's already narrow residential streets. My mind fixated on an image of Paige lying inert on those same hardwood floors, those same renovated light fixtures shining down on her bloody body. I pictured the killer standing over her with his baseball bat, dried blood from the other murders mixing with the still wet ooze deposited from Paige's wounds as he bludgeoned her until even the cracks between the hardwoods filled with her blood. The copper smell of blood seemed to mix in my nostrils with the yeasty smell of the basement.

My throat dried as I pulled in front of Paige's house and saw her black Volkswagen Jetta parked on the street. There were no open parking spots so I double-parked as close as I could without anyone inside Paige's house being able to see me—about four houses down. I popped the trunk and hopped out of my car. Inside the spare tire compartment I kept a snub-nosed .38. Spare tire, spare gun: temporary solutions, for emergencies only. I curled around the hood, raced over the sidewalk, and bounded up the cracked concrete steps to the front door.

I paused outside and to the left of the door, regrouping and forming a plan. Moving slowly while my heart pounded rapidly, I crept to the front window and then dipped down, placing my eyes at the lower diagonal to peek into the house. No movement, no lights on. The gray skies left the interior in dark shadows. I moved around the entire house, carefully looking in through the garden window jutting out of the kitchen. Nothing.

I duck-walked away from the house, toward a row of cypress trees that the neighbor had planted to serve as both property marker and natural fence. I moved as surreptitiously as possible back to the front door and tried the handle. It didn't move. I returned to the back door. Also locked.

I sucked in my breath, held the .38 away from my body, and kicked the door as hard as I could. The sound of snapping wood returned to me and the door sagged inward. But it didn't give entirely. Two more rapid kicks and it fell open.

No killer was waiting just inside the door with a gun pointing toward me. I dashed inside and curled to the left. I didn't stop or dive for cover behind a couch or overturn the dining room table to block an impending fusillade. I just ran straight through the kitchen, which I hoped was still as clear as it had been when I had peeked in earlier, away from the racket I had created with my kicked-in entrance.

The family room, a space that I couldn't see during my circuit of the exterior, waited ahead of me. I heard the cheap plastic clock above the stove ticking. In front of me, I heard muffled screaming.

Gun first, I turned the corner into the family room. My eyes scanned back and forth quickly, an open-eyed impersonation of REM sleep. My breath caught at what I saw but I continued visually searching the room. No killer in sight.

The family room didn't open to any additional rooms where the killer might be hiding. So that no one cold attack me from behind, I turned and walked backward into the room. Five backward paces into the room, I came even with Paige. She was bound to a tall-backed chair that had been brought in from the dining area. Her eyes gaped giant with fright. Duct tape covered her mouth. The silver center of the tape sucked in and pushed out quickly, her breathing panicky as she ineffectively tried to bring air in through her mouth. The killer had removed a swath of her hair, cutting from the center of her brow to about three inches back.

Paige had pulled her feet back underneath the chair, recoiling as far as her bindings would allow her. Directly in front of the chair, so close that Paige's feet would have been touching it if she hadn't tucked them back, lay Molly's mutilated body. It created a gruesome mockery of a loving pet resting at an owner's feet. The killer had positioned Molly with her chin resting on the floor, her dead and clouded eyes looking toward Paige. Molly's legs stretched out in front, one on either side of her snout. The killer had then crossed her legs, staged like a photographer would do if trying to capture an image of contentment. Except that the "X" meant to be formed by crossing Molly's legs couldn't be completed: both paws were missing.

Empty stumps with a gelatinous, blackish-red coating gaped toward Paige.

I untied Paige's hands and legs. The duct tape, wet with her tears, slipped in my fingers as I pulled it from her mouth. I reached with the back of my first two fingers to wipe away the tears leaking from her eyes. She pulled away, her head violently shaking back and forth as it escaped away from my hand.

"Is he still here?" I whispered.

She continued to shake her head back and forth. "No, no, no, no, no."

"Paige, look at me. Is the man who did this still here?" I asked again, not sure if her "no" was an answer to my question or a trauma response to Molly's dismemberment.

Her head slowed its shaking. Her eyes, shiny with the moisture of tears, turned toward mine. "Gone," she croaked. Her eyes dropped from mine. When they reached the body of Molly at her feet, she jumped from the chair, stumbling a bit, maybe as the circulation crept back into legs that had been bound tightly and frozen in place for too long. She backed away from Molly, and me, her left hand sideways over her mouth and her right hand waving. It could have been a movement to say goodbye, but I think she offered it as a stop sign, one of those gestures you give to tell the universe that you've had enough and need a break, just a short one. Those breaks never come.

Her retreat ended as she bumped against the rear wall of the family room. Pausing for only a brief instant, she began walking back toward us, so that it all looked like something from a wrestling match, where she hit the ropes, they gave momentarily, then propelled her back from where she came. Her eyes never met mine.

When she reached Molly, she crumpled to the ground. Her arms wrapped around the dog's body and her head turned to the side so that it could rest on Molly's back. She recoiled, slightly, then moved back once more to Molly.

"She's stiff. Cold," she said, more to herself than to me. I didn't reply. I didn't know what to say.

I let her sit that way while I went to get her a glass of water. I hoped that the coolness of the water might help her turn her attention away from the dog so that I could ask her more questions.

"Paige," I said quietly, gently tapping her on the shoulder, "I have water for you. Take a drink."

More automaton than human, she grabbed the glass. Her eyes brightened as the icy water hit her throat. She returned the glass to me, her eyes looking at me this time. They seemed as frosty as the water. She didn't say anything, but her icy stare didn't leave my face.

"Paige, I need you to tell me whatever you remember about the man who did this. What he looked like, sounded like, smelled like. Anything, anything at all, that he said to you." She turned toward Molly, then back to me.

"He wore gloves and a ski mask. Black gloves and a black mask." She didn't say anything else. I didn't say anything either. I knew from experience that sometimes the first words a victim says can unlock other ideas, that you can learn more by remaining silent and being patient for a few long moments than by rushing things and pushing ahead too soon.

"Soap," she added, her eyes lost to me as they looked at something only she could see. "He smelled of soap. So clean, I remember thinking. Like the soap had dried on his skin without being washed away. I smelled it even more than the leather of the gloves or the wool of the mask," she said, voice and eyes and mind faraway again.

"That's good, Paige. What did his voice sound like?" I asked, wishing desperately that I could hear exactly what she had heard, feeling oddly cheated that the killer's voice had hit her ears and not my own. Whatever the killer had told her, I believed, was intended more for me than for her. I would be hearing second-hand what should have been primary. She didn't respond but her eyes turned downward. "Paige," I repeated, "what did he say to you?"

"I can't be in your life anymore, Marcus," she responded, then turned quiet again.

"I understand, but I need to know what he said to you, Paige. This is important."

"That *is* what he said. He said that I need to leave you alone. He said that it's important that nothing takes you away. He said you were his orphan. He told me," she started and then broke down. "He told me that Molly was my warning. Then he cut my hair. I was so scared. He cut my hair and told me that every time I looked in the mirror I should remember him and what he did to Molly and that he would do it to me too if I didn't leave you alone." She started crying again, shoulders heaving but sobs so quiet to be almost, but not quite, silent. "I was so scared. He started breathing faster as he cut my hair. I was sure he was going to kill me."

"How would you describe his voice?" I asked, my own breath coming faster as I yearned to hear any other details she could give me about this man. I should have asked more about how she was feeling, I realized as soon as the words were out of my mouth.

"I don't know," she replied, anger in her voice. "He sounded scary. I was scared. I don't know. He was calm and slow-speaking for everything. Except when he cut my hair." Her eyes focused directly on mine again. "I thought I was going to die." Then something drained out of her voice and the flush in her cheeks seeped away. "He killed Molly. Why did he have to do that? Why did he have to do *this* to her?" she asked, pointing toward Molly's missing paws before quickly turning away.

I didn't have an answer and felt like shit for not being able to tell her anything helpful. I needed a primer on what to say to an ex-wife whose dog had just been murdered as an object lesson. Hallmark is amazing, but I don't think they have a card for that. Not even Shoebox.

"I'm sorry, Paige. I know how you felt about Molly." I moved to block her view of the dog. I put a hand gently on her shoulder, ready to hold her and let her cry some of the stress and anxiety out.

She slapped my hand off her shoulder. She started sobbing, gulps of air mixing with her words. "I hate you, I hate you, I hate you." Her words cascaded in a rush as her fists beat on my chest. "This is *your* fault, yours! He could have killed me, Marcus. I thought I was dead and all I could think of was you—not love for you but deep, dark hatred for you doing this to me."

She stopped again, her sobs slowly coming under her control. "I hate you for this, Marcus."

I felt my own voice crack as I scrambled for a foothold while I tumbled down the dark chasm that is reserved especially for pains that only those you have once loved can inflict upon you. "Paige, I . . . I'll get this guy. I'll get him and he'll pay. He's hurt me too. He shouldn't have brought you into this." I was lost again, out of words and ideas.

"Do you remember Molly as a puppy?" she asked, ignoring or not registering the feeble response I had mustered. "Remember how her ears looked too big for her face? Like when a kid first gets her permanent front teeth and her face isn't yet sized for them?" She smiled at the memory. Then it disappeared. Not faded as much as evaporated. "She was the best gift you ever gave me, Marcus. She was the best of anything we had together. I loved her all the more for that, for forcing me to remember that at one point you were connected to me and didn't hide from me."

She started to cry again, tears welling in her eyes and then slowly trickling down. She didn't brush them away, instead letting them roll from the corners of her eyes and over her cheeks until they curved toward the corners of her mouth. She probably could have tasted the salt from them. "She's gone and I want you out, Marcus. Out of my house. Out of my life. Out." She looked straight at me, the line of missing hair from her bangs zeroing in directly between my eyes. "It's your fault. Yours. Get out. Forever." I could see her shoulders shuddering as she put her arms around Molly once again. This time I didn't try to give her a hug or comfort her. I turned and left, feeling responsible and fragile and broken.

I called in the scene to SPD, then drove home dazed, filled with thoughts that crawled through my brain like worms, eating away the good memories that I had secreted and devouring the happiness that I had hidden to keep safe. When the worms were done devouring the good, they shit out the dark meconium of a despondency, newly birthed but familiar all the same. I saw myself as the bull in the china shop, crashing into and damaging everyone I came in contact with. I felt radioactive, could imagine a sickly yellow glow pulsing off my skin and making ill everyone I loved, everyone who I became close to, or even wanted to become close to. Like a perverse imitation of those crazy, curling paths in Family Circle comic strips, I carried a trail of infection everywhere I went, from Mr. Brey and Mike to Ash to Paige and Molly.

I wanted to know why, instead of waiting for me, Paige had returned home to the killer and all of this sickness. I realized, again too late, that the disconnect between Paige and me had been even larger than I wanted to admit. I saw now that it was total, a vacuum that sucked in words and gave back silence, that blurred gestures of goodwill until they were so distorted that you couldn't tell what they meant.

I felt responsible, not just for bringing the killer into her orbit, but also for my part in establishing a level of dysfunction so total that it sabotaged all communication and goodwill between us. I would have had more success protecting a complete stranger than her. Someone else would have trusted my warnings and not pushed back at them because of the messenger.

By the end of our relationship, Paige and I were alone, even when together. I hated myself for finding comfort in that emptiness, for first assuming and later accepting that two people always stare across an impassable gap, an unbridgeable space between what you need and what someone else can give to you. I took the easy route. I embraced the safety of not risking myself with Paige, held tightly to the idea that there is no emotional land of milk and honey between two people that can last for any length of time. So I pulled away and clapped myself on the back for my maturity in accepting that no one ever truly finds emotional fulfillment, that life does not offer a hidden jewel of delight, that life just is, that at root life is empty and lonely and isolating and sad.

I wrapped myself in this threadbare coat and called it warm, convinced myself that the holes pocking its surface weren't there. Then each time Paige pulled away, each time we hurt each other, I took it as further proof of my theory, a confirmation of my inability to love anyone else and for anyone else to give love to me. I became a coward, scared to risk giving myself to her, to something beyond me. Facing those shortcomings now made me fear that I would fail in the same way with Ash, would destroy it all because I was broken inside, defective at my core.

I pulled in front of my apartment, not remembering the drive home at all. I walked to my door filled with regret and unhappiness and a previously hidden bitterness that augured alienation and isolation. A sadness, sticky and tar-like, difficult to remove, pulled my arms down. My back slumped as if I had just walked out of the sea and my clothes were dripping with briny water, a soaking wool sweater heavy on my shoulders. I imagined wispy hands and long, bony fingers reaching up from the earth and grabbing hold, to slow me and fatigue me and suffocate me into submission.

I reached my door, fumbled my key out and turned the handle. Centered in the entryway was a small pillow, the kind a ring bearer might use. Atop it rested Molly's other paw.

Chapter Twenty

Molly's paw was a monstrous gift, but the thought that the killer had been inside my apartment again disturbed me even more. I already knew Molly was dead, had retrieved her other paw from a box, and had seen her lifeless body in front of my bound ex-wife. Shock value had been diminished. Knowing a murderer had been inside my apartment at least twice made my skin crawl in a way that can only happen from a violation of a space that you believe should be, must be, safe.

I moved through my apartment, gun ready, hoping that the killer was still there, feeling the despondency that had wrapped around my heart hardening into a black and brittle hatred, as though a furnace had been lit inside me that burned bright enough to transform anything that I fed it into anger and violence. I resented being a puppet, forced by an anonymous killer to dance this way then that way, bumping into and hurting those around me with each jerky movement.

The hate felt powerful, but I knew from experience that I had only exchanged one monster for another, that such a trade would only be temporary. The type of aggression coursing through my veins had, in the past, propelled me to acts that later remained only cloudy memories, indistinct in details but disturbing in their fuzzy outline, as though I had been drunk on rage and the desire to inflict pain on someone who had wronged me. It inevitably burned down into a sense of regret and shame that only made the original depression worse.

I completed my sweep of the apartment without finding any intruders. I put away my backup gun and poured myself a generous double of Balvenie Scotch. Drinking most of it in one pull, I felt the heat coat my throat and warm my stomach. I should have called Markeze, or the crime scene techies. Instead, I moved the paw to the side and left my polluted apartment. I wanted to see Ash, to find someone who I could share this with and find not just professional curiosity or efficiency but something as warming and comforting as the Balvenie now working through my system.

The Seattle rain fell gently but steadily, its trail more visible than audible. The headlights of passing cars shined in the rain like halos, the center appearing clear, with the corona hazy and undefined. I called Ash to tell her I needed to see her.

Ash's small, one-story house was located in Ballard, north of Seattle proper. It had a brick exterior painted white, a small lawn held in by a retaining wall that reached about four feet above the sidewalk that sat in front of it. As I walked to the door, the soft rain left miniscule, intact drops, glistening like crystals, on the hairs of my arm.

She answered the door holding two glasses of wine, the color a deep, inky purple. "You sounded like some alcohol might be needed," she said and led me inside. "We both could use some."

I wanted to tell her everything, and that scared me. I felt what I imagined some of the criminals I had interrogated had felt: a desire to confess, to tell all that pained and confused me. The desire to come clean with my own shortcomings burned in my heart, yet also momentarily singed my vocal cords.

I took a large drink of wine and plunged into a recap of the day, not holding back any details. I told her about my visit with the eerie old woman, about the package leaking blood all over my desk, about the paw and note, about finding Paige tied up with part of her hair cut out, about the killer entering my apartment at least twice and leaving the paw.

She refilled our wine glasses before speaking. "You're still holding back. Fill in the gaps, give me the emotion within all of this. Because I see it in your eyes. It's all there sitting behind a thin film, like something glowing underneath Saran Wrap, warping it with heat."

I drank half of my refill in one gulp, her words and the alcohol swirling like a cloud of bees in my brain. Her slate-green eyes refused to pull away, challenging me and being gentle with me all at once. I felt that look burn like a brand into my soul, into a spot that I would never forget, a place that I would be able to recall immediately, even upon awakening from a coma or when delirious on my deathbed. She spoke with her eyes, telling me that I would be safe with her and that she had her own pain and, for whatever reason, trusted me.

The scotch and the wine began to hit me, hard. They pulled my eyes back in my head, the room twirling briefly every time I blinked.

"Today," I started and then stopped, unsure how to explain what I felt. "Today stripped away the little bit of innocence I had left. I'd tried to hold a small sample of that back, locked away in some kind of Doomsday vault that even the job couldn't touch. It would be there, waiting for me when I needed it. Like those secret glow sticks that Superman found in his ice fortress. Something preserved for when I needed help. It's gone now."

She didn't say anything. Just held my eyes with her own, buoying me.

"Today forced me to see that Paige and I never had something real. That I held back from her; that she held back from me; that maybe there wasn't really love there to begin with." I finished my wine. "That's the spot that got me, that showed me all of the cracks in the ice fortress, that made it all come tumbling down." I could hear my words stretch out from the alcohol and felt foolish.

I stopped, searching for words for something that wasn't entirely clear even to me. I desperately wanted to explain it to her. I wanted to find in her a lifeline, a rope that could pull me out of the darkness that I felt turning my skin, and my heart, cold.

I started to reach for the wine bottle but reigned in that desire, grabbing the cork instead. With it gripped between my middle finger and thumb, I made a snapping motion. The cork shot out, spinning on the coffee table. I liked watching it spin, felt mesmerized by it. I knew it would stop, but the spinning seemed to lie about that. It seemed to thumb its nose at the inevitable. It wobbled more and more as it slowed until it fell on its side and rolled off the table.

I watched to see if she was ready to move away from her claim that she wanted to hear all of this. I feared that I would find only the gaze of pity or amusement normally reserved for freaks in the carnival. Instead, her beautiful, haunting eyes continued to hold the promise of understanding and comfort.

I wanted to stop talking, but I couldn't. Maybe it was the alcohol, or Ash's eyes, or the pressure of the last few days, or the hope that I could do things differently than I had when I held back from Paige in a doomed effort to keep both myself and the relationship intact through a policy of isolation. Whatever it was, I talked and felt a simultaneous repulsion and relief as the words hit my eardrums, hammering previously unspoken thoughts into my brain while releasing some of the pain that had been trapped the entire time they had remained silent to no one but me.

"He cut Paige out from me today," I said. "Don't get me wrong, Ash. I'm over her. Have been over her. What happened is that he made me look back and I saw how scared and withheld and weak I had been with her. I don't want that anymore. I don't want to feel like I'm holding back, don't want to feel like I've settled and feel my stomach turning over with fear and self-loathing and lost dreams of what I thought love was and what I thought I would feel from love."

"Marcus," Ash exclaimed, simply. She brushed my hand with the back of her fingers.

"Shouldn't there be an 'Oh' before that," I replied, grinning. "And you need to hold the back of your hand to your forehead at the same time. Overcome by 'the vapors' or the air or the heaviness of the self-loathing you hear escaping from my lips."

I stopped, pulled myself back from using humor as a defense. "Ash," I confessed, "I see something in your eyes that pulls deep inside me. It's like an echo of myself. I see that pain in you and I feel safe to share my own shortcomings with you. But I hear myself talk and I hate myself. I remind myself of Ryota, that it's all suffering and sacrificing and blah, blah, blah." I stopped, disgusted, feeling the oily coat left by the alcohol on my tongue.

She put her hands inside mine. I felt how thin her own hands were, the ridges of her knuckles pressing into my palm as her fingers gently nestled inside my hands. I rubbed my thumb over the curve of her fingers.

"Ash, I think you should get away from me. I think that, but I don't want that," I said, looking directly into her gray-rimmed eyes. "I feel like my world is shattered into pieces, jagged little ones that cut every time I try to put them back together."

Her gaze never drifted from mine. "Things that are broken can be repaired. They can be fixed." Her hands moved mine up and down as she talked, trying to pump her own confidence of repair into me.

I wondered to myself if the break could possibly ossify, burying the injury so that it would never be uncovered again, or if spidery, hair-line cracks would always remain and weaken the entire structure. Once broken, then what? I could only think of a Brady Bunch episode where a vase is broken by rough-housing and then glued back together to hide the damage. It, predictably, shatters at the lightest subsequent touch.

I turned away from Ash with this last thought, my mind registering embarrassment at something I knew she hadn't heard, but turning away nonetheless. I was tired. That was it, I realized. I remembered Paige's stop-sign gesture to the universe. I was worn out from fighting with life, exhausted from playing defense against a behemoth that I would never defeat. I yearned for that sense of acceptance, that peaceful feeling that you see in religious zealots. I always think they are nuts, but I can't help but admire the peace of resignation I see inside them.

I don't know how you find that when you've stuck yourself on a pin like a captured insect, one wing flapping desperately to find meaning, while the other wing flaps in a syncopated rhythm with the sad conviction that no meaning exists. Fighting with life is, always, a losing battle.

Rain collided, gently, with the windowpane. It carried a tenderness with it, I thought. The drops didn't burst apart as they hit the glass. Refusing to spatter, they struck the window and stuck, then pulled closer to one another as they wound their way down the pane in a curvy, chaotic movement that somehow pointed toward a greater, hidden pattern.

I wanted to tell Ash what I saw. I raised my finger, gesturing to the window. I know my mouth opened, but then I'm not sure. I don't know if she spoke first, or if I didn't speak at all. Her hand, fingers thin and delicate and wiry-strong, covered my lips.

She left her fingers there, shifting them slightly so that the tips lingered on my lips. "It's okay. You can rest," she mouthed. Her fingers on my lips became a conduit. As if the same electrical impulses that moved her were moving me, I felt my lips pantomiming the same words: "It's okay. You can rest."

I saw, more than heard, her speak my name, while her fingers pressed with slightly more pressure against my mouth. Her eyes, though, as always, got me. Got us. Her hand moved from my mouth, my lips imprinted with her touch. Her fingers returned to my skin, caressing away a tear from the middle of my cheek that I hadn't realized had escaped. Then her index finger, with a tenderness I had never felt before, followed the curve of my eye, softly wiping the moisture from my skin, unintentionally tickling my eyelash.

When I felt her finger move away, I opened my eyes to hers. The gray-green rims glistened with the dampness of her own tears barely held back. They looked overwhelmed, as though they were expending all their energy to toss me a lifeline while simultaneously trying to call out for her own salvation. I saw my own pain reflected, saw walls removed and a nearly desperate begging for me to save her. It was as if, despite everything I had told her, she still saw in me a spot of safety. I wanted to protect those eyes, love those eyes. Protect her, love her.

We somehow saw the best in each other. We saw ourselves, our pains and shortcomings and shared desire and common yearning to be better than we were, in one another's eyes.

I once more opened my mouth to speak, to try and communicate with words what our eyes had already said. She stopped me again. This time with her lips. I felt first the slightly oily thickness of lipstick. Then it gave way beneath the heat and movement of our kiss and I felt the naked tenderness of her lips. They offered a concomitant yielding and firmness that I found more intoxicating than anything I had drunk that night. Perhaps ever. I could feel her give part of herself to me, expose a raw compassion; I could feel her hold another part of herself strong. It made the weakness I felt from her all the more sensual. There was a trusting to it. Not so much a neediness as a willingness to risk herself, to gamble on me with what she had held back from others.

I broke away from the kiss, overwhelmed. The work her fingers had done to staunch my tears began to give way. I moved toward her, intent on answering the desire I felt in her lips with the longing I too felt, with the self that I had locked away from others for so long. She stopped me again, her left hand gently pushing on my chest.

"Shhhh." Her left hand continued to hold me back, my longing increasing with expectation and the first feel of her touch and her words. Her right hand moved to my face, fingertips once more softly wiping some of my tears away. Then she took her hands away. Her lips returned to my face, brushing my own lips, then moving to the cheek opposite where her fingertips had been and kissing away the salty tear that hung there.

She pushed me, gently, to the back of the couch, then stood between my legs. She bent down and kissed my neck. Then, still slowly, unbuttoned my shirt and pants. Standing straight again, she took off her shirt and unclasped the lacy pink bra underneath. She took a step back and removed her jeans as I in turn took off mine.

Her underwear had a lace top that hugged the curve of her hips. I started to stand to move toward her and she again moved me back, a gentle firmness to it all. She stepped out of her panties.

She leaned over me again to kiss me. Her hair, the ends touching my skin like electricity, moved over my nose and cheeks as she came closer. The swell of her breasts touched my chest, sending a shiver down my spine, then another one as her nipples pulled away from my skin. I felt a salty tear, this time from her eyes, drop on my neck as she leaned over me. Moving my knees together, she straddled me and took me inside her.

My hands found her hips and I felt a small shudder move through her body as I held to her curves. Her hair tickled my neck as we moved. I looked up to her face and found her eyes open, engaging my own. Her eyes held raw desire, a sexual longing that I felt even more powerfully with her gaze than with her hips moving in small and then larger circles on me. I wanted to close my eyes, lose myself in desire and forget about everything. But I couldn't. I couldn't lose those eyes. With her mouth curled in pleasure and her eyes wet with tears, she transfixed me. It was the most erotic moment I've ever felt, and also somehow one of the most protected moments I've ever felt.

The heat I felt between us was simultaneous physical and emotional, sexual friction combining with a melting into one another emotionally. I took my hand off the curve of her hip, feathering the touch of my fingertips over her stomach until I felt the curled edge of the cigarette burn branded into her skin. I wanted to understand more about her scars, be there with a gentle touch for her. Intense desire mixed with the sense that we were creating a mutual harbor from the world. With that realization, that hope, my eyes could no longer hold onto hers. I felt myself dissolve into her, felt my toes curl and my neck arch back and my mouth hang open as she squeezed tight on me and her hips shuddered once more.

Afterward, we curled together, our sweat mingling, on the couch. Neither of us spoke, keeping sacred in silence what words would diminish. I moved my arms tighter around Ash, hoping my touch would communicate what I couldn't verbalize. Her hands squeezed back on my arm. Her breathing grew slower and steadier. My eyes began to droop and my blinking became more rapid in my effort to stay awake. I wanted to hold onto the moment as long as I could. Despite my efforts, my blinking grew slower, my eyes held closed longer. I heard rain hitting against the window, remembered the way the drops pulled toward one another through some hidden law of gravity or attraction. I drifted off to sleep, with the heat of my body and Ash's body melting together.

Chapter Twenty-One

I awoke several hours later. It was as dark as tar outside and my mind was equally sticky as I processed where I was and what had happened. I stayed as still as possible, wanting only to snatch a few precious moments next to Ash and hear her even, peaceful breathing and feel her abdomen move up and down against my forearm. Finally surrendering to the fact that I wouldn't be going back to sleep, I carefully extracted myself.

I pulled on my shirt and stepped into my jeans. Shivering slightly in the night cold, I dashed to my car. I popped the trunk and found the extra set of workout clothes and shoes that I kept there.

I went back into Ash's home, changed, and returned to the outside. The air felt heavy and damp with pre-dawn moisture and quiet blanketed me.

I took off, my muscles soon warming enough so that the cold felt soothing and comforting instead of chilling. I felt my legs moving faster, my breath coming quicker. I pushed my pace until I could feel sweat curl down my nose and hang there, for an instant, before dropping onto my chest. My vision blurred momentarily as my eyelash caught a globule of sweat and held it. I resisted the urge to wipe it away. I felt the sweat as purification and ran to penetrate through the dark, goopy gunk that slowly, imperceptibly I had wrapped around my heart. I ran for a lightness, an air of something clean within myself that I hadn't seen, or been willing to see, in years. I didn't quite know how to clear a path within myself to reach back to it, but I wanted to run until I found it.

It was a feeling that instead of giving in to defeat I would rather, like the spinning cork, fight even as life pulled at me and slowed me down. The dazzling nature of continuing to spin in the face of loss, I decided, is its own way to fight pain, to try and right wrongs from the past that otherwise leave you dizzy with their oppressiveness.

Back at Ash's door, I let myself in as quietly as I could. I needn't have bothered. I heard shower water pulsing off of fiberglass in the master bath.

I entered the bathroom, a wave of moist heat hitting my skin. A smell of summer, something flowery, mixed with the steam hanging in the air. Ash saw me and smiled, the water painted on the shower door making everything shimmer slightly, like heat off of a summer road. She pointed to the bar near the shower door and I saw two towels hanging. I smiled back.

I peeled my running clothes off of my skin and entered the shower. Ash had already washed her hair and her normally tight curls hung loose. The water turned her auburn hair a shade darker. With her hair wet, her face appeared more open to me. She must have noticed my gaze.

"I look a bit like a wet poodle," she said, an embarrassed smile crossing her face as she ducked her eyes and head down. Only for an instant, though, and then she looked back at me and offered a fuller smile, no longer self-conscious. Both moments struck me as real: the awkward moment and the recovery of being okay with herself despite it. "What are you thinking?" she asked.

Water caromed off her shoulders and onto my chest. I saw again the freckle on her neck that had so entranced me at the bar. I saw more freckles forming their own constellation, starting from her left shoulder then moving over her breasts and dissolving into isolated points on her stomach. A quarter-sized birthmark, more brown than red or purple, colored the skin just below her right kneecap so that it looked as though she had fallen and scraped her knee on something muddy.

"I'm just realizing how much I don't know about you," I answered. "And realizing how much I want to find out." Steam curled around our bodies, caressing our skin in a sensual wrap. "I want to watch you brush your hair, dry your hair, put your makeup on, do the everyday stuff," I said, holding her shoulders gently with my hands and her eyes firmly with my own.

"What else?"

"I like seeing your hair wet. I like the idea of being around when your defenses are down. I want to show you the kind of intimacy and trust that comes in that moment when you step from the warm water to the cold air outside and you're wet and your hair is at its most poodle-like and you're naked and you feel vulnerable and embarrassed. I want to be there with you at that moment, and have you know, instinctively, that you are safe, that I am strong for you and my arms are warm for you and I am as safe for you as you were for me last night. That I love seeing you and want to be next to you even when you think you are at your worst."

Water rebounded off of our skin and jumped between our faces as I moved my head down toward hers. My lips found hers, full from the heat of the shower. Our kiss was hard, wild, teeth bumping together as desire moved us at an almost frantic pace. As gentle as last night had been, this morning was passion. My hands found her hips as my lips moved over her neck. I pushed her to the shower wall. She grabbed my lower lip between her teeth and pulled me closer. Her nails scratched into my back as I felt her breath move to my ear. Steam formed a cocoon around us. Sweat and water mingled together as we moved. Her right ankle hooked around my calf and I felt her thigh muscle tighten as she pulled me closer, deeper. She bit down on my shoulder as she would a pillow, moans muffled by my skin. We stayed in the water, reveling in the closeness, until the hot water tank gave out.

We dried off with thick gray towels that still held the scent from the dryer sheet, something fresh and airy. A drop of water hung onto the end of Ash's auburn hair, wavering for a split second before falling onto her shoulder and running away from my view down her back. I moved closer, brushed her wet hair away from her neck and kissed the freckle there that had always caught my attention.

I again saw the scar on her abdomen, the cigarette burn that I had seen and felt but not yet heard about. She saw me looking. She took my hand, moved my fingers to the scar again, as they had been last night. Touching the scar, something shot through my brain, a moment when what I saw in front of me connected to something else entirely.

"Son of a bitch," I said. "The body at the Market. Before I left for Kansas. Remember her?"

"Of course. She was bludgeoned." She paused. "Like what our killer does."

"I think it's even more than that," I said as I pulled on my wrinkled pants. "We need to get to the station and grab the file. Preferably before everyone else rolls in and wonders what two suspended detectives are doing in the files."

She smiled at me. A big, big smile. "Relax, Marcus. I've got a copy here. I haven't looked at the Market murder since all of this picked up speed, but I figured if we didn't get the serial killer maybe I could at least catch the guy from the Market. Still trying to prove my worth to Markeze."

I buttoned my shirt as I spoke, "I'll be right back. Gonna grab the genealogical folder from my car. We need it too."

Outside, the crisp air hit my lungs and my exhalation created a rolling fog. Seeing and feeling Ash's cigarette scar had turned my mind to the brands on the mini-bat. Burn to burn, scarred flesh to scarred wood. Everything mixed together in a giant 'son-of-a-bitch' jumble as I connected the dots between burns, bludgeoning, and being marked by the killer. It was all there. We had stared right at it without really seeing it.

Back inside, I found Ash in the kitchen. "You look through your folder and I'll look through this one. Pull out any crime scene photos in there and I'll do the same." The key, I thought, would be to combine what she held and what I held.

We fanned all of the pictures out on the kitchen island, creating a gruesome tableau of blunt force trauma and bodily mutilation. The violence captured in the pictures astonished me. I had the impression that each picture offered a moment frozen in time from the killer's mind, a still-frame of the anger and sadism that constantly boiled in there.

"She was definitely beaten to death. But what else are we looking at here that makes you so sure the woman from the Market is tied to our killer?" Ash asked.

"We need to look at this backward, see things again from a different angle than when we visited the scene. Look for signs of the killer who we know *now* in the scene we caught back *then*." I rearranged the pictures, putting them in chronological order, creating what I thought was a timestamp of the killer's movements.

"There, Marcus, there! The wall. We looked right at it and didn't even know."

"We couldn't have known. It didn't mean anything then. Just graffiti on a dirty downtown wall when we saw it the first time."

Positioned so that it sat above the body at the Market, the kanji for 'Truth' glared. There was other writing on the wall but seeing it this time, the kanji seemed to pulse with light, glow with an importance that previously we had no way of understanding.

Ash paused while looking through the case file for a name. "This woman, still no idea who she is?"

"I'm willing to bet this is Jamie Parks's mom."

Pushing the top photo aside, I uncovered the shot that tied together for me the branded mini-bat, Ash's scar, and the first murder scene. "Here," I said, tapping on the picture, "a single circular burn, on her hand."

"I remember, Marcus." Ash unconsciously moved her right hand on top of her abdomen, covering her own burn.

"He burned the mini-bat with something too. I found small circles on it."

"So he's giving us not just the symbols for 'harmony' and 'truth' but dots also. But what about the burn marks? Only this first body seems burned. If the others were burned, we would have noticed." She moved through the other photos, methodically but with obvious energy.

"Let's find the pictures of Mike," I said. "He was the next body we found, next in line." We turned our attention to his photos and I saw it almost immediately, something I had missed entirely the first time, either because I hadn't known to look for it or because seeing my near-brother in the picture distracted me or because the obvious violence and giant kanji carved into his flesh made it easy to overlook something so small. Whatever the reason, it now jumped off the picture, slapping me in the face for overlooking it in the past. "See them?" I asked Ash.

Mike's fingers, as Angstrom had noted to me in the Wichita hotel room, had been crushed. They were flattened, shards of bone breaking through the skin, the tips pointing at angles that fingers never touch in everyday life. It was brutal to envision the cap of the baseball bat rising and falling like a piston, destroying one finger at a time.

The back of the hand, however, appeared relatively unscathed. The undamaged portion of Mike's hand looked sinewy, even the skin on his hand thin from his meth addiction. His finger tendons looked like piano wire stretched beneath the skin, or thick strings attached to a puppet to create movement for the audience. Two small dots were positioned on either side of the tendon that traveled up to what had been his middle finger. Their shape looked too uniform, too circular compared to the surrounding damage, for them to be blood spatter.

"On his hand?" she was talking to herself, not to me. "Yes, I see it. Right there. On *his* hand, too. They don't look like burns but they're definitely dots." This time she was the one tapping the picture as she talked. "Two of them, Marcus. Two of them this time. It's a counting," she said, excitement in her voice and eyes. "One circle on the first victim, two on Mike."

"Except we're forgetting Mr. Brey," I said, feeling the same disappointment I saw register on Ash's face. "We don't have any pictures because it wasn't considered a crime scene and even if we wanted to exhume his body we can't because my brother cremated him. His death predates Mike's. He would be number one or two, depending on the timing compared to the body under Pike Place Market. Mike would be number three," I concluded. We sat in silence while we processed the discrepancy.

"I know you want to find some greater sense in his death," Ash began, balancing each word on her tongue before letting it out of her mouth, looking for the correct path to navigate through what she must have seen as emotionally difficult territory for me. "What happens if we entertain the idea that his death truly was accidental, no foul play? The count then holds between Parks's mom as the first murder and Mike as the second. The circles make sense that way."

"The circles would make sense but nothing else would," I replied. "We wouldn't get the link to the samurai sword, and the picture in Mr. Brey's pocket of the mystery Asian woman would become even more difficult to explain. Plus, he had the paper scrap with the kanji for "Harmony" on it. I don't understand why his death wasn't violent, why he evidently wasn't brutalized like the others. But he *has* to be connected to the other murders. I'm sure of it."

A long silence squatted in the air. The excitement from discovering another puzzle piece gave way to more confusion and discouragement at not seeing where the new piece fit.

"What about the kanjis?" Ash mulled. "We still don't know why there's a switch between the kanji for 'Harmony' and the kanji for 'Truth.' Is there a way to think about the number of dots changing as part of the same pattern that makes the killer change kanji? I have no clue what that pattern is but maybe we need to think about the dots and the kanji as linked."

"That doesn't work either," I replied, getting frustrated. "It holds for Jamie Parks because he has two kanji and two dots. But beyond him, it falls apart." I pointed to the pictures again. "Mike has one kanji, but two circles. Parks's mom also has one kanji, but only one circle. Worse, though Mike and Parks's mom each have a single kanji, they're different: 'Harmony' for Mike and 'Truth' for Parks's mom. And Mr. Brey had a picture of the kanji for 'Harmony' but we have no idea how many dots he might have had. It's too random to figure out and too important to the killer to not mean anything. We have dots, we have kanji, we have victims, but we don't yet have the connections," I finished.

"We're not getting any closer, are we?" Ash asked.

I felt lost, stumbling through an unfamiliar, dark room, holding my arms straight to avoid staggering into hidden furniture. I knew the answer was there, that it would all make perfect sense once I understood the whole picture, but for the moment I was tired of the confusion and the bruises from bumping into things I couldn't see.

My arm felt the light touch of Ash's fingertips. I could feel the heat from her body, from our bodies, fill the space between us. This time it was more unifying than sexual, as though we were a team, as though we could avoid some of the stumbling and bruises by guiding one another through the dark. She used her free hand to move the pictures around, rearranging the order to see if anything new jumped out at us. "We have too many bodies and too many questions," she concluded.

She was right. I feared, though, that before the pattern emerged in greater clarity we would uncover more of each.

Chapter Twenty-Two

We decided to stop at the station as early as possible, before Markeze arrived. I wanted to check with Nyssa for any lab results. I hoped we could locate another piece in the puzzle before word from the departmental rumor mill reached Nyssa regarding my suspension. I trusted her, believed she would help, but I didn't want to take any extra chances.

I pushed open the door to the lab and a strong, vinegar-like odor hit me. The smells, more than anything, always reminded me of being back in high school chemistry. I didn't do well in chemistry, more interested in a girl named Melanie than in reagents and chemical symbols. But the smell stuck with me, the lingering scent of things burning and things burnt, the harsh cleanliness I associated with acids dissolving metal. The powdery aroma of latex gloves mixed with it all, forming a unique potpourri that you find nowhere but in a lab.

Nyssa looked momentarily nonplussed when she saw us, then her confusion gave way to a friendly smile and I knew she would give us whatever results were available.

"You must be Ashlynn," Nyssa said, removing one of her latex gloves and extending her hand and her smile. My fears regarding the departmental rumor mill were off by a degree: word of my suspension might not have filtered down, but somehow my interest in Ash already had. I thought again of high school.

"I'm glad you got my message," Nyssa said, "because what I have for you is really strange."

"What message?" I asked as I pulled out my cell phone and found that the battery had died sometime during the night.

"I called as soon as I got to the lab this morning." She reached for a stack of papers on the top of a series of three interlocking wire baskets. She turned toward us, showing the excitement that science geeks feel when data gives back something they didn't expect.

"What I found is really unusual," she said, turning her head back and forth between the two of us, as if she were following an imaginary tennis ball over an invisible net. "Okay, the blood is canine. No big surprise there, given the inclusion of the paw." She was building to something and I thought it best to let her show off her stuff, not deflate the enthusiasm she felt. I stayed quiet. "The hairs were more interesting. Very unexpected. As you know, the baseball bat had two triangular shapes burned into it, each triangle comprised of two circles for the base and one circle for the pinnacle. I labeled these Triangle A and Triangle B. Taped to the left of each triangle were two hairs. I labeled these hairs A1, A2 and B1, B2.

"Nice system," Ash said. I silently agreed.

Seeing that we were following her logic, Nyssa continued. "We had matches for one out of two hairs in each of the pairs. The ones that did match, hairs A2 and B2 respectively, belonged to James Matthew Parks and Michael Paul Brey. According to the databases, Parks voluntarily offered a DNA sample during a rape investigation. He was cleared. The Wichita police supplied Brey's DNA record."

I tried to hold a poker face, understanding from Nyssa's telling that we still hadn't reached the best part. "What about the lone hair taped to the bat that didn't have a triangle next to it?" I asked. "I guess if the first two triangles were A and B, what about the lone hair in column C?" Nyssa's eyes lit up again.

"I'm almost there, but we're not done with the hairs corresponding to triangles A and B," she replied. "While I can't identify hairs A1 or B1, we do know that they have half of the alleles in common with, respectively, A2 and B2."

"Meaning?" Ash prompted.

"Meaning that they are genetically related. I can't give you a name, but I can tell you that they are very closely related—maybe a parent or a son or daughter."

Nyssa paused, letting her information sink in. Connecting the dots to the bodies we had found, I was willing to bet that A1 and B1 were hairs from Jamie Parks's mom and from Mr. Brey. The killer had collected hairs from each of his victims.

"Column C, the one with no burn marks at all, is the strange one," Nyssa continued, and I knew this constituted the highlight of her report. "I can't give you a name. The DNA doesn't come back as an exact match to anyone in the databases. But I can give you another solid familial connection, another close genetic match." She turned toward me, her finger tapping on the faxed report and her pupils slightly dilating with the last of her words. "The alleles are associated with you, Marcus. Half of the genetic markers resonate with the DNA from the hair sample you gave me."

Immediately after she spoke, Nyssa's pupils constricted, her brow furrowed and eyebrows moved closer together as she realized that she was, in all probability, telling me that someone related to me had been killed. The excitement of the science and the bunkered isolation of the lab suddenly crashed into the reality of me standing directly in front of her.

"I'm sorry, Marcus," she said. She turned her head and I heard a mumbled "shit," followed by "stupid, stupid."

I tapped her gently on the shoulder. "Not your fault. It's okay." She looked up at me and offered a weak, apologetic smile. "It's okay," I repeated. On my elbow, I felt Ash's hand, simultaneously registering support and urging me toward the door. "Thanks, Nyssa. You've been helpful. I mean it."

The sound of the lab door clicking shut behind us echoed in the hallway.

"You all right, Marcus?" Ash asked, her hand still on my elbow.

"I'm fine," I said absently, my voice coming out of my mouth without conscious control on my part. Speaking just to be speaking, to be in control when I didn't feel it. "I want to go back to my place and change," I said, pointing to my wrinkled clothes." I jabbed at the elevator button. Ash didn't reply but moved her hand from my elbow up to my shoulder and pulled closer as we waited for the elevator to open.

The drive back to my apartment was as quiet as the drive to the station had been an hour or so earlier. At my apartment, the stale smell of old cardboard permeated the air. The morning sun came through the front window, warming boxes that still, months after moving in, I hadn't unpacked. I associated the fusty odor with the run-down parts of life that I had become too tired to change, with things that I had intended to be provisional but that had, instead, started to calcify in place.

"Given Nyssa's information," I said, "I assume that either my father or my mother is dead. I'd say my father. I haven't seen my mother since I was seven years old. I don't know why our killer would murder either my mother or father, but unless he's a better detective than we are and somehow magically tracked down my mom, then the hair is from my dad."

"You okay?"

"I don't understand why there was no burn mark on the bat. What makes my father's murder the odd-sized jigsaw piece that doesn't quite fit with everything else?"

"But are you okay?"

"I'm confused. I feel like a little kid again. This whole thing has taken me to parts of my family..." I stopped, faltering. "It's placed me back inside a family that I don't know much about and had boxed away and given up on long ago."

"If it is your dad, Marcus, why hasn't anyone contacted you? Maybe he's all right," Ash suggested.

I pictured the dust on his coffee table, the disrepair to his yard, his drinking habits. "I have the sense that he might not be missed for awhile. Not seeing him for a few days here and there probably isn't completely unheard of." Plus, the killer said I need to become an orphan. I dug my hand into my pocket for my wallet, looking to retrieve the card from Angstrom, the Wichita detective. With my phone on the charger, I borrowed Ash's to make the call.

"Angstrom." Abrupt, all traces of the honey-toned voice that I had experienced in person missing.

"Detective Angstrom," I said, "this is Detective Marcus Brace, Seattle PD."

"Detective Brace," he replied, the honey sneaking back in. I pictured him smiling and leaning back in his chair as he spoke. "Something else you wanted to tell me about Mike Brey's death?"

"Actually, I remembered your suggestion that I tell you if I planned to leave the city," I responded. "I left. Two days ago. Thought you should know." Something about the guy made it hard for me not to bust his balls.

"How nice of you to inform me. I trust you aren't calling from Mexico to confess." He was joking, I think.

"I'm back in Seattle, working a case and would appreciate your help. Inter-departmental cooperation and all that good stuff." Before he could respond, I continued, "I'm hoping that you will bring to bear what I assume is the considerable influence that the Wichita PD has on a small Kansas town and check on my father's address for me. Possible homicide."

"Here's the problem: the last time we talked it was about the death of a man who, basically, was your brother. Now you're talking to me again, this time about what you say could be the killing of your father. I'm not thinking as much that I should help you as that I should investigate you further after all. You see the problem? See where I'm coming from?"

"Come on, Angstrom."

"I'm getting the feeling that you're leading me through a field of horseshit and I don't like my shoes dirty."

Keeping all of my chips to myself had run its course. Time to pay up, at least some of them. I hoped that Ash and I found ourselves far enough ahead of the wave that no one else would catch up with us before we finished.

"I'm going to send you some things from my end and see what you think. It's time we worked together," I lied. "I think we have a killer moving between your territory and mine. I've got a murder too close to that of Mike to be random. You'll see from the pictures—strange symbol on the body, blunt force to the head."

"Why is this the first I've heard of this, Brace?"

"We just got the lab work this morning," I said, giving a true answer as a dodge for what he really asked. "We have hairs collected, showing DNA that matches with Mike Brey and also DNA from someone who has genetic material close to mine. That's why I'm asking you to leverage the small town police about my father. You'll get the crime scene photos as soon as we get off the phone. I need that check on my father's place."

He sweated me in silence for a few moments. "What's the address? I'll see what I can find out."

I gave Angstrom the address and he promised to call me back as soon as he found out anything. I hadn't told him about Jamie Parks's mom or my thoughts that Mr. Brey had been murdered by the same guy, or what the killer had done to Paige and Molly.

"Mission accomplished?" Ash asked.

"Just about." I grabbed the genealogical folder and moved from the kitchen to the main room and my laptop. "Need to send these to the detective in Wichita and we'll see what he can find out about my father."

A sharp knock at the door echoed through the apartment.

"You mind checking on that?" I asked, as I worked to scan the images and attach them to an email for Angstrom.

Ash returned a minute later. "Here you go," she said as she re-entered the room, carrying a packing envelope. I took it from her and turned it over to see who sent it. No label on it anywhere, not even one with my own name and address.

"Ash," I began, "was anyone there? Did someone hand this to you?" I removed my backup gun and approached the door at an oblique angle so I would be less of a head-on target. Ash followed me, pulling out her own gun.

"No," she whispered. "It was just the envelope. It was resting right outside the door. You know how those delivery guys are always in a hurry. They drop the package and run unless they need a signature."

I nodded in agreement. "Except that there's no to or from address on this one," I explained. "Not your typical delivery service," I whispered, gesturing toward the door with my gun.

Chapter Twenty-Three

I pointed at the door, then pointed at myself and held up one finger, telling Ash I would go first. She nodded.

I flung open the door and exited low, keeping my body underneath anyone's initial eye level and spinning to the right. Ash followed directly behind me and moved to the left. Adrenaline dried my throat and bristled at my spine. The hallway was empty. Ash pulled open the metal door to the stairs. The stairwell was empty too. We held the door to the stairs open for a long minute, keeping quiet to listen for the echo of footsteps or the sound of another door clicking shut. Nothing. We were alone.

Back in the apartment, I locked the door. I left the envelope alone for the moment, moving instead past the unpacked cardboard boxes to the window. No one in a deliveryman outfit lurked on the street below. No one stood by a tree across the street in a dark trench coat. No one looked up, ready to wave at me with an insane smile and then dash away. There was just empty street, an old couple walking together on one sidewalk and a female jogger moving by on the other sidewalk.

"Looks clear," Ash said. She spoke normally, but after the tension and the whispering and the straining to hear even the faintest sound in the stairwell, her voice exploded in my ears. We moved back to the envelope.

"At least we know it's not a dog's paw," I suggested. "He only took two from Molly and we already have both of them."

"And the envelope is too flat," Ash added. "Doesn't look like anything bulky could be in there."

"Let's hope we're free from body parts of any kind," I said, imagining my father's finger or ear waiting for me in the packing envelope. I broke the seal, squeezed the sides of the envelope slightly to make an oblong opening, and tipped it toward the table. A piece of paper slid out. Nothing else followed.

Anxiety mingled with excitement as I saw the same angular penmanship from his previous missive and I realized that I was staring at another direct communication from the killer. Ash moved behind my left shoulder to see the message.

My Dear Marcus,

You surprise me. And disappoint me. I thought you would have contacted me by now. To thank me for the favors I have done for you. To return what is rightfully mine. I understand it's not your fault. We are both history's bastards, tainted in the blood by weak and illegitimate parents. Bastard parents who ruined innocence, who wriggled free of what was rightfully theirs to carry, who cast their burdens onto us.

I grow weary waiting for you, though. Prove yourself to me, Marcus. Bring me what is mine and cut your pain out of yourself. Bleed out of your veins the stain that is theirs, not yours.

"Who is this guy?" Ash asked, breaking the silence. I was thankful for her voice, for pulling me away from the disturbing sensation that someone whom I had, to my knowledge, never even seen, thought of me as his bosom buddy in a war against bastard parents and tainted blood.

"He seems to think we're old pals," I replied. "His language bothers me," I continued as I thought through his words. "He's reversing the idea of illegitimacy, bastardizing parents and keeping the kids sacred. And here," I said, pointing near the beginning of his note, "he says 'favors,' plural." I stopped.

"Your father," Ash replied, filling in what I had left blank. "It's not just Paige, is it? You think he means what he did to Paige, plus whatever happened to your father."

"I guess he could mean Paige and Molly as two favors, but I don't really believe that. So, yes, I think he's telling me that he killed my father and is angry that I didn't respond as soon as I received the bat with my father's hair on it." I wasn't sure what else to say.

"I'm sorry. Marcus."

"I hated my father, Ash. He was shit for giving me away. But now it feels even more empty, unfinished. I don't even know if I wanted it changed but there's no chance for that now. Ever."

Ash and I stayed like that, resting in silence and thinking through the case and, for me, navigating through pain that stung as much personally as professionally.

Ash spoke first. "The message is creepy, Marcus. But no address label on the envelope means he knows you. He stood right outside the door. He knocked on the door when we were right in here. And I think he knew that. He's watched you, Marcus."

"Which means he's watched you at times, too." I felt a sickness and anger move through me as the killer's presence polluted what had been a magical night for me with Ash. The mere thought that he was anywhere in our proximity, that he even knew I was at Ashlynn's last night, bothered me, tarnished the beauty of what had felt vaguely sacred to me. A claustrophobic sensation crushed me, making me want to flail in a panic against a box put onto me by a killer whom I couldn't see but who could see me, who watched me from shadows.

My cell phone, still plugged into the outlet while it charged, buzzed and brought me back. I checked the number—Angstrom already returning my call. I mouthed his name to Ash as I picked up the phone.

"That was quick," I said. "Either really good news or really bad news to be that fast. What'd you find out?" I asked, not letting my voice carry any of the emotion or anxiety that I had been feeling. The cool, collected detective.

"It's the really bad variety, I'm afraid. Your father's dead. The local police found the body a few days ago. No notification to you because they didn't know your father had any children."

I tried swallowing away the cotton feeling lodged in my throat. "Email me the pictures, Angstrom. Same guy who killed Mike?"

"I don't have the pictures yet myself. I'm waiting for our own inter-departmental hoops to be navigated. I'll send you copies when I get them. But it doesn't sound like the same guy to me."

"What did they tell you?" I asked. "Describe the scene to me."

"They were shook up, not used to something so violent," he began. "Your father had been bound to a chair, his legs tied to the legs of the chair, his arms to the arms of the chair." I thought of how Paige had been tied, forced to look at Molly.

"Anything placed in front of him?" I asked. "Something the killer intended for him to see?"

"Why are you asking? Have you seen this before?" Angstrom answered. "I didn't see anything like that in the other pictures you sent me. I'm doing you a solid with this, and I appreciate that it must be hell to hear that someone murdered your father. But don't screw with me again on this." He stopped, waiting for my response.

"What I saw before wasn't a murder scene, Angstrom. I don't have any pictures of it, so there wasn't anything to send to you. My ex-wife was tied in a similar manner. She wasn't killed. Supposed to be a warning to her, or to me, I'm not sure. The son of a bitch killed her dog and put it in front of my ex-wife."

"What the hell are you caught up in?" Angstrom replied.

"I don't know. Tell me more about the scene. How'd he die—head crushed, like the others?" I asked, keeping my focus on the killer, remaining professional. I jotted notes for Ash while I talked, trying to keep her in the loop about what Angstrom reported to me.

"No blunt force trauma. Had his throat cut. Deep. He bled to death."

Angstrom continued but I didn't hear what he said. An image filled my mind of my father choking on his own blood, gasping for breath or for words that this taciturn man finally wanted to let out.

"Say that again, Angstrom, the part after my father's throat being cut," I murmured.

"I said that you were right: the killer arranged the scene for your father. The local guys said that the coffee table had been moved, placed in front of him, length-wise. A bottle of bourbon sat on it, with an empty glass turned upside down on the top of it."

"Bourbon, or scotch?" I asked. "My father drank scotch, not bourbon."

"They said bourbon, but I don't have the pictures yet to see for myself. They found a coffee mug sitting at the other end of the table. They think that's from your killer, that he sat and drank coffee and watched until your father bled out."

"So the killer made him stare at a bottle of bourbon with a glass on top of it?" I asked, confused.

"And there was a Bible. Bourbon and Bible is what they told me. There was a passage circled in blood. Probably your father's."

"Which passage?"

"Exodus 34:7. You familiar with it?"

"Exodus 34:7," I repeated, partly for myself and partly for Ash. She looked at me blankly and shook her head. "It's been awhile since I made it to Sunday school."

"I didn't know it either," he answered. "They recited it to me over the phone, but I won't get the biblical language right. Something about sins of the father and punishing the children."

"I'll look it up," I said. "Anything else unusual, anything else at all?"

"That's it. I'll send pictures as soon as I get them."

"Thanks, Angstrom. I owe you. One more question," I added as an anomaly popped into my head. "How'd they find his body? He was a drunk. The kind of drinker who it wouldn't be unusual if he dropped out of sight for a day or two on a bender."

"Delivery guy called it in," Angstrom answered. "Approached the door with a package and saw the scene from the front window."

"Shit," I said.

"Shit what?"

I didn't know how to tell him about the package delivered to me at work, or the one outside my door, without him knowing that I had still held back on him. I didn't want to risk the tenuous rapport we had just developed by admitting that I had kept a card or two from him.

"Shit that a delivery guy found him and not some close friend that I didn't know about. I guess I hoped he wasn't as alone as I thought he was," I lied.

"Sorry, man," he said, buying it. I felt bad about the lie. Despite our rough first encounter, Angstrom had turned out to be a pretty good guy.

"Send me the photos as soon as they cross your desk."

"Will do." He clicked off.

"What's with the Bible reference?" Ash asked as soon as I closed my phone.

"This all goes from strange to stranger," I replied. "The killer left a Bible in front of my father, with an Exodus reference circled in blood. Angstrom said it was probably my father's own blood used to make the circle."

"You have a Bible around here?" Ash wondered, looking around my meagerly decorated apartment. "We need to know what's so important about Exodus."

I moved toward one of the unpacked cardboard boxes warming in the sun. "Believe it or not, Ash, I actually do have a Bible. And it's not even a Gideon copy I swiped from a hotel," I joked, as I rifled through the box of books. I'd kept a Bible from my youth all of these years, packing it with me any time I moved. "Despite my joke to Angstrom," I said, "I did in fact attend Sunday school. Many, many years ago. My mother gave me a Bible to take with me. It's in here somewhere."

It served as the last tangible link I had to my mother, and I had never been able to let it go. For many years I thought of it as evidence that, despite abandoning me and my father, my mother was actually a good, saintly person. Eventually, that dream passed and I wondered if she had just used Sunday school as a convenient excuse to spend time away from me. Either way, I couldn't bring myself to get rid of her gift. It had my mother's handwriting on the inside cover, where she penned the briefest of messages ('To my son, Marcus. Love, Mom.'). I thought of it as part of her. Part of her that she had wanted to give to me. Not the part of her that ran away and left me.

"Maybe this is the message that gets us to the killer," Ash proposed as I flipped through the Bible's thin, translucent pages.

"Exodus 34:7," I said, moving my finger down the page:

> [God], keeping steadfast love for thousands, forgiving iniquity and transgression and sin, but who will by no means clear the guilty, visiting the iniquity of the fathers upon the children and the children's children, to the third and fourth generation.

"Serious Old Testament stuff," Ash said, "an eye for an eye, tooth for a tooth, and then some."

"We need to figure out what it tells us about our guy, why he kills, and how he picks his victims."

"And why he thinks you two are somehow psychological siblings," Ash added.

"Yeah, that too," I agreed, squirming slightly inside. "He definitely wants to drag me into his world. And he definitely likes to think of himself as though he's my mentor. It's a strange mix from him. He wants to be honored for the anguish visited upon him and also admired for his strength to fight back. The Exodus excerpt makes me think that the suffering part is from something his parents did. It's the same type of vibe I got from the last message, where he made the parents into bastards and marked himself as innocent and pure. It's like there's something passed down to him that he has to carry but doesn't think he deserves."

"I see what you're saying. But flip it around a little bit. Take him away from being the one suffering," Ash suggested. "If, for the sake of the quote, you place him in the position of God, then the first part is about forgiveness and acceptance granted to those who follow him. Kind of what he seems to feel with you," Ash finished, her finger tracing delicately along the words.

"And if you take the second part," I continued, finding a new way to see the quotation, "you better not piss him off because he will not only hurt you but hurt your children and your grandchildren and your great-grandchildren."

"Right, payback not just to you but to future generations, like a mafia vendetta passed down."

Something Ash said resonated for me. I closed my eyes to focus, to see what I felt but didn't quite understand. I opened my eyes, excited and afraid at the same time.

"Generations, Ash," I repeated, my hands lightly moving to her shoulders in my epiphany. "It's counting, but not a linear progression."

"What are you talking about, Marcus?"

"The dots. We thought the circles on the bodies were some kind of counting but it couldn't be a linear progression because the bodies jumped around with the number of dots they had: one on Jamie Parks's mom, which seems like the first body, two on Mike, but then only two, again, on Jamie Parks. If it's counting, then why not three on him?" I asked. Not waiting for an answer, I continued. "There are two circles because it's not counting victims; it's counting generations." I stopped, waiting to see if I had explained it well enough.

Ash's pupils dilated as she saw it too. "So one circle for Jamie Parks's mom because she is generation one for the revenge plan. Two circles for both Jamie Parks and Mike, because, regardless of what order they are killed in or when the bodies are found, they're second generation, heirs to revenge."

"Exactly!" I replied, feeling slightly guilty for the excitement that the breakthrough generated within me. Then my excitement dissipated, rushing out of me like a balloon suddenly punctured. "And if I had to guess, I would bet that Mr. Brey had a single circle somewhere on him. If Mike's the second generation of revenge, then he must have been the first."

"But it still doesn't make sense that Mr. Brey wasn't brutalized like the others. What made him different? And," Ash continued, "why does the killer use dots and not numbers? I mean, if it's counting, why not numbers?"

"I get what you're asking. I don't know. Numbers would definitely be easier," I agreed. "But the counting makes sense this way. I don't know what made Mr. Brey different for the killer. I'd like to know. I really would," my voice grew softer and I trailed off.

"I get that he was really special to you," Ash replied. "Like the way your father should have been, right?" Her mention of an obscured father-son relationship awoke another breakthrough for me. It latched onto the drops-as-generations idea and shot a surge of fear through me.

"Jamie Parks has a kid," I blurted. "One of his gossipy neighbors told me and Ryota about him. That kid is in trouble. We have to find him; he's the third generation, the next in line if the killer finds him first," I finished, out of breath.

Before Ash could reply, my laptop interrupted with an incongruously cheery "beep," alerting me that Angstrom's pictures were in my inbox. I sent the images to the printer. Ash started with a photo showing the far end of the coffee table, where the killer's mug sat. I left a picture showing the details of my father's death sitting in the printer tray. I wanted to ground myself before I looked at my lifeless father. I turned to the photo of the open Bible and scotch. Not bourbon. The yokels, evidently, didn't know their alcohol as well as the Brace family did.

Ash's eyes continued to rove through each quadrant of the picture she held, taking nothing for granted. I left her at it and picked up the picture of my father, the emotionally tortured man who died after being physically tortured. I remembered seeing him at my last visit, a man enfeebled by a past he could never make peace with, his interior life hollowed out by the emotional pain that had eaten away like a cancer at his thoughts and memories and ability to function in the present. Part of me expected that this last picture of him would show his face in peace, maybe even a smile curling his lips slightly with the realization that all was finally at an end, an odd smirk that would have perplexed the killer.

Death, however, is never that orderly, not even remotely concerned with irony or poetic endings. The duct tape binding him to the chair pulled at his arm hair, tugging skin that had lost elasticity with age into wrinkled bags around the tension created by the tape. My father's face was curdled in surprise and pain. His lips were parted open slightly, suggesting a final attempt to gulp in air or scream out his final breath. The only thing I saw resembling a smile was the curved cut on his throat. Below the cut line, blood covered the rest of his neck and flowed onto his shirt. His eyes, grossly large, bulged with panic.

I put the picture of my father down. Seeing that Ash had moved on to the "Bible and bourbon" picture, I picked up the one showing the other end of the coffee table. In its own way, this photo disturbed me as much as the picture detailing my estranged father's murder. The local detectives had surmised that the killer had sat here, drinking from a mug and watching my father bleed to death, watching as he struggled against the duct tape and his eyes protruded from their sockets and his face grew ever more pale as blood spurted from the cut on his throat.

I looked again at the mug, picturing in my mind the killer calmly sipping at his drink, his slurping mocking the gurgling of blood that bubbled out of my father's throat. My hand gripped the picture tighter, my back straightened, then my spine immediately curled downward as I examined the image in closer detail.

"Ash, look at this," I said, as I dropped the hard copy and went to the laptop to call up the image so I could zoom in.

"What do you have?" she asked.

I opened the image, talking while I clicked to enlarge a portion of the mug. "It's not coffee," I said.

"What do you mean?" she asked, and I could hear my excitement rubbing off onto her as well now.

"Angstrom might not have known. He hadn't seen the pictures when we talked, was just relaying info second-hand to me. See it? There's a string showing at the far side of the mug. It's not coffee. It's tea. We have other links to teapots and chakins. I want to know what kind of tea the killer was drinking," I said. I zoomed in even more, the grainy pixels transitioning to clarity as the computer worked.

"Holy shit!" Ash exclaimed. "That's the tea I talked to Ryota about at the station while we waited for you to get back from the Xerox machine. That's the tea you found at Jamie Parks's house. That's the tea that Ryota's father makes. We have to find Ryota. He might be our killer," Ash finished, her voice dropping.

"It gets worse," I said. "Ryota looked surprised when the neighbor told us Parks had a son. He also asked me yesterday if I had heard of any leads on the Parks kid. We've got to find not just Ryota but also this kid."

"And hope that finding one isn't the only way to find the other. We don't need to see any more of this," Ash quietly finished, pointing at the crime scene photos of my father's death.

Chapter Twenty-Four

We rushed out of my apartment, with the images from Angstrom and the killer's latest missive now added to the burgeoning genealogical folder. I rode the accelerator hard every chance I had. I realized how very little of Ryota's past I knew. I felt sick to think that he could be behind this; I felt sick remembering the wry smile on his lips after I hit him.

As I careened around a corner, Ash pulled out her phone, her free hand bracing against the dashboard.

"Who you calling?" I asked.

She didn't have a chance to respond, her call answered almost immediately after she dialed. "Mills," she said, "this is Ashlynn. Marcus and I are on our way to the station. You seen Ryota around?" she asked. A moment's pause, then she continued. "If he shows up, tell him I have a breakthrough on the Parks case but need to ask him a question. Don't mention Marcus, though. That's important. After their thing yesterday, I don't want Ryota to leave me empty." Another, longer pause. "Will do. I'll tell him. Thanks, Mills." She hung up.

"What's up?" I asked.

"Mills hasn't seen Ryota today. But she said she'd keep him around for me if she could. She also said to tell you that they have a good lead on Paige's attacker. A neighbor saw a delivery truck drop off a pet carrier. Mills thinks that might be the guy, that he carried Molly's body in the pet carrier to get her inside Paige's place."

"Definitely fits," I replied. "The delivery aspect, I mean. There's been a package addressed to me at the station," I said, remembering Matt flipping the box to me. "And the letter outside my door at home, and a delivery guy called in my dad's death. Might also explain how the killer got in to see Mr. Brey without any sign of forced entry."

"And how he managed to get behind Jamie Parks to club him on the back of the head," Ash suggested. "We couldn't figure out how someone with a bat could get behind him so easily, remember? If he had hidden the bat in or behind a package, it might make sense."

"So what's Ryota doing, moonlighting as a delivery man somewhere?"

Once at the station, the elevator seemed even more interminably slow now that we were in such a hurry. "What's the plan if Markeze sees us?" Ash asked. "Do we tell him we think Ryota is the killer?"

"Let's just find Ryota," I answered as the elevator completed its slow climb. "No chance that Markeze will believe 'Right-Way' could do this. He'll just think I'm being a shitball toward him because of our fight yesterday. We need to get Ryota ourselves. If we see Markeze," I added, "tell him we're retrieving some personal stuff from our desks."

We found the bullpen nearly empty when we entered, Mills the only one present. "You had company while you were away," Mills said. "Some guy named 'Stimmy' came looking for you. Said to tell you he couldn't be sure but he thought he saw someone trying to get into Jamie Parks's apartment. I asked him for a description but he didn't have anything helpful."

I turned toward Ash. "Ry and I talked to him in the hall of Parks's apartment complex. Kind of an ass and just helpful enough to not be helpful: sees a guy but no description." I turned back toward Mills.

"Thanks for the relay, though. Still no Ryota around?"

"Nope," she said.

My desk phone flashed, alerting me that I had voicemail waiting. I punched the button to retrieve my messages. Mrs. Lump, even her voice heavy and overbearing, greeted me with the first message.

"Hello, Detective Brace. This is Shannon Sullivan, Jamie Parks's neighbor. You talked to me the other day. I wanted to apologize again for my husband. I know he wasn't very helpful. Just be glad you don't have to live with him. Anyway, your partner came by to see if we had any news on Jamie's son. Tell him I hope the ice pack I gave him helped his lip, by the way. Poor man. Anyway, I didn't have any news on Jamie's poor kid, but I wanted to follow-up and see if there's something else I should know. I only have your card and number, by the way. Don't you think I should have your partner's number too? Time is of the essence for these things, right? Stop by again if you need anything else. I'll make sure my husband is better next time."

The pieces were coming together. Ryota must have gone to the apartment complex after I punched him. Guilt wrapped around me as I considered the possibility that hitting him had started some murderous impulse rampaging through his blood. The fact that Mrs. Lump hadn't been able to tell him anything about the missing kid certainly qualified as good news.

The second voicemail was from Chief Tibbs. He must have called first thing when he got to his office: the voicemail stamp noted an incoming time of 5:01 am, just after 7:00 am St. Louis time. I dialed to return his call.

"Chief Warrant Officer Tibbs," he said, confidence wrapping each syllable.

"Chief, this is Marcus Brace, returning your call from this morning. Thanks for the quick turn-around."

"Not a problem. It's always good to have an excuse to run my people about and test their efficiency with the files."

"I appreciate it. What do you have for me, Chief?" I asked.

"The highest rank achieved by Adam Brey was Corporal, Military Police," Chief Tibbs began.

I interrupted, confused. "Military Police? Are you sure?" The stories Mr. Brey told us about his father always resonated with reverence and adoration for an overseas hero, a man who had fought the Japanese on the frontlines with valor and sacrifice. Nothing, ever, about being an MP.

"Positive, Detective Brace," Tibbs responded. "Adam Brey served with the military police from 1942 until June of 1946, stationed during the war in Eden, Idaho and afterward in Tacoma, Washington. He received a dishonorable discharge after striking a superior officer."

I was flabbergasted. Chief Tibbs's report moved my understanding of Adam Brey from war hero to military reject in the space of less than a minute. Mr. Brey's father, it seemed, hadn't ever participated in any overseas campaigns. Idaho, certainly, was no Japan.

"Thank you, Chief Tibbs," I finally replied, flipping absentmindedly through the genealogical folder until I landed on the family tree.

"Detective Brace, I hope it was a help. Call me if I can help you again."

"We're even," I replied, still on autopilot with my responses.

"No, we're not." He hung up.

Mr. Brey's fascination with WWII paraphernalia and stories had disappeared shortly after he helped Mike with his tenth grade family history project. I didn't think much about it at the time, except that I was secretly happy that I wouldn't have to hear more about family histories, which always made me feel ashamed for my own lack of family. Maybe Mr. Brey, through the course of his research for Mike's project, had discovered what I had just found out, had dug down and discovered that what his own father had told him about his war service was bullshit.

Ash put her hand on top of mine. "What did he say?"

I pulled my hand out from under hers, then realized what I was doing and brought it back, wrapping my palm around her fingers from the side. "Mr. Brey's father wasn't a war hero, wasn't even in any battles. He received a dishonorable discharge, after serving during WWII in, of all places, Idaho."

I showed her the family tree and its names, blank slates upon which you could write almost any story, craft any narrative of noble lineage, brave forefathers. Until, that is, you learned of a different narrative from someone else. "I feel bad for Mr. Brey," I said. "I always thought he and Mike had a great family. But by the end, Mike had disappeared from him. His own father wasn't what he thought he was either."

I saw a small spot of dried blood on my desk, smeared on one side where the paper towels must have wiped along the edge but missed getting all of it. An idea hit me.

"That old woman, the one you first mentioned to me on the phone."

"Yeah," Ash said, waiting to hear more.

"Sumi Yoshinaga. She was here the day I received the package."

"You think the old woman brought it?" she asked, incredulously.

"No, no, no. Matt the postman gave it to me. I'm thinking more about when she left. I didn't finish my talk with her. She was so adamant about seeing me, and only me, right?"

Ash nodded in affirmation. "Absolutely. When you were back in Kansas she refused to see anyone else, only wanted to talk with Marcus Brace."

"But we *didn't* finish our talk. We barely got started. She got up and left right in the middle of it."

"So what changed?" Ash asked, picking up my line of thought. "If she was desperate to see you but didn't get to tell you what it was about, why not come back? Why leave in the middle of your talk?"

"Exactly. Here's the best part. Ryota wasn't here when she came in and started talking to me. Once he came out of Markeze's office and walked toward us, *that's* when she got up and hustled out of here."

"Then you got called into Markeze's office."

"And when I came back out, the shit broke loose with me hitting Ryota and I forgot all about her."

"We need to find her."

"We find her, maybe we find Ryota," I concluded as I reached toward the corner of my desk. Still sitting atop the metal mesh tray that I used more as a storage bin for junk that I didn't know what to do with than an actual "in" box, sat the brief information I had recorded from the old woman. "Here it is, contact info for Mrs. Yoshinaga."

Ash picked up the genealogical folder, pushing it gently into my chest. "Let's go," she said.

We made the short drive to Mrs. Yoshinaga's house in silence, the only sound that of the tires running across wet pavement and throwing water onto the underside of the car. I put the car in park and turned toward Ash.

"Once we get inside, I'll talk to her and try to keep her attention focused my direction. You see if you can get away to look around the house. Look for hints of Ryota, or anything similar to what's been sent to me or found on the bodies."

We exited the car in front of a small, one-story house with tan brick exterior. Several decades of settling had cracked the mortar in spots. Only the cracks gave an indication of age, however. Everything else looked well-tended to.

I knocked lightly on the door. I was just about to knock again, but then I heard footfalls, almost a shuffling. Mrs. Yoshinaga started to pull the door open but stopped halfway, both she and the door frozen, movement incomplete.

"Good morning, Mrs. Yoshinaga. May we come in?" I asked, smiling and gently nudging the door to help it complete its trajectory. Her hand fell off of the door as it moved. For a moment, she seemed to shrink into herself. Her eyes became hooded and her spine arched even more than the significant curve that age had brought to it. It passed, however, and a sense of resoluteness pulsed toward us.

"Hello, Detective Brace. I've forgotten your name, Miss," she said to Ash but turned back to me without waiting for a response. She offered it as a statement of fact, not a social apology or an invitation for Ash to fill in what was missing. Ash returned a polite smile and kept the focus on me, letting the old ghost woman drive where we were going. "You should come in. Both of you." She moved to the side, letting us pass into her house before shutting the door.

Ash and I stopped a few feet inside, waiting for Mrs. Yoshinaga to lead us. All the lights were turned off and Seattle's weak winter sky wasn't doing much to help. The temperature inside felt cool, barely warmer than outside. A bulky brown sweater, the fabric knitted in large loops, wrapped around Mrs. Yoshinaga. At least one or two additional layers peeked out from beneath the sweater's collar. It all gave the impression of a woman who sacrificed the free use of utilities to save money. Mrs. Yoshinaga walked us to a sitting area.

"Take a seat," she offered, pointing us toward the couch. "I'll get some tea," she said, not waiting to see if we would be interested. I again had the impression that she didn't intend her abruptness as rudeness but rather that it grew out of some kind of ease and comfort she had with who she was and what she had seen over the years. I liked her.

Ash followed her to the kitchen. "Mrs. Yoshinaga," she began, "could you please point me to the bathroom?"

Mrs. Yoshinaga reappeared a few minutes later, carrying a black-lacquered tray that held a small iron teapot and tea bowls. "Genmaicha," she said. "Green tea with roasted brown rice." As she poured, steam curled and disappeared into the room from each tea bowl, like confused whirlpools that circled up instead of down. She pushed Ash's empty tea bowl to the side.

"Thank you." I took a sip. The liquid scalded the tip of my tongue. Her house, though clean, breathed a slight musty odor that mixed with the earthiness of the tea, the two smells consolidating into a different fragrance altogether. It made me think of an old church, a space well-worn, made of stone and redolent with the smell of snuffed candles and the soft hiss of whispered prayers and chants. "Mrs. Yoshinaga, we never finished our conversation from the station. Why did you come to see me and how can I help you?" I asked.

"I'm sorry, Detective Brace. I've wasted your time." She sipped at her tea.

"No waste, but I would like to tie up the loose ends and be able to close the file I opened." I smiled. She didn't bite. "If I can't close this, then I have to send it up the line and you'll have to start all over with someone new."

She didn't move to dismiss me or tell me I was offering her a lie, though I think she knew I was. Her silence, I thought, grew from an internal evaluation of whether she wanted to believe me or not, whether she wanted an excuse to talk. I had the impression that she too felt a bit confused about whatever had impelled her to seek me out in the first place, that her reticence would crumble if we could land on the right note.

"Tell me what's worrying you, Mrs. Yoshinaga. When you left the station, you left quickly. Not out of anger. More like fear."

Her milky eyes blinked. "I thought you might be trying to hurt someone close to me. Then I thought maybe I was wrong. That you might be hurt instead. I was obviously mistaken on both counts, because you're both fine." After a long wait, during which time our eyes never left one another's, she added, "you can close your file now."

"Who are we talking about, Mrs. Yoshinaga? Who would I be trying to hurt? And why do you think that he might hurt me?"

"You can close your file. You're both okay," she said again.

"Mrs. Yoshinaga, I don't want to hurt anyone. That's not why I'm here. I also don't want to be hurt by anyone. Why would someone hurt me?"

"He's been through enough. He's lived through more than his share of sadness." This time she started to rise and I knew I was losing her.

"Please sit, Mrs. Yoshinaga. Let's have some more tea." I pointed toward the teapot in a gesture of truce. She nodded, sitting back down. "I recently discovered what a chakin is, Mrs. Yoshinaga, and I've also learned that a seemingly simple pot can be a container for history, not just tea."

She nodded again.

"I like that, Mrs. Yoshinaga. I like the idea that heirlooms hold stories and carry a sense of belonging inside of them, that seemingly empty pieces can be formed and glued into a unique family bond."

She looked appraisingly at me, as our everyday conversation turned deeper.

"I must sound over the top. It's just a teapot, right?" I chuckled, self-deprecating. "I think a lot about family. I didn't really have traditions and dinners and things like that as a family when I was young. Thought about it a lot, though. Still do." I pulled out the genealogical folder, shuffling through the contents for the picture found with Mr. Brey. "I've become interested in genealogy. Just the last few weeks really. A new hobby for me." I closed the folder. "I even have pictures of people and I don't have any idea who they are." I smiled again as I showed her the picture of the unknown Asian woman.

Her hands faltered. Tea sloshed onto the carpet. She set the cup and saucer down and took the photo from my hand. As she stared at the face, her hands shook violently. After a few seconds, her breathing grew more regular and her hands settled into a slow but steady tremble, the photo fluttering up and down as if being moved by a current of air that no one else could feel.

"Where did you get this?" she asked.

I watched the wizened woman sitting in front of me. Her skin looked thin and translucent, like glue or half-melted wax hanging loosely from where muscle should have been. From fear or excitement, her eyes burned bright beneath the milky overlay of age. The rest of her seemed wispy, ready to disappear as quickly and quietly as the steam that had evaporated from our cups of tea. I felt as though I were staring at a ghost, someone filled with memories that I could never guess at, someone who was here but not here.

"Let's start with who this woman is," I replied. "We'll work our way to where I found the picture."

She nodded, focused once more on the face in the photograph. "I haven't seen this picture in years, decades," she said. "She was my best friend. Kana Ohkuma. I think this is her wedding photo. Why is her husband not in this picture?" she asked. Tears slid slowly down her face.

"Who did Kana marry?" I asked.

"Kana and Natsuo. We all grew up together. We shared skinned elbows and dirty knees from playing together on our parents' farms. Kana and Natsuo had something even then. He never made fun of her when the other boys did. I always knew they would be married. Not in the way that they were," she added, "but I knew they would be husband and wife."

"What do you mean, 'not in the way that they were'?"

"They had their wedding license already. The wedding should have been on the farm. Kana's mom had planned the baking for weeks. Then it all changed and they ran out of time. We all ran out of time. Too much to do, to try and save. The wedding was lost, so they ended up getting married in camp instead. A marriage ceremony should make you happy, but theirs made me sad. I felt sorry for them. It was a shame."

"What camp are you talking about, Mrs. Yoshinaga?" I asked, uncertain of what she wanted me to see as she spoke.

"The internment, Detective Brace," she replied, looking down at the floor before pulling her eyes directly toward mine. "Our internment during World War II. We were given two weeks to report, two weeks to figure out what to do with a lifetime spent building and growing. Just two weeks notice before 'relocation' for everyone of Japanese descent. Two weeks, Mr. Brace."

Her rheumy eyes caught mine, though I couldn't tell if they focused on me at all. I neither stirred nor said anything, knowing my silence would help Mrs. Yoshinaga move back, fall into memories. I wanted to be there with her, to not just hear but also feel the past that she described. I needed to retrieve the past in order to see clearly where my foot would land with the next step.

"It was all lost for Kana and Natsuo. Lost for the rest of us too, but most immediately for them. They spent their first night as husband and wife in a shanty sitting in what used to be a horse stable. The smell of straw and the odor of sweat from where horses had lived mixed with the sourness of all of us crammed too close together. A homemade sign hung on the door of their barrack, requesting privacy for the newlyweds; their first taste of married intimacy was marked off from the rest of us by warped plywood and parents uncomfortably trying to shoo children away to give them space."

Her eyes looked around the room, pulling away from the past as she worked to wrap herself in the bubble of the present. "I've learned something, detective. A trick of memory or an error of time: I'm sorrier for them today than I was back then. I feel even worse for the people we became than for the people we were."

"What do you mean, Mrs. Yoshinaga?"

Her left hand curled around her tea bowl; her right palm wrapped around them both, so that it looked as though she were cradling the cup, keeping it safe, offering a prayer.

"Innocence and how it's lost, Detective Brace. And what happens when it's lost and after it's lost. We were all so innocent, so naïve as we stood in front of a gaping mouth of cynicism. Maybe that's why we were able to be so innocent," she mused. "The scale of the cynicism and hurt and rejection was so great, maybe we all just shut down, not wanting to see what was right in front of us, devouring us." She sipped at her tea before continuing. "We ignored the present. We focused on the future. We believed it a mistake that would soon be fixed. That if we acquiesced to internment it would prove that we were good Americans. We were willing, you see, to sacrifice to prove that. We imagined our lives returned to us in just a few more weeks or months. We hated what we saw there, what we found there, but we made it better. We decorated the ramshackle buildings, constructed our own furniture from scraps of lumber. We took it and made the best of it."

"Like with the wedding and even the honeymoon," I said.

"Yes, I suppose so," she replied. "I no longer know whether I should smile or cry for it. It's beautiful and pitiful all at once, isn't it?" she asked.

"Do I sound too naïve, Mrs. Yoshinaga, if I say that life is often like that, all mixed up, the strands of joy and pain too tightly wound to separate?"

"You don't sound naïve. You sound scarred."

"Scars prove healing," I replied.

She looked carefully at me. When she spoke I wasn't sure if she had made a decision about what she saw in me, or about what resided inside herself. "Some scars are too horrible, too deep and wide and ugly for people to move beyond. That's what the camps did: they wounded, then the scars continued to grow for years and years afterward."

"What camp were you in, Mrs. Yoshinaga?"

"We were assembled first, temporarily, at Camp Harmony. They later turned the site into the Puyallup Fairgrounds, as if to make something happy out of, or erase, our trauma. All that's left is a small memorial and an even smaller display case in the Fair Museum. Do you like the irony of that, Detective Brace? That something that grew out of so much discord and hatred and fear was first called Camp Harmony and later turned into a Fairground."

It was my turn to not respond. 'Harmony.' My brain raced, neurons firing as I realized that Mrs. Yoshinaga had just given me the key to one of the kanji.

Chapter Twenty-Five

"Mrs. Yoshinaga," I began, trying to calm myself, "you said you were at two camps. Was the second one called Camp Truth?" I asked, wanting all of the pieces to fit.

"There was no Camp Truth, Detective Brace. Is 'Harmony' not ironic enough for you? No, we stayed at Camp Harmony until we were transferred to Camp Minidoka. It wasn't any better. Worse, certainly, for Kana and Natsuo."

"Tell me about Minidoka, then, Mrs. Yoshinaga." I needed the next link, in both her story of the past and also the murders taking place in the present.

"Barren. Windy. Dust blowing into my eyes, pebbles ricocheting off my skin, leaving stings that I would rub after I was once again inside and protected. It looked desolate, dead. We gave it life, Detective Brace. Cultivated crops there, turned the emptiness into something worthy. They auctioned it off after the war, after we improved it and made it something valuable. Japanese Americans couldn't buy it. We couldn't bid on the very land that we made good."

"What made it worse for Kana and Natsuo?"

Disgust pushed into her face, stretching the loose skin surrounding her mouth into an eerie, disturbing mask of revulsion.

"At Minidoka, we found a devil," she said. "I thought he must be the reason why the ground had died, why nothing wanted to grow. The wind picked up everything negative about the camps, within the camps, hidden inside us, and blew it around the mountains until it all came roaring like a cyclone into this man's heart. He lived in coldness and emptiness and hated us. He enjoyed hating us. You could see in his eyes that he was made of hate and would never let it go. Implacable hatred, Detective Brace. I'd encountered racism before. We all had. But not like this, not like him."

"And Kana and Natsuo?" I asked again.

"Everyone avoided this devil as much as they could. His eyes roved over the bodies of the women. He didn't hide his stare; he *wanted* us to feel him staring." She shook again. "I felt it several times myself. It made me lower my head, turn in the opposite direction, and shuffle away. My palms would sweat, my chest tighten." She swallowed several times before continuing. "The men would see these things happen. He liked that part as well. They couldn't do anything. I think it made the men feel helpless, small."

"Did he do anything to the men?" I asked.

"Anything he could to make them feel weak in front of him. He would get in their way and not let them pass, laugh at them. Mock them, make comments about their manhood. He never saw us as Americans at all. We were playthings, animals for him to tease and hurt."

"Were there others like this?"

"Yes, some. Some who would be like him when they were with him, when they all congregated together. None like him to the same degree, though." She put down her tea. Her hand shook, from age or from the memories, as she wiped at the side of her lip. Then her lip started shaking, as if she were passing something contagious from body part to body part. Her voice caught the contagion as she began to speak, the sound from her throat crackly and broken.

"I was walking with Kana and Natsuo back to the barracks after dinner. We saw a girl, young, cornered by him outside, near the back of the mess hall. We watched, scared as this devil put his hand on the girl's shoulder, rubbing up and down her arm. She was a child, fourteen. We had never seen him touch a girl or woman in our camp before. When the devil touched her, Natsuo moved forward. Kana and I grew terrified as he approached. Natsuo didn't say anything, didn't confront or challenge him. Just put his arm around the girl and huddled her away, as quick as he could."

"Did the devil follow?"

"No. But I saw his eyes as we left. I grew cold inside, Detective Brace. That night I didn't sleep. I thought he would kill Natsuo that night."

"But he didn't?"

"No, nothing happened. After that, though, he began to harass Natsuo more violently than before. Pushed him down and spat on him. He punched him, broke his nose. He threatened to have Natsuo transferred to Tule Lake, where they sent the 'danger' cases, those who resisted and complained about the internment."

"No one did anything?" I asked.

"The man running our camp was weak. He wasn't as evil or so full of hate, but he didn't do anything for us. Repairs would not be completed. Food supplies would run low. He dismissed us, ignored us the way some men do dogs they keep but don't want to be concerned with."

"He didn't see you as people," I said.

"No. For him we were something to keep alive and tend to because that's what the government made him do. We were an obligation. And a resource. The crops in the surrounding area were going to go to waste. With the war effort, there wasn't enough manpower to harvest them. That year, Detective Brace, Japanese American labor saved the sugar beet crop. We were given work furloughs and we saved the crops."

"Like you did with the camps, the wedding—taking the bad and rescuing the good hidden within it." She slumped again, any pride that she might have felt from her story mysteriously punched away.

"The devil can turn the wheel in the opposite direction. Our devil pulled the bad out of the good." She said no more. Her eyes closed. Her breath rattled in her chest.

"What do you mean?" No answer. Her eyes shifted underneath her thin, veined eyelids. "Mrs. Yoshinaga, what do you mean?" She opened her eyes, looked into mine, and spoke slowly.

"You had to apply for a work furlough to leave the camp and rescue the beet farm. Natsuo didn't. Guards walked him to the truck and put him on board just as it prepared to pull away."

I swallowed, fearing I knew where this was going.

"He was gone all day. While he was away, the devil raped Kana. Twice. She told me about it later, much later. The devil raped her in the morning. She hadn't moved when he found her after lunch and raped her again."

"Did Natsuo come back?"

"Yes. Unharmed. He jumped from the truck and ran to her, told her he had been sick to his stomach with fear all day. She didn't tell Natsuo what had happened. She buried it within herself, walled it off and kept it away from him. She told him she was fine."

I didn't speak, wondering how Kana could possibly have functioned that day, could possibly have been able to withhold the news from her husband. I didn't know if she hid it to protect an already emotionally and physically captive Natsuo, or because she felt a misplaced sense of shame, or if there were some other reason entirely.

"That same night several of the guards got drunk, including our devil. They were always bad when drunk, but this night was the worst of our entire time in camp. They came and pulled Natsuo into the night. We found him the next morning in the gymnasium, curled on the floor unconscious, his hair matted on the side with blood, his clothes covered in large patches of it as well. His body was bruised all over, both eyes swollen shut. He spent almost a month in the hospital."

"Did you find out what had happened?"

"He wouldn't talk about it. I think he was afraid. Kana told me later that they had beaten him with a baseball bat. He was lucky to live."

Everything spun again. The picture of the unknown Asian woman and the kanji for 'harmony' and the baseball bat all now fit together. This was revenge, coming decades after the crime. The verse from Exodus ran through my mind. Revenge visited upon not just the perpetrator but upon the children coming after, unto the third and fourth generations. A sick feeling flooded through my stomach as more pieces connected for me.

"Where was Minidoka located?" I asked, closing my eyes while I waited for the answer.

"Eden: another painfully ironic name, don't you think? Minidoka was in Eden, Idaho."

I kept my eyes closed, thinking of the genealogical folder. The picture of the family tree mocked me. I saw the trunk gnarled and twisted, roots poisoned, branches heavy with bitter fruit. Adam Brey had been stationed stateside during WWII at Eden, Idaho. Mr. Brey, as close to a saint as I had ever known, and his father was the devil from Minidoka? Could it be?

"What was his name? The devil from the camp, do you remember his name?" I asked, my voice quiet. I wanted to look at the floor while I waited for her answer, but I forced my eyes to find hers and not let go.

"Of course I remember. I'm sure all of us remember." She hissed the name, her eyebrows angling inward while her upper lip curled in disgust. "Corporal Brey."

Chapter Twenty-Six

Her answer punched the air out of me. All of this, even down to Molly, stemmed from an outpost in Idaho that before this morning I had never heard of, revenge for events that occurred decades ago.

I had uncovered at least the outlines of motive, but there were still pieces missing. As I looked at the shriveled woman in front of me and thought of the violence she had seen and experienced, that sense of ghost music flooded over me again. The echo was present, easy to hear, but the original call remained hidden.

"What happened to Kana and Natsuo? What happened with the devil?" I asked. I couldn't bring myself to say the name Brey in association with what I had learned, preferring instead to keep him more evil spirit than my own quasi-forefather.

"He left them alone after that night. He picked on others, but he never touched Kana or Natsuo again."

"Are you sure about that?"

"Yes. I am sure. I carry them with me. Sometimes I think I understand more about Kana than she ever did about herself. Yes, I am sure he never touched them again."

She looked ready to say more. I waited, keeping my eyes locked on hers.

"Natsuo withdrew into himself after being released from the hospital. He was smaller. He lost weight while he recovered, but it was more than that. He walked with his eyes on the ground, his spine drooping. He didn't speak and his cheeks grew hollow because he wasn't eating. We all worried about him."

She stopped, putting her hands back in her lap, permitting herself a sedate smile as she continued. "Then one day he was back. I found him beaming, eyes filled with light that had been missing for weeks. He and Kana were expecting a child. Most in the camp were excited: the couple who had married during internment now would have a child. There were some, those whose disillusionment with our country festered during internment, who didn't celebrate, who thought it appropriate that their child be born in prison, to learn immediately what their country truly thought of them. But for most of us, those were happy months, something else for us to focus on, something else to help us think of the future and not the present. The war couldn't last forever. I liked imagining their child learning to walk outside of the guarded gates that had become part of our life."

I saw Ash standing at the entrance to the hallway, behind Mrs. Yoshinaga. I shook my head slightly and slowly at her, telling her to stay where she was and not disrupt Mrs. Yoshinaga's story.

"Did anything happen to the baby?" I asked, still searching for all of the pebbles tossed years ago that had sent ripples outward until they collided with the present-day Brey and Parks families.

"The baby was fine. They had a son, Takashi, born in March 1944. So you see, I was right," she smiled again, "the war ended and he did learn to walk and run outside of the camp."

"And you never heard from the devil again?"

"No. I don't know what happened to him," she answered. "His presence lingered with many of us, though. We didn't find it easy after the war. Many of us had lost our land, our farms. The wealth that families had worked to accumulate over the years had, for many, been stolen away while we were in the camps. Racist comments continued to bombard us; each time I heard them, I thought again of the devil we had known in the camp. I think Natsuo did as well. That sense of happiness I saw in him after he learned of Kana being pregnant slowly leaked out of him. He never again returned to the man I knew before the camps, never again became the man who strode over to protect that girl. That beating, that camp, took away his sense of being a man."

"No one should have to experience what he did, what all of you did," I said.

Mrs. Yoshinaga didn't respond right away. She looked as if she were searching for the right response, debating with herself. Then the uncertainty disappeared and I saw resolve and the beginning of tears mix within her rheumy eyes. I had seen this type of look, minus the milky eyes, many times before, when someone had decided to let go of a great weight and confess a secret. I looked her in the eyes, and waited. She sucked a deep breath in through her nose, exhaled it through her mouth.

"Natsuo didn't learn of the rape until years later. I don't know how Kana managed to stay so hidden from him emotionally. She kept it her secret. She never even told me until after Natsuo's death. She held it in tight all those years."

"How did Natsuo die?" I asked, knowing that she had already determined to tell me and was waiting for only the slightest encouragement.

"Hanged himself," she answered. "After he finally found out that his son was not his, was actually the bastard child of the devil we knew in the camp."

"When did he find out?" I gently prodded.

"Takashi was three years old. Kana never told me why she finally confessed to Natsuo. Takashi always looked very light, his skin ashen as though he had encountered a ghost. Natsuo drank a lot. Maybe when drunk he tried to disown the child to hurt Kana, only to find out he had stumbled on a truth he never wanted to know. Maybe they had a fight and she blurted it out before she knew what she was doing. It doesn't really matter, does it?"

That smell of snuffed candles wafted toward me again. "No. It doesn't matter," I answered, the echo from the original event growing louder in my ears.

"Natsuo's death broke Kana, tore down whatever wall she had been able to construct to keep her own pain back. She lost her ability to be a mother to Takashi. That's when she told me everything: the rape, why Natsuo hanged himself, how she feared she too would kill herself. I still feel shock, anger at myself for not seeing that something had been eating her from the inside out all of those years."

She stopped speaking again, the sound of water slowly dripping from the kitchen faucet into the basin counting time for us. "She left," Mrs. Yoshinaga suddenly said. "Kana went away and left Takashi with a friend who couldn't have any children of her own."

"It was you, wasn't it?" I asked. "You're the friend who couldn't have children."

Mrs. Yoshinaga rose, smoothing her pants with her hands as she did so. "She sent a letter, telling me she couldn't come back. Takashi became more my child than hers. I took him and he became mine. I took him and tried to shelter him from a past that should never have been." Her jaw jutted out after she spoke these last words, as though the sense of ownership over Takashi represented the most important part of anything she had thus far told me. "Excuse me." She rose and shuffled out of the room.

Ash passed Mrs. Yoshinaga as she entered and the old woman exited. Mrs. Yoshinaga didn't offer a word to her. Ash stood above me, excited. "Follow me, I have to show you this before she gets back."

She led me toward the rear of the house. The hallway felt dark and narrow, as hallways often do in older homes.

Ash directed us to the room at the end of the hallway. I saw a full-sized bed, a dresser, and a desk, all shining with the lustrous auburn of cherry wood. Not much else. Over the desk, however, hung one photograph, perfectly centered.

"Look closely," Ash said, a smile of satisfaction showing.

I stared into the eyes of four people I assumed were Japanese

American. It was a family photo, the poses artificial, as though each person had been instructed exactly how to hold his or her arms at ease. The photographer had arranged them in the shape of a diamond. In front, a boy sat, cross-legged. He looked around ten, an age when you could see both the child he had been and hints of the teenager he would become. Behind him a man and a woman kneeled next to one another. Their interior shoulders touched, their outside arms reaching so that the man's right hand and the woman's left hand rested on the boy's shoulders. The boy's parents, unquestionably. At the back of the photo, an elderly woman stood, so short that even standing she barely eclipsed the others. She had one hand carefully placed on the shoulder of each adult in front of her.

The woman in the back row was Mrs. Yoshinaga. There were fewer wrinkles and the eyes weren't milky, but it was her.

"She's holding back," Ash said decisively. "She hasn't told you anything about Ryota yet. We know Kana got pregnant in the camp and that was WWII. Takashi would be, what, nearly seventy years old at this point? Senior citizens don't go around bludgeoning people to death, some of whom are half his age. We're still missing a generation. We need to know how Takashi is tied to Ryota," she said, pointing to the child in the front row.

"We need to get back to Mrs. Yoshinaga."

We found her sitting on the sofa drinking another cup of tea while she waited for us. "You saw his room." Her voice sounded measured, calm, as though she were merely confirming something she had already foreseen or accepted.

"We're missing part of the story, Mrs. Yoshinaga," I replied. "What happened to Takashi?"

"Takashi, *my* son, grew up and married and had his own child. We never heard from Kana again."

"So you saved him." Ash said.

"No. I didn't save him as I had hoped. There were times, especially when he was mad, that I would catch glimpses of that white devil inside of him. His temper, his rage, was terrible." Her mouth pulled back involuntarily as she finished, making a straight line out of her lips before they moved back into place.

"Tell us about his rage," I coaxed. "What are you remembering?"

"The devil within killed him," she answered. After a small pause, she added, "the devil's killing the rest of us now." Her cataract-covered eyes looked to the ground, maybe searching for comfort or maybe stilling anger or maybe because that part of the carpet held a stain that I couldn't see from my angle.

"Tell me what happened to Takashi," I said, letting his name hang in the air.

"Takashi is better than his story," she said, looking up again and refusing to turn away. "What he did and what happened to him didn't come from him; it was the devil from the camp in him. He carried a stain. He was good, but ruin was passed down and carved into him from the camp. None of it was his fault."

"It was all stacked against him. And against you," I confirmed, looking for the string to help her finish the story that she didn't want to tell. She nodded at me, a half smile of gratitude directed my way.

"He died in prison. He hanged himself, like his father also did," Mrs. Yoshinaga said as tears once again brimmed in her eyes.

"Why was he there?" I asked gently.

"His wife died. September, 1985." I waited for more. Nothing else came.

"That must have hurt you terribly," Ash said.

"She was a good woman. Good for Takashi. A good mother too." Mrs. Yoshinaga's eyes moved to the ground again. This time, however, she looked up on her own, without any prompting. "Takashi beat her. The devil in him made him beat her. It wasn't his fault. It was the devil he carried inside his blood." She was crying now. Silent tears. Tears that spoke both to the sadness she felt and also, I suspected, to recognition that the excuses she had constructed were thin, inadequate, a Maginot line vainly trying to ward off psychic trauma. She closed her eyes as she finished. "He'd hit her before. Many times. I don't know why except for the devil in his blood. This time she fell and hit her head on the corner of the table. She died."

Her tears came down in more force. Her body shook, silently. No words, no sobs, no loud catching of her breath. She fought with everything she had to try and not let any crevice of weakness show.

Then she spoke, her voice creaking on the first syllables. "Their son saw it all. My arms wrapped around him to keep him safe but we both saw it. Ten years old and he saw his mom die." Her sobs found voice now. The sound of air sucking in to her lungs and exhaled in quaking gusts made her words harder to follow. "Even with that I think he would have been okay. But his father died in prison later that year. I tried to protect him, to protect both of them. But how do you protect someone from what is inside them?" she asked, panic and failure on her face. "How do you wrap your arms around them tight enough to still what burbles where no one can see?"

"You can't," I answered, thinking of the snakes that slithered around my mind and how they were mine and no one else's. "It's not your fault. That picture in the bedroom at the end of the hall," I added, trying to bring her focus back to a happier image and prevent her from shutting down, "all of you look so happy. The boy in the picture. How old was Ryota when it was taken?"

"What do you mean?" she asked, nonplussed. "Who's Ryota?"

Chapter Twenty-Seven

"Takashi's son isn't Ryota?" I was lost, had been sure Ryota wasn't just a poor partner but was a murderer.

"Shinji. My grandson's name is Shinji."

"Why did you leave the station before we finished talking?" It obviously wasn't because she saw Ryota approaching my desk.

"I see his father's anger in him. I see the devil grinning at me again." Her tears fell into and traveled down the causeways mapped by her wrinkles. "I found your name on a piece of paper. I thought maybe you were harassing him. His temper got worse: he broke things, yelled at me, hit his own head against the wall." She stopped and looked at me, pleading. "I saw his handwriting on the package you had at the office, the one leaking. But you're all right, aren't you? You're right in front of me and fine. Shinji's been better too. He's calmer, happier. So it was just the delusions of an old woman." Another smile. "He's found himself, Detective Brace. He's found peace with the past. He even brought me a gift. I think as an apology for how he's been the last few months."

"What gift?" Ash asked.

Mrs. Yoshinaga smiled again, this time gesturing toward the iron teapot. "We've been drinking from it, detectives. He somehow located the tetsubin stolen from my family when we were sent to the camps. My father asked our neighbors to watch over a trunk of items that we couldn't take with us to Camp Harmony. We never saw the trunk again. We thought we could trust them. We were wrong. But Shinji found not only our tetsubin, but even our matchawan, the tea bowls we've been drinking from." She continued to smile and point at the tea service in front of us.

Ash and I looked at one another. We had been drinking Genmaicha from tea bowls that Shinji had reclaimed after beating Jamie Parks to death. I swallowed, my brain expecting to find the taste of blood lingering from the tetsubin and tea bowls stolen so violently.

We now had the link between the Parks family and the Brey family. The two families weren't directly connected; they didn't know one another, yet each family had a tie to Shinji. The connecting spokes were Shinji and the generational lineage of pain passed down from the internment.

"Mrs. Yoshinaga, where is Shinji?" I gently asked, trying to offer a smile rather than the disgust I felt when imagining the taste of blood in my mouth.

"I don't know." Her smile faded. "He hasn't been here for several days. He kissed me on my forehead and told me he needed to restore balance and I haven't seen him since."

"Those were his words?" I asked, growing simultaneously excited and worried, "'restore balance?'"

"Yes," Mrs. Yoshinaga answered. "I told him not to talk in riddles, that his father liked people to be direct. He gave me another kiss on the forehead and walked out the door."

I opened my wallet and gave her another one of my business cards. "If you see or hear from Shinji, give me a call. Immediately."

She nodded her head in agreement. Then Ash and I left the ghostly woman to her memories and the interpretations of the past that she had erected to try and keep herself and Shinji safe.

As we walked to the car, Ash asked, "where are we going? Where's Shinji?"

I climbed into the car, slammed my door shut, and looked toward Ash. "Puyallup," I answered. "It all comes back to Puyallup."

Chapter Twenty-Eight

"How can you be sure he's in Puyallup?" Ash asked as I drove down I-5 and over to WA-167, heading southeast of Seattle.

"It's part of his message," I answered. "He said he's going to 'restore balance.' I don't think he's trying solely to punish; I think these murders are about something larger for him, some attempt to rebalance things, the 'truth' and get back to 'harmony.' He's going to the Fairgrounds, back to the site where the internment started for his family. We need to find the Camp Harmony memorial that Mrs. Yoshinaga mentioned."

"Do you think he knows about the kid? Does he have him?"

"He wouldn't head back to Puyallup unless he was ready to complete the cycle he's started. It's part of the rebalancing mission he's set for himself."

"'Unto the third and fourth generations,'" Ash mouthed.

"'Unto the third and fourth,'" I agreed.

We made the drive to Puyallup in a little over an hour. Moving through the streets of Puyallup felt unnaturally slow after flying down the freeway.

"I get that Shinji is on some sort of revenge quest," Ash said, breaking the silence that we had carried for the last several miles. "But what happened in the past, what he's trying to fix, it's so much more complicated than that."

"For him it's simple, direct: all of this is payback for what happened to his family, what they went through during the internment. As he sees it, the internment caused every tragedy and misstep that followed for his family." I stopped, trying to figure out how to put into words that I could understand Shinji while simultaneously see the flaws in his reasoning. "He was dealt a terrible hand. The internment was terrible, his grandmother getting raped was terrible, having the man he would have thought of as his grandfather kill himself was terrible. Having his father beat his mother to death was terrible. Having family heirlooms stolen was terrible."

"So it's okay?" Ash asked, incredulous. "That makes it okay that he cut off your dog's legs, that he killed Mr. Brey and everyone else?"

"No. Not at all. I just get how for him it's easy this way. It makes all of that pain easy to deal with if he can think of it as a destiny that needs to be addressed and rebalanced. It's even easier," I said, "given what I think Mrs. Yoshinaga spoon fed to him all these years: the 'devil' started all of this; it's not him but the 'devil' that is to blame. It's the devil within his DNA that is to blame. That's what he always heard. It's the ghost in his genes."

"Like the ghost music you told me about. That echo you can hear but can't quite place," Ash replied.

"Ripples hitting us from pebbles dropped decades ago. The aftershocks smack us even though we were never present for the root cause. We're hit with the reverberations, scrambling to see where they came from and what they mean. Good sometimes, bad sometimes, just like ghosts. Echoes from the past are absolutely like that too."

"So he blames what happened in the past, then takes on some biblical generational revenge plan that moves retribution from history onto future generations." Ash said.

"Echoes and ghosts," I replied, as I pulled into a large nearly empty parking lot.

The Puyallup Fair always reminded me of Kansas, transported me back to my youth and the Hutchinson State Fair: farm animal contests, cheap carnival rides that you hoped had their safety inspections up to date, overpriced corndogs and greasy elephant ears and snow cones that, by the time you reached the bottom, never had enough flavored syrup left. It was the kind of place, at least in my memory, where you had your first kiss as a young teenager or tried to work up the courage to talk to the freckled, pony-tailed girl who kept glancing coyly at you while she used the ball of her foot to grind a loose piece of hay into earth already hard-packed from being trampled by countless visitors.

I wondered how many other visitors had walked on this ground, inhaling the smell of funnel cakes coated in powdered sugar, remembering their own past, and never suspected it had also been the site adopted earlier by the War Relocation Authority. We walked over a space that exhaled an uncanny palimpsest: the trauma of internment layered with the celebration of small-town, farming Americana.

We passed the Fair's grandstand, silence weighing where my ears were used to hearing the noise of the crowd. Positioned at a natural corner of the fairgrounds, out in the open yet also unobtrusive, the memorial stood. No killer hid behind it, ready to pop out and cackle maniacally at us.

"This is it? Ash asked doubtfully.

"I guess so," I replied, looking at the plaque for assurance. The memorial itself was small. Beautiful as an artistic endeavor, but much smaller than I would have guessed. But, then, how do you capture something like the internment within a sculpture? The artist tried to answer that impossible task with a cylindrical monument about ten feet in height, shapes cut into it that allowed light to play through, the top reminiscent of a wide belt. It sat atop a pebbled concrete slab about two feet in height and was surrounded, also on top of the slab, by matching pebbled concrete pots, empty basins of dirt during this winter. I assumed during the Fair they would house flowers.

"Now what?" I asked. "No killer, no kid, no shoot-out at the OK Corral."

Ash stepped onto the concrete pedestal to get closer to the monument. She played absentmindedly with the shapes carved into it, curling her fingers within the interior of the memorial. "To the museum," she replied, hopping down. "Let's look for the exhibit about the assembly center."

The lights inside the Puyallup Fair Museum were darkened, but the lock to the door had been broken. Ash looked at me. Not knowing where inside the museum the Camp Harmony exhibit would be located, I pointed an index finger at my chest and then gestured to the left, then pointed at Ash and gestured to the right. She nodded in agreement, then reached to the small of her back and pulled out a Beretta 9 mm.

Hoping for an unobtrusive entrance that would give us a chance to gain our bearings and reconnoiter the building, I pulled the door open as slowly as possible. It swept open with no more sound than a quiet swoosh of air. Inside, nothing moved.

I crept to the left, hugging the wall and keeping my arms locked in front of me in a triangle frame to brace my weapon, ready to fire if needed. I moved past displays that held pictures of an earlier era: farmers clad in overalls and old tractors and the kind of Chevy trucks that inspire Mellencamp songs. No signs inside the acrylic cases pointed with large arrows to show me where to find the killer. I crept on, concentrating to keep my breathing slow and in control.

I was surrounded by shadows and displays sealed behind glass to prevent touching. Without the bustle of other visitors, the space seemed dead and vacant. Its effort to venerate the past felt eerie. Rather than making history feel alive, it made it feel as though the past were trying to suck me down, trap me, smother me. I had a fleeting image of walking through a bog, my feet sinking into the muck, a tremendous effort required to pull them free and keep moving forward.

I reached the edge of the museum's left perimeter and swung to my right. As I turned the corner, a searing pain surged through my right shoulder. My gun clattered to the ground as I instinctively reached toward the pain. Another severe ache hit just above my left pectoral and radiated onto my left bicep. I crumpled to the ground, registering with an initial clinical detachment the maroon stain of my own blood creating a small puddle beside me. My heart rate spiked as the shock and objective disinterest passed and I was brought back to panic and reality by the killer, by a voice that I had heard before but could not yet place.

"I'm glad that you're here, Marcus. Sorry about the shoulder. But after all I've done for you, the gun is really pushing it. That's a nasty cut." He chuckled, soft and low. "There's irony here somewhere, Marcus. Does it hurt more if you know that the cut comes from your dad, or from Mr. Brey? Help me out with this one, since you are, after all, the one bleeding." His words didn't make sense, the pain pulsing through my shoulder and upper chest making his already obscure phrasing even more difficult to decipher.

I felt his hands grab under my armpits to pull me upright and prop my back against the wall. Folded in half, I looked up, toward the dark ceiling and the face of the man who had killed Mr. Brey and tortured Mike. His features remained momentarily hidden in the shadows. I saw, however, a sword hanging parallel to his right leg.

"You've been back to my apartment again," I uttered, my voice hoarse. "That's the sword my father gave to me."

"Bravo, Marcus. Yes, your father told me all about that. Mr. Brey gave it to him, he gave it to you. How's it feel, Marcus, to be exchanged for a sword, your body bartered for a blade?" He looked at me with what I took as pity. "I'm afraid I have news that will cut even deeper: the sword's a fraud. It's no grand souvenir from WWII. It's nothing. It's something you'd find at a mall, a tourist item, a fake." His voice rose with his anger.

"I understand your earlier babbling now. I get it. I've been wounded by a sham," I said. My words sounded slower to me than I imagined saying them, as though a lag existed between mind and body. "Bought at a place called something like the Sword Emporium and manufactured in China but real enough to damage. You're using a fake WWII artifact to redress real wrongs."

He chuckled again. "I'm glad you see it, Marcus. It's important you see it clearly. We take their lie and use it to cut out the other lies. Maybe it's poetic justice and irony all wrapped together. What do you think?" He moved forward, his head covered this time by his shirt as he pulled it above his arms to remove it. He grabbed me again and the pressure that his hands put on my injured shoulder made my eyes squeeze shut. I rotated my head backward in pain and then down toward the pool of blood on the ground. My chin came to rest on my sternum. He pushed his shirt onto my wound, taking my hand in his and moving it toward my shoulder so that I could hold the shirt on the cut. I opened my lips, jaw still clamped tight, sucked air against my teeth until they felt dry, then forced my head up so I could see his face.

"There. That will staunch the bleeding. That gun, Marcus," he continued, shaking his head slightly from side to side while he scolded me like a schoolboy, "that gun really wasn't necessary."

It was that sense of the schoolboy that made me open my mouth in recognition, my eyes squinting at the realization. I tried to laugh but only a dry cough emerged from my throat. My chin dropped toward my chest again, this time from a sense of defeat and critical oversight. "You. I stood right next to you, directly in front of you."

I looked up again to find a smile waiting for me. "Yes. That was fun, Marcus. Not something I expected. But very fun nonetheless."

"We were so close. Right next to you," I mumbled, more to myself than to him. I raised my head again, looking into the face I had seen in the hallway next to Jamie Parks's apartment after coming out of Mr. and Mrs. Lump's residence. I stared into eyes I had appraised before, that had, I realized, appraised me before.

"Stimmy. You said your name was Stimmy. You gave the same name when you spoke to Mills at the station. Why lie about your name, Shinji? I've talked to your grandmother." This time I smiled at him. "I know you now too."

"Yes, I lied about my name. A lie, but a fun one. Henry Stimson. You should know your history, Marcus. Stimson was Secretary of War at the time of the evacuation and internment. The irony tickled me." His eyes turned cold again, reminding me of how he had challenged me with his stare outside of Parks's apartment.

"I thought you were a student heading off to class. The backpack you had," I finished, trailing off not from the injury to my shoulder but to the professional wound I felt.

"That *was* fun, wasn't it? You've finally figured out what I hid in the backpack, haven't you, Marcus?" He seemed excited. "Good. I thought you would, hoped you would."

"The tetsubin and matchawan," I said evenly. "Your grandmother's heirlooms."

He clapped his hands, smiling down at me. "Exactly."

"She served me from the teapot earlier today," I said.

"Don't blame her. She doesn't know how I procured it. I'm glad, though, that you drank from it, shared a part of my family."

"You must have been in Parks's apartment while we were next door with the busybody neighbor and her husband," I said, finally understanding how the teapot worked its way back to Mrs. Yoshinaga.

"Close one, wasn't it?" he smiled. "Right in front of you and you still couldn't rattle me. Of course, to be fair, I'd seen you before and you'd never seen me."

"Kansas," I stated. "You saw me at Mr. Brey's."

"Oh yes. I saw you storm off after meeting with that piece of shit quasi-brother of yours." His eyebrows curled toward his nose as he continued. "I worried about you. You left in such a rage. I couldn't imagine what Mike must have said to you."

"He paid though, didn't he?"

"Of course. Not for you, though, Marcus. Not for you."

"No," I replied, "for your grandma's 'devil,'" I said, trying to stare him down. "For the man you carry within you, who still courses through your veins, his DNA riding your bloodstream."

He laughed. A forced laugh, shrill at the high notes and brittle on all the rest. "He's what brought us together, Marcus. Grandpa Brey, the rapist devil. Yes, he's in my blood. But you became part of that family too, didn't you?"

"Mr. Brey was a good man. You must have seen that as well, to be so merciful to him and so violent with Mike," I said, tears in my eyes.

"Mr. Brey, I agree, was unfortunate. I wanted to ignore him. I wanted to let him live. Because of you, Marcus. Because of what he did for you. He took you in, tried to save someone otherwise abandoned. I appreciated that he tried to atone for the guilt passed onto him. You understand, don't you, that *you* became his effort at atonement: take in the neighbor orphan to make up for the bastard orphan left behind by his father." He stopped for a second, assessing me. "Even so, he remained guilty. He still carried the stain within him. I was easy on him, but he was still marked, still part of that lineage whether he wanted to be or not."

"Why not kill me too, then? If I was adopted by that line and, as you say, became part of the family, then why not kill me?" I stared at him, searching for an answer. "Why am I different?" I asked, hearing the echo of the same, desperate question that I had asked myself countless times while growing up.

"Don't you *feel* the link?" he asked, eyes wide. "You and I are united, victims, abandoned children who find themselves, now, as family." Sweat beads slipped from his forehead onto his eyebrows as he talked. "Abandoned and alone and alienated, that's us. We're history's bastards, Marcus. Orphans of chance, both tossed to the side as garbage to be forgotten. Never acknowledged by the rest of the world. Boxed in through no fault of our own but not seen truly by others. Not even our pain seen. Our anguish overlooked by everyone else but throbbing out from us like secret magnetic waves. Pulsars of pain, Marcus."

"I like that, Pulsars of Pain. We should start a band," I managed through teeth grinding together against the throbbing in my shoulder.

"You're disappointing me, Marcus. You're not understanding the importance of what's happening, of what we're doing here." A look of excitement replaced his disdain, his eyebrows moving up and eyes glittering with excitement. "This will help you see it. You made your entrance just in time. Say hello to our guest, Marcus." He moved to the side, opening space for me to see who had remained hidden behind him.

A boy, maybe ten years old, sat on the ground, his back propped against a display case and his feet tied together straight in front of him. He stared with eyes pulled wide from fear and horror. I saw, next to him, propped against the side of the same display case, a Louisville slugger caked with dried blood.

"The Parks kid," I said, feeling the breath deflate from my lungs.

"The last of the line, Marcus. The final stone to overturn. Let's see what creepy, crawly bugs lie beneath, hidden to everyone else." He smiled, lips curling into the glee of the passionately insane. He moved to the display case. Once there, he trailed the tip of the sword across the kid's cheek, drawing a thin, slightly curved line of blood. He transferred the sword to his left hand and picked up the baseball bat with his right.

I struggled to get to my feet but he moved back to me before I managed to do more than send another current of pain flashing through my shoulder and chest. He held the bat straight out in front of him, as though he were knighting me, and pushed it against the top of my injured shoulder, crumpling me to the ground. A scream, quiet because the breath in my lungs had already escaped, crawled out of my lips. As he pushed me down, I saw the end cap of the bat, stained from where he had plunged it up and down onto Mike's hand, shattering bones and tearing skin. Feeling my wound pressed on by the same bat that had soaked up Mike's blood made me feel closer to the Breys than I had ever before felt.

I looked again at the Parks kid, who seemed close to hyperventilating. His pupils had dilated so much that the irises appeared nonexistent. Assuming we made it out of this, I wondered how he would ever recover.

Shinji's voice brought me back. "Don't try to get up, Marcus, unless you want to help me." The scowl on his face transformed into a broad smile. He moved to clap his hands in glee, instead settling for quietly knocking the flat side of the sword against the barrel of the bat. "I've just had the greatest epiphany, Marcus. You *can* help me. You can be a part of this too."

"I won't help you."

"You will." He moved the bloody point of the sword in front of my face. "This silly, imposter sword. This cheap lie is from your adopted grandfather, Marcus. My bastard grandfather, Adam Brey. He lives in it still. It's him; it's you; it's me." He turned his head toward the Parks boy and then back to me, his shadow jumping in exaggerated motions. "I was going to beat him to death." The bat tapped hard against the ground, Mike's dried blood pounding into the concrete with each sharp "bap, bap, bap." He looked momentarily confused then once more determined. "I still will." A final, cracking "BAP" echoed through the building as he drove the bat to the ground. He stared into my eyes. "That has to be how he dies, by the bat. You understand. It's purifying that way."

"Your own blood sacrifice," I said, wanting to keep him talking. "Your warped attempt to make up for your grandfather being beaten by a bat."

"Good, Marcus, good." He smiled again. "Better than you think, even. We're going to cleanse the ground here, Marcus. And you will be a part of this."

He moved closer to me. The sword pushed against the side of my neck. As he moved near, he slid his palm along the blade, so that the sword never moved. Neither did the funhouse smile plastered on his face. Feeling the steel press against my neck, as though it were looking for my carotid pulse, I wondered how he kept the blade from slicing his hand.

He held his right hand, palm up, in front of me. Moving his hand down the blade hadn't left him unscathed at all. He had never intended that it do so. His smile, if possible, now curled further at the corners as I saw blood leak from fingers sliced by the sword.

He kneeled closer to me. His skin smelled like the granulated soap I remembered from elementary school. His breath carried the odor of wet wood. He held his index finger directly in front of me, the base of the finger just above the bridge of my nose, the pad of the finger hovering between my eyes so that I saw double. He pressed his bloody print onto my forehead two times. His finger squished and slid slightly with each bloody dot he left upon me.

He looked approvingly at the marks he had made. Then he raised his index finger to his own forehead, marking himself with two irregular, burgundy circles.

"We're all in this together, Marcus. No one gets immunity." He pointed to his forehead, then to mine, then toward the Parks boy. He had three dots on his forehead, though his circles were black, drawn in by marker or paint. Those marks had been planned; my marks and the killer's own marks were evidently improvised additions.

"The dots again," I said, feigning indifference and weariness. "No new tricks?"

"Not dots," he responded, angry. "Drops, Marcus. Drops." His anger disappeared once he saw my confusion. "You haven't figured it out, have you?" he asked.

"I get it," I replied. "Three dots. Excuse me, I mean three *drops*. It's counting. Three drops for three generations. 'Unto the third generation,' and so on and so forth."

He looked angry again. "Stop being coy, Marcus. This isn't a game." He tapped the sword blade against my neck to emphasize his point.

"Ok," I said, tilting my neck away from the blade. "Why not use numbers to count the generations? Why drops?"

"You're right about generations and the counsel from Exodus. But you're missing the other part of it. That disappoints me, Marcus," he responded. "I thought you, of all people, would figure it out. You studied Emerson, didn't you? Surely your literature training included Ralph Waldo?"

He even knew about my brief tenure as a literature major. He had invaded my life in ways that I never suspected.

"Listen carefully, Marcus." His voice shook with passion. As he recited Emerson's words, I realized we were inside the central nerve of all of this:

> "'How shall a man escape his ancestors, or draw off from his veins the black drop he drew from his father's or his mother's life?'"

Silence hung heavy after his brief, intense recitation.

For Shinji, the black drops tied it all together. They were black holes that he used not only as a simple system of counting but also as symbols for an unwanted inheritance, an unbidden branding of the soul that he turned into his personalized killing symbol. The black drops became tokens of a biological accounting, markers of a perverse retribution against the present generation for sins they somehow carried inside their bodies, passed through the blood, from generations past. I saw Shinji staring at me expectantly. With bloody fingerprints on his forehead and an eerie smile hanging on his lips, he had transformed himself into the love child of an illicit union between Exodus and Emerson.

He once more pointed the sword at me and then toward the boy. "It's time that you accept your guilt in all of this, embrace the complicity you inherited. I'm going to cut his throat. With your sword. The cut comes from your family. We'll see him bleed. We'll watch as his blood falls to the floor in penitence and reparation. Then, just before he passes out," he continued, hefting the bat to his shoulder and smiling broadly, "I'll crush his skull and complete the cleansing." The Parks kid threw his body back and forth against his bonds. His head wasn't restrained and moved faster than the rest of him, so that he looked like a rag doll tossed around by giant, invisible hands.

The killer laughed as he watched. Then he turned toward me. The smile left his face, replaced once more by the scowl. "That annoying partner of yours isn't here too, is he, Marcus? Don't lie to me. I've lived a life of lies. I see when someone lies to me." He stared intently at me.

"No. Ryota's not here." I held his gaze, my eyes drying out as if a fan were directed at them as I willed myself not to blink. "We had a falling out."

He smiled again. "I believe you, Marcus. I'm not surprised," he added. "There's a part of me that hates him as much as I hate this boy." He kicked with his heel at the shoes behind him. "Ryota's also Sansei. Just like me."

"Not just like you."

"No," he laughed, "you're right." The laughing disappeared. "He's a coward for accepting what was passed to him. Meekness and powerlessness, that's his inheritance. I've watched him as well. The more I saw of him, though, the more I hated him." He looked as though he wanted to spit. "Maybe the internment stole his Issei grandfather's manhood, as it did to my own ancestor. But Ryota has done nothing to challenge the weakness inside him."

"His father's tea?" I asked. "You left signs of that on purpose, didn't you?"

He smiled. "More fun, Marcus. I wanted you to find me, but not right away, not while I had so much work to finish. Besides," he added, "Ryota needs to see that the universe punishes passivity, that the submissive are pulled into events they would rather avoid. They get steamrolled. He still believes that you must follow the rules, that obedience is the only option. His naiveté makes me sick. There's no such thing as innocence, is there, Marcus? We're all marked whether we want to be or not. We're disfigured by the weight that those who came before us pile onto our backs."

I heard scuffling coming from behind the Parks kid. I needed to keep Shinji's attention focused my direction. "There's still innocence," I began, not sure where to go, searching equally for myself as I searched for an answer for him. "This kid didn't even know his father. Up until a few days ago, I don't even think you knew this boy existed." A tidal wave of guilt crashed into me with the thought that I had helped direct Shinji to the child. "I remember your face outside the Parks apartment. There was a moment of shock in your eyes, wasn't there, that Jamie had a boy? You didn't know. The boy isn't a part of this. He never was."

"He *always* was! As soon as he was born he was!" he shouted back, bending his face closer to mine, as though in prayer. "I knew you were part of my fate at that point, Marcus. I knew I was right that you were meant to be involved with this." He smiled at me again. Even in the darkened room I could see sweat tracing down the bridge of his nose. "You gave him to me." A bead of sweat dripped off his nose and landed on my hand. "No one, absolutely no one, is innocent."

"You're wrong," I replied. "There's more than that." I felt my own sweat cooling on my forehead. "We're all born neck deep in the shit that came before us. I get that. But maybe we make ourselves innocent. Innocence isn't given. It's earned. It's how you respond to what that you inherit, to the shit that chokes you and threatens to drown you. It's about whether you're strong enough to shovel a path through the shit you find yourself in, or whether you give up and add to the pile, choking everyone who follows even more."

"Yes, Marcus, yes!" he shouted with a glee I hadn't anticipated my words would engender. "That's what I'm doing. I'm stopping the spill of lies gushing like a waterfall from their mouths. I am the fire that burns it all away, that shows the purity beneath. I am the one who resets the system. I rebalance the register. I reveal the truth." He looked at me again, his knuckles white with the pressure he placed around the sword and bat. "Do you see it now? To clear away the sins passed down by the parent, we clear away the child. To punish the parent, we destroy the progeny." The display case rocked back and forth behind us as the Parks kid buckled forward and back in panic. "It's good you have no kids, Marcus, to pass along the stain. It all ends here. We purify it all here, now."

"NO," I shouted back, hoping like hell that I hadn't imagined hearing that shuffling behind him. Then I thought I heard something from around the corner behind me as well. I wondered if you could have auditory hallucinations. "No," I repeated, "What came before does not predetermine the present and the future. Nothing is ironclad, total, sealed so tightly that escape is impossible. The child is not responsible for his parent. The son is not, cannot be, his father."

Panic pumped through my chest, my face dropping toward the ground as I finished shouting.

I felt the coolness of steel lift my head, the point of the sword digging just above my Adam's apple. The voice sounded quiet, almost pitying. "You feel the same as me. I hear it in your voice. How do you love yourself, knowing that those who gave you life consider you a mistake, an error best left forgotten and not acknowledged? I'm right, aren't I, Marcus?" The blade of the sword moved from my throat to my cheek, almost caressing me. "What I do today, with this blade and this bat, frees us of all of that." The sword moved away from me, slicing vertically through the soft flesh of the Parks kid's cheek. Then it moved back to me, once more at my cheek, preventing my head from moving. "See it, Marcus," he demanded. "See what we're doing here. We're purifying ourselves of the sins of our ancestors, sins we have been burdened with but didn't ourselves commit." The sword gently tapped my cheek. "Watch the blood drip down the boy's cheek. Watch as we bleed the past out of the present."

I watched. He didn't give me a choice, but I don't think I could have pulled my eyes away even if a sword hadn't been pressed against my head. I felt my heart race, my breath catch, could imagine my own pupils dilating. A soft, tinny chuckle echoed toward my ears.

"See it, Marcus. See the cut. Understand how the father circulates in the blood. See that we are nothing more than a pained remembrance of horrors past."

I understood what he was saying. I understood that this was supposed to be my initiation, my full entry into a shadowy part of my soul that I had previously, at certain dark moments, brushed against before pulling back in fear and shock. My shoulder continued to pump blood. I felt myself getting weaker. I felt my father dripping down my chest. I looked at the killer and saw part of my reflection, the part of me that felt lost and worthless and wounded; I looked at the Parks kid and saw part of the abandoned child I once was. The blood slid an irregular path down the boy's cheek, a maroon teardrop that called forth all of the pain I had held hidden inside my heart. I understood that pain as I had never before let myself understand it. I saw my heart clearly, recognized the fear that lurked within it, faced frailties that skulked in the usually darkened fissures.

I found myself inside these fissures and caverns, byproducts of an emotional erosion that had slowly carved the shape of my pain. It had been hollowed out through a drip, drip, drip process so slow that it was imperceptible, silent even while I lived through it. I thought of Ash and felt my heart squeeze tight, my eyes pull shut. Erosion eats away, patiently and calmly, counting time and pain drop by slow drop. As blood oozed from the cracks between my fingers, I understood that erosion had also taken place in my heart, salty tears patiently dripping down and leaving me hollow, my being crisscrossed with cavities that collected as aquifers of pain.

I saw eyes of fear staring at me, witnessed the Parks kid's labored breathing. I thought of Ash's eyes, windows that had silently spoken more to me than any words ever uttered. I thought of the last images I had of my father, shrunken from the man I recalled as a child, his soul atrophied with anxiety, terrified to act in the present because he couldn't escape the past. I saw all of that and my own fear washed away, oozing from my body along with the blood that continued to drip from my wounds. Fright gave way to a warm tingling and my own choppy laughter, broken from the spasms of pain that each chuckle sent through my injured body.

"What are you laughing at, Marcus?" Shinji asked. His eyes betrayed confusion. I heard, as though a distant echo, a snort. A moment later I realized it was I who had snorted. His anger brought me back. "Shut up," he shouted. "WHY do you laugh?"

"It ends here," I replied, feeling the aftershocks of the laughter in my belly. "You've freed me." He looked pleased again. Triumphant. I wagged my index finger at him. "Not in the way that you think, though. No, no."

Chastised, he looked angry. "You're right, Marcus. It does all stop here. The line ends here—mine and yours. Ours." His eyes burned with hatred, shone with resolve.

"I'm finally free, Shinji. Let the pain and the fear go. Let the love remain," I muttered.

His pupils narrowed. "You think you're ready, Marcus? You think you can face it better than your father did?" he asked. "I know you're curious about how your father confronted the sword, how he responded to the reckoning I brought. When I was younger," he continued, in a softer voice, "I wondered what my father thought in the moments before he hanged himself. What went through his mind after he made the final move, what did he want to say as no more breath entered his lungs? He didn't break his neck, you see. He must have swung back and forth, slowly suffocating. I've seen it millions of times in my mind. What did he think? What would he have wanted to tell me?"

I still didn't say anything.

"I did you a favor, Marcus. Killing your father was a bonus, just for you. He wasn't even part of my original plan. No bat for him, since he wasn't part of my line of lies, wasn't tied to the Minidoka devil. But I had fun watching him bleed."

I didn't respond.

"You know what your pathetic shell of a father said as I cut him?" he taunted. "I watched his final breaths, Marcus. I know. Ask me and I'll tell you." He almost begged.

Up until a few moments ago, a pint or so of blood ago, I had been desperate to see the secret that Shinji waved. I now recognized that it was fear that had made me desperate, not to hear my father's voice or understand his tortured soul, but frantic instead to hear that he felt sorry for abandoning me, frenzied to hear that it was a mistake and that he loved me. I remembered how he had begged of me to hear any crumb about my mother as I left his house. It was fear, I suddenly understood, that made me my father's child. Fear and anxiety had been my inheritance.

I didn't want that anymore. I didn't want to be beholden to whatever answer my father might have given with his last breaths. It didn't matter. What mattered was what I did with the fear he had bequeathed to me. Would I continue to nurse it? Could I accept it, let it scar over, and grow from it? I felt my eyelids shut, my lips move slightly with the start of a smirk, my head tilt back and expose my throat.

Above it all, more important than anything else, I thought of Ash. I saw her in my mind. Those eyes, those bewitching gray-green eyes. I felt, more than remembered, how we soothed each other's pain, how we were attracted to that pain and were helping one another move past that pain. The memory burned alive within my body, moving from cell to cell, nerve to nerve, leaving a trail of serene heat inside me, filling the cavities carved by erosion. I understood the fear in my soul. I faced the pain in my heart. Love remained. I remained. Even if for only a few moments more, I remained. More complete than I had ever felt before.

"No," I said. "It doesn't matter what my father told you. I don't need it."

He moved close to me, his breath shallow. Quick exhalations came from his nostrils and ricocheted off my cheek. He opened his mouth to speak, a smell like that of sodden wood and rotting leaves battering my nose. His words came in a whisper.

"He didn't love you. He never loved you." He moved away from me, his voice rising with his head. He took the sword from my throat and pointed it toward the Parks kid. "First him. Then you. Then me. The last thing to echo in your ears will be the sound of this child dying, the gurgle of blood from his neck."

He turned toward the child. Gripping the sword with both hands for the cutting stroke, he dropped the bat from his hand. It fell vertically, the end cap clanking against the ground. It bounced off of the concrete floor and started its return arc, the handle tilting down and the barrel arching up. It landed again, the handle and barrel clattering back and forth in a faster and faster staccato until its movement suddenly ceased.

Shinji's arms reached up and back, so that the sword tip pointed behind him. He started to cut down diagonally, moving toward the child's throat. Everything around me suddenly sped up incredibly fast, the world collapsing into synesthesia as my brain melted together sights and sounds that were too much to process. Then the strands separated once more, leaving me in the wake left by the boomerang momentum of life hurtling past at breakneck speed and then slowing to a near standstill.

The killer's sword, my sword, carved through the air. As the blade fell, multiple screams sliced my way. The child shrieked, squeezing his eyes shut and turning his head as far away from the blade as he could. The killer remained silent, focused. I realized I could also hear myself scream, shouting for the killer to stop and knowing that he wouldn't.

As my brain picked apart the various strands bombarding it, I recognized more voices adding to the combination of screams. I heard Ryota before I saw him, both his voice and body throwing themselves toward us from a spot to the right, midway between me and the killing scene. Mouth open wide, Ryota hurtled his body toward the spot that the sword approached. His right shoulder flattened into the pedestal base of the display case. Picture-perfect tackling form. In slow motion, I saw the rest of him momentarily continue forward and rotate slightly in the start of a circle as his shoulder stopped and the rest of his body didn't. The display case teetered and fell to the ground. Glass shattered as it landed. The papers inside spilled out, a few of them fluttered up before weaving their way to the ground. Ryota landed on top of the Parks kid, his body covering the boy. The sword missed its intended mark, continuing through empty air until, moving down a foot or so on its arc, it sliced into Ryota's back. Ryota's head arched up in pain, another scream gushing out of his mouth.

I dropped my hand from my wound, reaching for the bat that the killer had dropped. I tried to stand but had trouble moving after losing so much blood. I pushed the end of the bat into the ground, using it as a cane for leverage, and forced myself up. Fresh blood spurted from the cuts on my chest and shoulder. As I moved toward the killer, Ryota flipped over. He scrambled to get to his feet. The sword swung again, this time cutting into Ryota's left arm. He collapsed on the ground, his arm already covered in blood and hanging lifeless at his side.

I stumbled forward. Only a few feet from the killer, I crumpled to my knees. His back was to me. He moved the sword toward his right shoulder as he loaded for the next swing. I leaned forward on my left hand, my right hand still clutched tightly to the bat. Pointing the bat toward the killer, I lunged forward and rammed the end cap into the back of his knee. His legs buckled forward, his torso arching back in response.

My blow was weak, my body failing me. He regained his balance as I fell. I rolled over onto my back, looking directly into his face. He laughed, yet also looked hurt that I had moved against him. He raised the sword again, his face changing. He looked at me, not in anger, but with the kind of disappointed pity that an adult reserves for a child who fails to understand something that has been explained over and over again. He readied to swing. I wanted to strike at him with the bat but my arms wouldn't respond. I barely managed to raise them up in a final gesture, of defense or surrender.

I heard more screaming and Ash's voice hit my ears. The killer looked toward her. I followed his eyes. She stood about five feet behind us, gun pointed at the man standing above me. Shinji looked back to me. He smiled. He let go of the sword, straightening his back but never letting go of my eyes. I heard Ash scream at him again, urging him to raise his hands.

He raised his left hand. His right hand stopped midway up. The gun he had taken from me rested in his waist band. He smiled at me again. His brown eyes filled with tears, then his pupils dilated and he reached toward the gun. Ash fired. Plumes of blood erupted from his chest. His mouth opened, lower jaw spread wide. His right hand moved away from the gun and started to move toward where the bullets had entered his body. Before reaching his chest, his hand fell. His body toppled over, temporarily landing on top of me, forcing my breath out, before the momentum of the fall carried him to my side. His eyes were empty, ghostly. I wiped at the spot on my chest where the killer had fallen. I found my hand covered in red. I didn't know if it was my blood or his.

I heard big, heavy sobs bubbling out of the Parks boy and moans of pain coming from Ryota. Ash ran to my side and kneeled down, putting one hand onto my wound to staunch the bleeding and the other hand behind my neck to support my head. I felt the palm of her hand on the back of my neck, her thumb rubbing back and forth through my hair. Just before I lost consciousness, I looked into her eyes, full of all of the words yet to be spoken and all of the ideas and feelings that already silently vibrated the string between us. I felt those vibrations connecting us, heard the call of my heart reverberate in hers, origin and echo at last united.

Epilogue

The rain disappeared today, one of those anomalous, impossibly bright days during Seattle winter that makes you realize just how much your body has been missing the sun. Temperatures in the fifties. Perfect running weather. I moved through the forest trail, the air tasting good and feeling clean in my lungs. My body burned comfortably from the effort. For the first time in ages, the sensation of my feet moving and my sweat pouring down felt clean and pure, as I continued the process of exorcising hurts that had over the years calcified within me.

After the events at the fairgrounds, I felt fortunate to be running at all. Before Ash had a chance to radio for the paramedics, I fell unconscious. By the time we arrived at the hospital, I had slipped into a coma. I awoke three days later and spent the next eight days recovering in a lumpy, antiseptic-smelling hospital bed.

Ryota didn't spend as long as I did in the hospital, but his recovery continues. The cut on his back required sixty-eight stitches. It's ugly but no major damage. Shinji's other strike, however, sliced through Ryota's bicep muscle and tendon. He still can't move his arm. It rests in a sling, hanging loosely, helplessly at his side and he'll probably never regain full movement.

He's a hero in the department now, though. People still call him "Right-Way," but instead of mocking sarcasm it now carries respect. He gets pats on the back when he moves through the bullpen, arm suspended in its blue canvas carrier.

Ryota's overwhelmed by all of it. He simply saw a report waiting on his desk that the Parks kid lived in Puyallup and drove down to follow-up. Inside the kid's room he found the killer's calling card: the kanjis for "harmony" and "truth" next to three black drops, all transcribed on top of a micro-fiche article that described the conversion of the stable grounds to an "assembly center." Good police work combined with good luck, but not much to do with me. Throwing himself in front of the sword didn't have anything to do with me or even the Parks kid. It was merely the thing to do whether you loved the person or hated the person. For Ryota, sacrifice is second-nature.

We talked in-depth after I got out of the hospital. He told me his family had also been interned, in California. He grew up hearing stories from his Nisei father about how his grandfather felt betrayed, that his family had followed the rules only to see them bent and perverted to justify the internment. I came away from our talk with the sense that Ryota did things the right-way, perhaps even became police in the first place, to prove to himself that things could be okay, that the law could be decent and moral and as pure as possible.

He's changing now, or at least trying to. I keep that to myself, though. The department needs the image and story of "right" sacrifice. I don't know what they'd do with the irony that his last, best sacrifice might be the impetus for abandoning those same ideals. When I visited him after being released from the hospital, he talked to me about living for everyone else except himself and that he couldn't do that anymore. His marriage had been falling apart over the last several months. That's why he'd been missing work: to make it to counseling appointments, trying to save what was dead because it's what he thought he should do. I wouldn't be surprised if, now that he's changing, he left both the department and his marriage. He wants to find whatever piece he's been missing. His details are different than my own, but the empty feeling is similar.

On the forest trail, I moved my running pace faster, yearning to feel the sweat drip from my forehead and pull out what I had always preferred to remain buried or ignored. The majority of my life, ever since my mom ran out and my father then abandoned me to the Breys, I had spent trying to move forward, away from my pain.

My feet kicked across the soft ground. Sunlight sneaked through alder leaves and pine needles to speckle the forest trail. I listened to the heavy cadence of my breathing, complemented by the sound of my shoes digging into and then pushing off of the trail, leaving my prints behind. The trail split at the 3-mile mark and I looped around the post, beginning the return leg of my out-and-back run.

My chest ached, not from the run but from the mark left by the sword. All these years I had been desperate to run away from my scars but this particular one pulsed with pain, refused to be chased away by endorphins as my body bounced over the forest floor. The scar, an up-to-down diagonal slash on the left-center of my chest, transfixes me. I stare at it in the mirror while the shower water heats up. Changing clothes at the gym, I look down at it with my chin tucked into the hollow at the base of my neck. Ash has rubbed her finger over it. I have too. Its texture makes me think of a petrified worm, frozen just below the surface of my skin. My finger feels the bumps and nodules of the tissue scarring beneath the surface, but the wound itself remains numb to the touch, so that I'm not sure if it is dead or alive. Bright red in color when I was in the hospital, it shines pink as my recovery continues.

I think about Shinji every time I think about my recovery. The transfusions I received at the hospital, blood from someone else mixed with my own blood, saved me. Shinji talked about blood itself carrying inherited sins, so that we need to bleed the past away, cut it out and let the wounds hemorrhage. Leach therapy to solve emotional wounds.

I've decided that he was close to it after all. We do carry past sins, our own as well as those passed down to us, but not as Shinji thought or feared. They're not in the blood, or on our genetic code, but the past and its sins remain very much alive and they do indeed constitute an inheritance. Each one of us is living history.

My breath heaved in and out of my chest as I ran and considered the balancing act that we perform every day between past and present. All these years, I had been running a race I could never win, trying to outpace scars that I carried inside me with every step. I had plowed forward, out of balance, at the expense of the past. Tilt too much in the other direction, though, and you sacrifice the present and future to reify the past until it suffocates you. My father lost his last breaths that way, smothered by what he could never forget or move beyond, pinned to the past as the present cartwheeled by.

I don't quite know where to place Shinji. He certainly ensnared himself in the past. I sometimes even wonder if he wasn't, spiritually, the adopted child of my father, the son who fully appreciated the weight of the past in ways that I had, futilely, attempted to disregard. I imagine my father looking into the eyes of his killer and finding, at last, a kindred spirit, a soul who similarly misunderstood the hold that the past can have over us. An accidental pairing that makes perfect sense.

Yet I also believe that Shinji's warped efforts to destroy the past by killing the present exhibit the manic energy of the caged animal, that he was desperate to escape the trap of the past. For me, he stands as a violent, disturbed emissary of remembrance. He manifests, for me, the horror and violence of forgotten memory, of that within ourselves and our culture that we want to ignore but that ultimately explodes uncontrollably if we bastardize the past and neglect to address it.

The most egregious error, I've decided, is failure to recognize that we are all misbegotten. We are all accidents, bastard products of chains of chance so enormous it boggles the mind to consider. One different turn here, one missed turn there, and all is different.

As my feet dislodged the mulch and dirt of the forest floor, I returned once more to erosion. It can hollow out from the inside, but it can also strip away the outermost layer and uncover what would otherwise have remained buried. Erosion tears apart from above and from below, wearing away the surface and carving interior caverns. There is no stable ground, no spot for your feet or heart to rest for very long.

That seems appropriate. The loss of stability is how it should be. It's impossible to live exclusively in the present, impossible to reside solely in the past, impossible to dream solely of the future. Those walls of containment, or internment, inevitably break down, crumble at weak spots to show us that they are never as tightly constructed as we assume. Or hope. There is no moving forward to avoid the past, no resting in the past to ignore the present. Neither exists without the other.

The trauma levied by Shinji showed me a new understanding: a spiraling relationship between past and present. Moving forward, I now think, means being strong enough not only to move back but also strong enough to not get stuck there. We need past and present to boomerang into each other. Their collisions fill in our gaps, complete our narratives and smooth over the jerky spots in the time-lapse movie that we all live. You don't escape history; you don't avenge history. You live history, every day, scars and all.

I look inside myself and see things changing. With Ash, I'm risking more than I ever thought possible, more than I ever thought was within me; yet I feel less fear in doing so than I have ever felt before. In the past, I loved out of fear. I believed that love and fear remained inextricably mixed and I lived with the fear more than the love. I gave myself to others so that they wouldn't want to leave me; I gave myself to protect myself. With Ash, I'm learning of a new love, of love not driven by worry or fueled by fear. She does that to me. Those eyes do that to me. She keeps the world at bay for me and I try to do the same for her. We're each other's safe harbor, a spot where we can recharge and rebuild our hurt selves.

I've thought too about the love given to me by Mr. Brey. I suspect Shinji was right, that in part Mr. Brey adopted me as a token of atonement. He could have done more, I realize. He could have reached out to those his grandfather had victimized. But no matter how or why it started, the caring he gave to me never felt tainted by guilt or fear. No matter what shortcomings or qualifications accompanied his decision to take me in, he made my life better when he didn't have to. He took the past and those sins given to him and did his best to make something change for the better in the present.

I've made that lesson my true inheritance. I owe that to Mr. Brey. I think I owe that to Shinji as well: I want to believe that while past sins cannot be erased, they can be confronted and the scars tended to as carefully and tenderly as possible. I tried to locate any children or grandchildren related to Kana and Natsuo, to the genetic line begun with the rape at the internment camp. There are no others. That line is dead.

Every Wednesday, I visit Mrs. Yoshinaga. It was tricky at first, with Shinji's death hanging between us. But we're starting to move beyond it. Every Thursday, I drive down to Puyallup to spend time with Jamie Parks's kid. Kevin is his name. He's living with an aunt and uncle. They seem like good people, but Kevin's still shaken up, filled with fear and confusion about what happened at the fairgrounds. I've made it my own personal Big Brother program to let him know that I will be there for him, that he's not been abandoned. I also want him to hear about the past and learn about the wounds formed years ago that culminated with him tied to a display case that memorialized the Puyallup assembly center.

Last Thursday, I drove Kevin back to Seattle, where we picked up Mrs. Yoshinaga and then the three of us caught the ferry to Bainbridge Island. We watched the wake of the large ship, enjoyed the sun gleaming off the water, and looked with interest as the docks slowly melted away. The Space Needle, standing tall as the popular and national repository of Seattle culture and history, grew smaller and smaller as we floated across Puget Sound.

Once across, we visited the now defunct Eagledale ferry dock and located the granite marker that memorializes the 227 Bainbridge Island residents who, on March 30, 1942, became the nation's first Japanese American residents forced into internment. The three of us sat at the water's edge, underneath a giant western red cedar with branches as big as the trunks of smaller trees. I rubbed my hand over gnarled bark that, perhaps, some of those leaving to be interned had gently touched as well, a loving glance of fingers to the last living thing they would feel on the island that they had made their home. How different their ferry ride must have been from the one that we had just experienced.

On the forest trail, my feet pounded over loose bark and carried me to the crest of a hill. My legs burned now. My breath came in short gulps that told me I was pushing hard, nearing the end of my out and back loop. I thought again of erosion and my image of the ground dissolving beneath my feet, opening to reveal a chasm of fire and molten earth. I had always tried to run a step ahead of disaster, keeping my feet churning to keep myself just out of reach of the destruction and pain that I felt threatened at every footfall. I had, always, been running away.

I thought of Mr. Brey and Kevin and Kana and Natsuo and Takashi and all the lives destroyed by the internment and, later, lives destroyed by the killer. I thought, most clearly, of Ash. I no longer run out of fear, or to try and outpace it. I am trying to run toward, not away. I feel something bigger, better out there. I want to chase it, run myself into connections and memory and a type of love that I had never before seen clearly or had the courage to embrace.

Whether we want to face it or not, we all run toward the future while running alongside the past. Nothing happens in isolation, broken from the chain of history. Life is a clause, every event or thought or action dependent on something else, tied to some other, often hidden, motivation or person or event.

I broke from the forest, the trail transitioning back to sidewalk. I smiled, taken by the thought that relationships are like clauses as well; we are separate, yet tied together, simultaneously linked and delineated by the slimmest of margins.

I finished my run, recalling the final words carved into the granite memorial that Kevin, Mrs. Yoshinaga, and I looked at on Bainbridge Island. It ends simply, a hope transcribed in both Japanese and English. "Nidoto Yai Noni, 'Let it Not Happen Again.'"

Acknowledgements

Writing a book is a funny thing. What feels at times like a very solitary activity is actually filled with quiet connections to others who have great impact on the final product. One of the beauties of having a work published is that there is finally a chance to let others know how helpful those quiet connections have been.

I'd like to thank Sunny Frazier for taking the time to help out a new writer. She's offered suggestions and support to a number of writers, and I have been fortunate to be included in that group. She was a strong advocate of *Ghost Music*, and I appreciate her time, dedication, and encouragement.

A huge thanks to Oak Tree Press for giving *Ghost Music* a chance. The community of writers at OTP is amazing. Thank you for welcoming me to the group, showing me the ropes, and for believing in my work.

Makiko Okuma was a great neighbor, and I peppered her with suggestions for character names and random questions about Japanese American culture. The help was hers. Any errors are mine.

Rob Carnahan is probably my oldest friend. He and his wife Merri dug into old military contacts and knowledge that helped me when the novel took a turn toward St. Louis and the government's storage of military personnel records. Thanks go to both of them.

Mike Wacker let me bombard him with questions about DNA and biology. He's another one of the really good guys out there. And here again, any errors are solely my own.

Dave Andersen is the best editor I know. He can't give anything a quick edit. And that's a good thing. Beyond the editing, Dave is a fantastic friend. "Diamond," thanks for the editing, for the laughs, and for the beers and bar time.

Katie Knappenberger helped not only with transcribing final edits but also with timely emotional support and humor. "Live you homey."

If I hadn't attended grad school at the University of Washington, this book never gets written. Caroline Simpson introduced me to Michi Weglyn's *Years of Infamy* during a seminar, and the description of the internment barracks and saving the sugar beet crop caught my attention well before I thought about becoming a novelist. Ross Posnock helped deepen an appreciation of Pragmatist philosophy that had initially been sparked by Bob Antonio at the University of Kansas. The opportunity to teach a modernist/postmodernist class, meanwhile, gave me time to think further about how the past and present interact.

Finally, my children Aidan and Kiera have changed everything. I tell people that writing is my "cave painting," my way to record in some way that I have been here, and lived, and felt. Aidan and Kiera, you two are the true record of that. But I love the idea that you will someday read this book and know me in a slightly different way than before.

About the Author

Patrick Linder was born in Wichita, KS and moved to the Seattle area in 1997. Awarded a Mellon Fellowship for Humanistic Study, he earned his doctorate in American Literature from the University of Washington in 2005. He now works as Communications Manager for RootMetrics.

Also an avid runner, Patrick has competed several marathons and values his running as time to disconnect from everyday life and rummage through new ideas and old emotions.

Patrick lives with his two children in the Seattle area, where he likes to run the forest trails with his dog (Baxter the Vizsla). He is currently at work on the follow-up to *Ghost Music,* again featuring Seattle Detective Marcus Brace.

Made in the USA
San Bernardino, CA
27 October 2013